The Red Mohawk

Anonymous

Cover Design by BespokeBookCovers.com

ISBN 978-0993257704

Books by Anonymous

The Book With No Name
The Eye of the Moon
The Devil's Graveyard
The Book of Death
The Red Mohawk
Sanchez: A Christmas Carol (short story)
The Plot to Kill the Pope

The author can be found on Facebook and Twitter as Bourbon Kid.

"Every day I'm the hero in my own personal movie. Some days without realising, I show up in other people's movies. And they almost always cast me as the villain."

Anonymous.

Prologue

Randall Buckwater had agreed to stop swearing when he got married over thirty years ago. But as he slammed his foot down on the accelerator and reversed back down the bridge as fast as he could, he came mighty close to screaming out a few *F* words. Instead of cursing he did the next best thing. He screamed out the lyrics of Jeffrey Osborne's *On The Wings of Love*. It wasn't a particularly logical thing to do and it wasn't something he would ever admit to later when questioned about the incident, but he was in a state of shock. And panic. It was already clear to him that the horrific image he had just witnessed would replay vividly in his mind for the rest of his life. And *On The Wings of Love* would never sound the same again.

Yet the evening had started off so slow, so mundane, so run of the mill.

One

Randall and his new partner Pete had been on bridge patrol for four hours when the sad news came through. Marjorie Buckingham had passed away. The sweet old lady had been ill for months and had finally lost her life after a vicious bout of pneumonia. Chief O'Grady had radioed it through to them just after two o'clock in the morning.

'This is it then,' said Randall to his young sidekick. 'Your first chance to change the sign.'

'Whoop dee-doo,' Pete replied sarcastically.

Their squad car was parked to the right of the bridge just inside the county line. It faced down the highway, waiting for any vehicle that might come their way hoping to cross the bridge. The sign Randall had referred to was the Population board that stood proudly on the state line. At present it read:

B Movie Hell: Population 3672

'Just switch the two around,' said Randall. 'There's a one on the other side.'

'I don't give a shit what's on the other side. I'm not going out there just yet.'

'Why not?'

'Because there's a fucking big rodent out there,' Pete moaned.

'No there isn't it. Come on, this is a big moment. Your first time changing the population. You should be proud. I was the first time I did it.'

'What was the population of B Movie Hell back when you first did it?' Pete asked.

'Two thousand and forty four,' Randall replied. 'Of course, back then it was called Sherwood County, a much more sensible name for a town.'

'B Movie Hell is much cooler though, ain't it?'

'I don't think so.'

'That's because you're an old fart.'

Randall stared across at Pete who was sitting in the passenger seat looking totally disinterested in just about everything. Pete was a good kid by all accounts. He had a heart of gold, but he also had shit for brains. He was nineteen years old, but with all the emotional maturity of a ten year old.

In his quieter moments Randall wondered if he had been the same at that age. He rationalised that it wasn't possible. As a nineteen year old, Randall had already married his childhood sweetheart and was well on the way to becoming a father for the first time. Heaven forbid a moron like Pete became a father any time in the next five years.

'There's definitely something out there,' Pete said, squinting hard through the windscreen.

'It's just a stick. It's not moving.'

'I reckon it's a squirrel. Fucking huge one too. Are they carnivorous?'

'They only eat nuts.'

'In that case I'm definitely staying in the car,' said Pete.

'I'm telling you, it's a stick,' said Randall. He didn't need to take a closer look at it like his partner. Instead he stared in fascination at his young apprentice. This idiot was convinced he could see a squirrel in the woodland. There were no squirrels in B Movie Hell. Never had been.

The woodland that Pete was staring into was on the other side of the county line, thirty yards outside of B Movie Hell, in Lewisville County. But even so, Randall was damn sure there were no goddamn squirrels there either.

It was an indication of how slow and quiet the night had been that they were debating whether something in the distance was a squirrel or a stick. But Randall had long ago given up the idea that the role of a local cop would ever have anything in common with the cops on TV or in books. The most excitement he had was negotiating 'donations' to his retirement fund from hapless motorists stopped for broken tail lights and tyres that looked a bit low in air pressure.

'It's definitely a squirrel,' Pete insisted. 'See that fuzzy tail? That's a squirrel.'

The older cop caught himself shaking his head in disbelief and bewilderment as he looked at his gormless buddy. Talking was Pete's downfall. But he didn't do himself any favours in what he looked like, either. He had a typically ridiculous young person's haircut. It was one of those stupid birds nest styles that looked like it should have a pair of antlers sticking out of the top of it. It covered half of his face and was probably to blame for his greasy skin and spots. The gormless look was capped off by the fact that Pete never seemed to be able to close his mouth. His bottom lip was always hanging down, giving the impression he was about to say something, but coupled with his constant squinting (the kid clearly needed glasses) it just added to the "brain dead" look.

'Shoot. I think it's gone,' Pete declared, squinting some more and pressing his face closer to the windscreen.

'It was never there. So, you want to go change the population on the board now?'

Pete shrugged. 'Not yet,' he said while fiddling with his crotch. 'That squirrel might come back in a minute. With reinforcements.'

Randall looked away and stared out of the window on his side of the car. He had one hand still rested on the steering wheel even though they were parked. He had no idea why he did it but he always kept a hand on the steering wheel whether the engine was on or not.

'Okay, let's just say for arguments sake that there is a squirrel out there,' he said. 'It's got to be less dangerous than dealing with drunken fights in town.'

'At least a drunken fight would provide a release from the boredom of sitting here all night,' Pete complained.

'You're missing the bigger picture,' said Randall. 'There's money to be made out here on the bridge.'

There was a pause before Pete asked, 'How so?'

'If you're a difficult enough sort like me, people will slip you a few dollars to let 'em through quicker.'

'You take bribes?'

Randall turned back to face Pete. 'Donations,' he said. 'I like to think of them as donations to my retirement fund.'

'When are you retiring?' Pete asked.

'Five more years. I'm getting out at fifty-five. Thirty-six years on the force is long enough, I think.'

Pete frowned. He was clearly trying to do the math.

Randall shook his head and returned to staring back out of his driver side window. There wasn't much to see. One solitary streetlight lit up the end of the bridge that led into B Movie Hell.

On night patrol they were lucky if one car *a week* came their way. That's what drove officers crazy. The boredom, the waiting and the pointlessness of it. Randall had gotten used to it over the years. The only time it was tough was when he was breaking in a new partner like Pete. The banal conversation was often more soul destroying than the silences.

'How much do you charge people to cross?' Pete asked.

'As much as I think they can afford.'

'What's the most you ever got?'

'Fifty bucks.'

'Shit, really?' Pete sounded impressed. 'I bet I can get a hundred.'

Randall turned back to face him and caught sight of him scratching his groin area for the hundredth time that night.

'Whadda you need the money for?' Randall asked. 'Buy some cream for that itch you got?'

'What itch?'

'You've been scratching your junk all night. You're starting to creep me out.'

Pete grimaced and stopped scratching himself for a moment. 'Think I might have picked up something at The Beaver Palace last week.'

Randall raised a quizzical eyebrow. 'You've been going to Mellencamp's?'

'Not regularly or nothin' but you know, every once in a while.'

'You wear a hat though, right?'

'A hat?'

'You know what I mean.'

Pete looked confused for a few moments, before he suddenly cottoned on to what Randall meant. 'Oh yeah, but not the whole time. I mean, this one chick last week she had some sores on her face. Think maybe I caught something from her.'

Randall shook his head. 'Jesus, Pete. Don't you get to choose which girl you go with?'

'Yeah,' Pete blushed ever so slightly. 'I hadn't been with this girl before though, so I thought it would be rude not to.'

'I thought you said you didn't go there often?'

'I don't, but I think I've done all the girls there at least once now.'

'How many girls are there?'

'About thirty or so. They haven't had a new one in for a while. Think they need to freshen things up a bit.'

'Don't let Mellencamp hear you say that.'

'He's not as bad as you think y'know. He's always been really friendly when I've met him.'

Randall scoffed. 'Of course he has. You're one of his customers. And that means you're in his debt.'

'I don't owe him anything. I pay up front. That's one of the rules.'

'Sure. And what happens when you pull him over for a broken tail light, huh?'

'He's got a broken tail light?'

'No. But if he ever does you won't be able to bust him for it.'

'Why not?'

'Because he'll tell the whole town that you like having your balls tickled with a feather duster.'

Pete looked surprised. 'Who told you about that?'

'No one, I was just speculating.' He looked closer at his young partner's face. 'You like having your balls tickled with a feather duster?'

'No.'

'Well, anyway,' said Randall, not wishing to dwell on the thought of his partner in a compromising position with a cleaning utensil. 'My point is, stuff like that can come back to haunt you. If Mellencamp gets you in his back pocket, one day he'll come calling on you for a favour you won't like, and you'll feel obliged to say yes when you know you shouldn't.'

Pete laughed and then scratched his nether regions again. 'Yeah, right.' He suddenly sat up straighter as if he'd been jabbed in the stomach with a hot poker. 'I'm gonna have to take a piss,' he said.

'What about the squirrel?'

'What squirrel?'

Randall let out a deep sigh and reached for a button on the car stereo. He turned it on, and recognising the tune that was playing, he turned it up loud. It was *The Greatest Love of All* by Sexual Chocolate. 'Just change the number on the population board before you go will ya?' he said.

'I'll do it on the way back. I'm busting.'

'Fine. But hurry up before someone else dies.'

Pete opened his car door, but before climbing out he looked back at Randall. 'When I come back, you think maybe we could listen to a station other than EMM for once?'

'What's wrong with EMM?'

'Eighties Movie Music? There's only so much of that shit I can take!'

'But it's the local station. Gotta support the locals.'

'Don't you want to listen to something different for once?'

'Like what?'

'How about a bit of rap?'

'What the hell is rap?' Randall actually knew full well what rap was, but he enjoyed pretending not to know about such things, just to see how much it wound Pete up.

'*Christ,* Randall. When I get back I'm gonna introduce you to some serious gangsta rap.'

Randall turned the radio up another notch and watched his young sidekick hurry off across a stretch of grass towards the dark woodland up ahead. Pete soon disappeared out of sight behind some tall trees. It was a safe bet he wasn't just going for a piss. He probably needed to scratch or inspect the rash he seemed to have picked up at The Beaver Palace. The thought of it made Randall shudder. He wondered whether he and Pete's hands had touched at any point in the night. Satisfied that they hadn't, he indulged himself in a good sing-along to *The Greatest Love of All* and a less than memorable Wild Stallyns song that followed it. By the time it finished and the airwaves had been replaced by adverts, at least five minutes had passed. There was still no sign of Pete returning from the woodland, so Randall decided to try and surprise him by finding some rap on the radio. He flicked through several stations before he finally found some rap music. Ten seconds of it was all he could stomach before he twisted the dial on the stereo again. That was when he found Jeffrey Osborn singing *On The Wings of Love*.

He hadn't heard the song in years but he remembered instantly how much he had enjoyed singing it at the top of his voice as a young man. Secure in the knowledge that Pete was the only person within hearing distance he wound down both windows on the car and turned the stereo up to the max before bursting into song, dueting with Jeffrey Osborn on the chorus.

He half expected to see Pete come rushing out of the woods to see what all the noise was about. So while singing for all he was worth, he peered over the steering wheel into the darkness of the trees for any sight of his partner.

But there was no sign of Pete. Or any movement at all in the woods for that matter.

The song was going into the final verse, so he decided to flick the headlights on in the hope of catching Pete's attention. The lights were only on for a couple of seconds before he finally saw some movement. A tall, broad shouldered man walked out of the woods and into the bright white light that was emanating from the car's headlamps.

But this wasn't Pete.

It was a much larger man. As this man strode into the centre of the light Randall got a real good look at him. And it caused him to stop singing *On The Wings of Love*. His face froze in mid song as he stared at the sight before him.

The man who had come from the woods stopped in the centre of the light as if he wanted Randall to get a good look at him. He was wearing black jeans and a shiny red leather jacket over a black vest. His face was ghastly, or at least it appeared that way at first, until Randall eventually processed the image correctly in his mind. That was when he realised he wasn't looking upon a face made from skin and bone. He was looking at a rubber mask. A *dirty yellow mask* designed to look

11

like a human skull. It had an evil grin and several of its teeth were blacked out. Protruding up on the top of the mask was a two inch high strip of red hair that ran back from the front of the forehead like a Mohican or Mohawk. And through two eyeholes in the mask, a pair of vivid black eyes stared right back at Randall.

Two more things caught Randall's eye before he started up the engine and slammed the car into reverse.

The man in the yellow mask was holding a long sharp silver blade in his left hand. And the blade was covered in blood, a stream of which was dribbling onto the ground.

In his other hand he was carrying a human head, holding it by a fistful of its thick brown hair. Randall's eyes opened wide as the image took up a place in his memory bank forever.

It was Pete's head.

Two

'Nobody puts Baby in the corner.'

Baby had heard Patrick Swayze utter that line a thousand times. Even now it still gave her goose-bumps. It represented so much more than just her favourite line in *Dirty Dancing*. Deep down she believed that one day a real man just like Johnny Castle would come and sweep her off her feet, make her feel like she mattered, and take her away from The Beaver Palace. She dreamed of being whisked off to a happier, friendlier place. Somewhere like the holiday resort in the movie would do just fine.

She had picked up the nickname Baby not long after arriving at The Beaver Palace. It had been an appropriate nickname too because up until recently she had been the youngest girl there. She was nineteen now and her crown as the youngest girl in the Palace had been inherited by her friend Chardonnay, who was only seventeen. But the name Baby was a keeper, not least of all because no one had ever called her anything else. And it made watching Dirty Dancing just that tiny bit more special for her. She tried to model herself on Jennifer Grey, the actress in the movie. She was a similar build and she owned a pair of white jeans that she wore most days. The major difference between the two of them was that Jennifer Grey didn't have a bright blue birthmark on her left cheek. Baby had one and it stood out a mile. She remembered how as a ten year old she had once spent half a day and two bars of soap trying to wash it off. Birthmarks don't go that easy though and as the years passed she had grown used to it and accepted it. Clarisse, the madam at The Beaver Palace always referred to it as a beauty spot. Baby had learnt to think of it that way too. Anyway, birthmark or not, she suspected that most of the other girls at The Beaver Palace were envious of her. Everyone wanted to be Baby, the one in *Dirty Dancing* that is, not the one currently watching it in her room. On her own.

There was a knock at the door. Baby paused the movie because she didn't want an interruption ruining the dance sequence at the end, and she loved to hear every second of Bill Medley and Jennifer Warnes singing *Time of My Life*. She rolled off her bed and walked over to the door. Before she even reached it, the handle turned and it opened. Chardonnay poked her head around the door.

'Hi Baby. Whatcha doin'?'

'Just watching a film.'

Chardonnay had her long brown hair tied up in a bun on the top of her head. She was naturally beautiful and had the most divine olive coloured skin. She stepped inside and closed the door quietly behind her. 'Have you seen the news?' she asked.

'No. Why?'

Chardonnay was one of the few girls who loved her job at The Beaver Palace. Unlike Baby she had no aspirations to ever leave. She loved the work and she loved living in B Movie Hell. She grabbed the remote control from Baby's bed and pointed it at the television. She was about to press a button when she spotted Patrick Swayze on screen.

'You watching Dirty Dancing again?' she asked.

'There was nothing else on,' Baby lied.

Chardonnay smiled at her and jumped back on the bed, propping herself up against baby's headboard. Baby jumped back onto the bed and snuggled up alongside her. Both of them were wearing their pyjamas. Baby compared her flannel Tweetie Pie pyjamas to Chardonnay's silky leopard print ones. Chardonnay was so much more grown-up and sophisticated.

'You know you should try watching Coyote Ugly some time. It's just as good,' said Chardonnay.

'Nobody's better than Johnny,' said Baby.

Chardonnay shook her head and grinned. 'But Patrick Swayze's dead now. Adam Garcia from Coyote Ugly, he's still alive. And he's still hot.'

'Well then you can have him. I'll stay with Johnny.'

'Fine,' said Chardonnay, flicking through the channels on the remote. 'But if Adam Garcia shows up here one day, I'm holding you to that.'

Baby was slightly irritated by Chardonnay's channel flicking. The Dirty Dancing DVD was paused so she wouldn't be missing anything, but even so, she hadn't given her co-worker permission to channel flick. 'What are you looking for?' she asked.

'The news. Wait, here it is. Look!'

Baby took a look at the television screen. She was only afforded a small portable television in her room but even on the tiny screen, she recognised a face on the display behind the newsreader. 'Is that Pete Neville?'

'Yeah,' said Chardonnay. 'Someone's murdered him.'

Baby put her hand over her mouth. 'Oh my God. What happened? Pete was a real nice guy.'

'They aren't saying too much at the moment but Sophie said she heard he had his head cut off by a masked madman.'

'What?'

'Seriously. The news haven't mentioned the decapitation bit yet but they did say the killer wore a mask.'

'Have they caught him yet?'

'No,' said Chardonnay turning to Baby with a fake look of horror on her face. 'Just think, he could be coming here. Who knows whose head he'll cut off next?'

Baby gave her a playful shove. 'Don't joke about things like that!'

'It's exciting though isn't it?' said Chardonnay. 'I don't think we've ever had a serial killer in B Movie Hell before.'

'I don't want one *now* either. I won't be able to sleep now you've told me about this.'

'Doctor Bob had the right idea,' said Chardonnay.

'What do you mean?'

'He left town on vacation this morning. He's gone to Fiji for two weeks.'

'Really? So who's giving out pills and stuff now?'

'Clarisse I guess.'

Baby was pleased to hear that Doctor Bob wasn't around, but she hid her feelings from Chardonnay. 'Oh. Scary isn't it? There's a killer on the loose and our doctor has gone to Fiji.'

Chardonnay giggled. 'It won't make much difference. If you get your head cut off, Doctor Bob wouldn't be able to sew it back on anyway.'

'Ooh, that's horrible. You shouldn't even joke about stuff like that.'

'No one's listening.'

'Maybe not, but joking about it is tempting fate.'

Chardonnay giggled. 'You scare far too easy. If you want I could stay in here with you tonight?'

There was something about the way Chardonnay said it that suggested she was keen to stay with Baby. And the fact she was wearing her pyjamas and already pulling the duvet back hinted strongly at a desire to stay. Baby didn't mind. It made sense that nobody would want to be on their own knowing that a masked murderer was in town. In fact, the more Baby thought about it, the more grateful she was to have some company.

'Okay,' she said. 'But you gotta watch the end of Dirty Dancing with me.'

'Fine,' said Chardonnay. 'But when it's finished we're watching Coyote Ugly. I need to introduce you to this film.'

'What's it about?'

'You'll like it. It's about a girl who runs off to start a new life in New York. She gets a job in a bar and falls in love with this really cute guy.'

'I'd love to go to New York.'

'Well tonight Baby, we're going with Adam Garcia,' said Chardonnay jumping up from the bed and heading for the door to go fetch the Coyote Ugly DVD. As she opened the door she added, 'unless that masked killer comes and gets us first!'

Baby smiled politely. She didn't care about the masked killer that much. She was much more interested in the news that Doctor Bob, The Beaver Palace's in-house doctor, was out of town.

Three

The phone seemed to have been ringing for hours. Jack Munson had incorporated the ringing noise seamlessly into his dream. He opened his eyes and the first thing he saw on his bedside table was a half empty bottle of navy rum. His cell phone was next to it, its stupidly loud old-fashioned ringing tone blaring out. He reached over and grabbed it, lifting his head from his pillow, immediately feeling the full effects of the previous nights alcohol intake.

'Yeah,' he mumbled, blinking his eyes to try and wake himself up a bit more.

'Hi Jack. Please tell me you're not hung over.'

'I'm not hung over.'

'Good, because I need you to come in to the office. I've got something for you. Something big.'

Jack rubbed his forehead and tried to estimate how much extra sleep he could get away with. 'Okay, give me a couple of hours.'

The voice on the other end hesitated a moment before replying with a sense of urgency. 'Jack, I need you right now.'

'Okay. Give me an hour.'

'I can give you thirty minutes. Call me back on this number when you arrive.'

The line went dead. Jack let his head fall back onto the pillow. 'Fuck,' he mumbled to himself.

He closed his eyes and made a feeble attempt to grab an extra thirty seconds of sleep, knowing that even if he were able to, it wouldn't be a good idea. The voice on the other end of the line had been his old boss Devon Pincent. Pincent hadn't called him in over a year. He hadn't worked in almost *three*. If Pincent had a job for him now, then it was going to be something extremely important.

Something serious.

He sat bolt upright, his head dizzying momentarily. Then the training kicked in. The "old school" reactions came back instinctively. He rolled out of bed and staggered to the bathroom. He needed to shower and brush his teeth at the very least. That would leave him twenty-five minutes to get dressed, jump in the car and race down to headquarters to meet Pincent.

He turned the shower control valve to unmercifully hot and scrubbed hard in an effort to wake himself up. It worked. He began to slowly feel more awake. He hadn't had to do this in a long time. For the last few years when he woke up with a hangover he did everything at a leisurely pace. But the years of training in the Special Forces came back quickly. When he needed to be sharp and alert his body and mind had an incredible capacity to perform under any duress. And a hangover didn't really count as any kind of duress. His mind began to focus on all the things he would need to take with him. His gun, his passport, some fake id's, and his security pass to get into the building, as long as it hadn't been revoked. He had been assured that it wouldn't be without his knowledge.

While brushing his teeth, he began to mull over the possible reasons why Pincent had called him. Three years ago the unit had told him his services were no longer required. He was a dinosaur they'd said. Stuck in the past. His methods no longer appropriate. And then there was his drinking. That had become a problem. As he'd gotten older he'd found it harder to cope with all the things he'd seen and done as a young man. Done for his country and for the greater good. One thing in particular had haunted him for the longest time. He had made a mistake that could never be undone. A mistake that replayed over and over his mind like a broken record. Only alcohol could ease the pain and make him forget, even if it was just for a few hours.

When the department had placed him on indefinite leave his drinking and his attitude had been listed as factors. He knew his judgement was off, the drinking had seen to that, and if he was honest, his attitude hadn't been great either. But that wasn't all. Times had changed. Technology had changed. Muscle wasn't required any more. Not his kind anyway. Modern investigative work required more technically minded people. Younger people. Honest people who didn't cover up their mistakes. Or drink to forget them.

He trawled through his old work clothes in his wardrobe and picked out a pair of grey trousers and a black shirt. Neither of them fitted quite as well as they used to. He was a touch heavier around the waist and the chest. Where once there had been solid muscle, there was now what he called "slightly softer muscle". In his more self-aware moments, he guessed others would call it flab. The top button on his shirt wouldn't do up, so he decided to leave it undone and go without a tie. He slung on a loose fitting brown suede jacket and took a quick look at himself in the mirror. He had become a washed up older version of himself. He looked like shit.

In his younger days Munson had almost always been in a relationship. And the thing he missed most now that he was old and single, was having a woman make him breakfast in the morning. These days all he had for company was his rum, and rum wasn't a good cook.

Polishing off a bottle of the stuff the night before didn't help put him in the mood for cooking his own breakfast either.

As he slipped his watch onto his wrist he realised he didn't even have time to make himself a coffee. Instead he took a large swig of rum from the bottle on his bedside table. It might just be the last chance he would get to take a drink all day, so it was now or never. Damn, that stuff tasted good in the morning. He was about to put it back when he found himself wondering if he'd get a chance to buy any more later. Probably not.

He screwed the lid back on and slipped the bottle into the inside pocket of his suede jacket.

Better safe than sorry.

As he was making his way down to the parking lot beneath his apartment block he still hadn't figured out why he had been suddenly called up out of the blue. His brain hadn't quite shaken off the feeling that there was a layer of cotton wool on it, stifling it from connecting the dots. The rum hadn't provided any inspiration either.

He started the engine on his black Lotus Esprit and drove out into the backstreet behind his apartment. Maybe it was the sunlight that did it, but suddenly his mind cleared completely. It occurred to him that Pincent had said, "*I* need you". Not *we,* not *the unit,* not *Your Country.* Nope.

I need you.

That could mean this was something unofficial, something for an outsider, someone who could be trusted. Maybe he was needed to track down a mole in the department? Or maybe something he and Pincent had done together years ago had come back to haunt them? He hoped that was not the case.

They had done at least a hundred "off the record" jobs between them in the good old days. In these modern times of full disclosure there was every chance they could go to prison for just about any operation they had carried out in the past. Pincent had overseen or authorised most of them. Jack had been his secret right hand man. In the old days he had been known as *The Ghost* because no one ever saw him in the flesh. Jack Munson was the most secret agent of them all.

In the old days.

Four

The drive across the city to get to headquarters had gone by in a blur of beeping horns and stop signs. Munson ignored them all. That was one of the curious oddities about drinking rum for breakfast. The rum brought out his innate ability to drive from one place to another without any concentration or awareness of his surroundings. And yet every time without fail, he ended up exactly where he wanted to be, and usually with a few minutes to spare. On this occasion he had actually arrived at his destination about twenty minutes late, but he put that down to the ridiculous timeline set for him by Pincent.

A security guard had been waiting for him outside the building and led him through the reception area to the elevators. The place hadn't changed much.

When the doors opened on the eighth floor, the first thing he saw was Pincent's face. His old colleague was standing directly in front of the doors waiting for him. He looked run down, his features all craggy and weathered from the stress of the job. His hairline had receded an extra inch too. He still had a fairly decent clump of grey hair on his head, but these days his forehead went a lot higher.

'Is it taking you a lot longer to wash your face in the mornings?' Munson blurted out, courtesy of the rum.

'What?'

'You're receding a bit.'

'Have you been drinking?'

'No,' Munson said defensively, before adding, 'I just didn't have time for breakfast. I had a few drinks last night and my stomach's a little unsettled. Some breakfast should sort me out. Any chance someone could rustle me up a bacon sandwich?'

Pincent didn't even crack a smile. His sense of humour seemed to have deserted him. Another noticeable change in him was his clothing. He was better dressed than Munson had ever seen him before. He wore an expensive charcoal grey suit with a smart white shirt and a dark blue tie. One thing about him hadn't changed though. His expression gave away nothing. That was one of the great things about Pincent. His poker face.

'This way,' said Pincent. Without waiting for a response he turned and headed down a long corridor. Munson followed him all the way into a meeting room at the far end.

'Take a seat,' said Pincent, closing the door behind them as Munson stepped inside the room.

Inside was a long marble meeting table with six black leather seats running along either side and one further seat at the end. Sitting in one of the seats on the far side of the table was a smartly dressed, tanned lady of Latin descent.

'Hi,' said Munson. 'I can tell just by looking at you, you're from either Jacksonville or Baltimore. I've got a good eye for these things. Picked it up in the field of duty. So which is it? Baltimore isn't it?'

'Close,' the woman replied. 'I'm from Verona.'

'Don't let him fool you,' Pincent butted in. 'He's just warming up. Jack's always cranky and a bit off his game when he hasn't had anything to eat.' He nudged Munson. 'Jack this is Milena Fonseca.'

Fonseca was wearing a black figure-hugging suit with a black blouse and had her dark hair scraped back into a ponytail. Munson took a silent guess that she was a field agent in her early thirties (and maybe secretly wished she was a cat burglar). She had chiselled features, high cheekbones and big brown eyes. He liked her right away, solely because of the eyes. Munson was a sucker for brown eyes.

Fonseca didn't get up from her seat. 'Nice to meet you Jack,' she said outstretching a hand. He took her hand and shook it firmly but briefly as he sat down. Pincent pulled out another chair and sat down next to Munson.

'Milena's fully briefed and will bring you up to speed with all our intel when you leave.'

'Where am I going?'

'You're both going to a place called B Movie Hell. Before that though, you'll be making a stop off at an asylum first.'

'*B Movie what?*'

'Hell.'

Munson frowned. For a minute there he thought maybe he'd had too much rum, but Pincent had confirmed it. He'd said B Movie Hell. 'What's *B Movie Hell* when it's at home?' he asked.

'It's a hick town in the middle of nowhere. Used to be called Sherwood County.'

'A perfectly good name.'

'Indeed. About twenty years ago a rich benefactor named Silvio Mellencamp moved in there. He used to work in the film industry. When he moved to Sherwood he changed the name of the town to B Movie Hell.'

'I didn't know you could change the name of a town when you moved there. Have I been missing out on something?'

'No, Jack. But Silvio Mellencamp made an absolute fortune as a movie producer in the eighties and early nineties. When he moved to

Sherwood County he invested a lot of that money in the local businesses. He turned the whole place into a shrine to his favourite films. I've never been there but I'm told the whole place is a tribute to movie clichés from the eighties. They've got a Nakatomi Towers, a Rocky Balboa statue, a McDowell's restaurant, you name it.'

'I have no idea what you're saying right now.'

'Don't worry about it. It's not important.'

Munson shifted uncomfortably in his chair. Even though he had maintained his fitness and kept his weight down (to a degree), his clothes were even tighter than he'd realised when he first put them on in a hurry an hour earlier. He twisted his chair away from Fonseca for a moment and adjusted his trousers. After all, there was no sense in drawing attention to an ill-fitting crotch area.

'What kind of movies did this guy make?' Munson inquired. 'Anything I might have seen?'

'Porno,' Pincent replied. 'He was one of the biggest producers and distributors of the porn industry when VHS tapes were big. When DVD's came along he's one of the few that realised his days were numbered. He sold up and got out of the industry. And as I just said, he moved himself down to Sherwood County, invested a lot of his money in the local businesses and in turn, the townsfolk let him change the place completely, including the name.'

'*Townsfolk?* That's a good word,' said Munson. 'It's not used often enough these days, if you ask me. I'm picturing bearded people with pitchforks.'

'Well then you're about right,' said Pincent.

'So then what do you need from me?' Munson finally asked, still unable to fathom the relevance of all the talk about porn and B Movie Hell.

Pincent took a deep breath. 'We've got a major problem Jack. *Actually, I've* got a major problem, and I need you to clean it up.'

There was a knock at the door.

'Come in,' Milena Fonseca called out.

The door opened and an elderly woman with grey hair wearing a blue tunic backed in, pulling a hostess trolley with her. For the next two minutes no one spoke as she unloaded some coffee and pastries onto the table for them. When she was done, Pincent thanked her and she let herself out.

As soon as the door was shut, Munson grabbed a cup and saucer and began pouring himself a coffee. Fonseca poured herself an orange juice while Pincent took the opportunity to get down to business. 'Ever heard of Operation Blackwash?' he asked.

22

Munson took a sip of his black coffee. It tasted quite spectacular. He hadn't had decent coffee in a long time. He answered Pincent quickly so that he could take another sip. 'Nope. Never heard of it.'

'Well, that's a relief. Sort of,' said Pincent. 'Although it does mean I'm going to have to explain it to you.'

He took a second sip of the coffee and then congratulated Pincent. 'Great coffee.'

'I know.'

He took another sip. 'Should I have heard of Operation Blackwash?'

'Definitely not.'

'But you thought I might have?' The caffeine was kicking in rapidly. Munson could feel his mind sharpening with each passing second.

'You're a clued up guy,' Pincent went on. 'But this was a top-secret project from years ago. Anyone who was involved in it would automatically deny all knowledge of it, even under intense interrogation. We had good people on board. The best.'

'I only found out about it this morning,' Fonseca added.

'Me too,' said Munson. 'So is it safe to assume that Operation Blackwash has gone to shit somehow?'

'Like you wouldn't believe Jack. I need you to clean it up. And fast.'

'So tell me what information I need to know and I'll get on it.'

Pincent gave one of his brief fake smiles. 'Good. Let me cut right to it,' he said. 'Operation Blackwash was the brainchild of a headstrong idiot in the department some years ago. Some dickhead who watched far too many spy movies thought we could create an elite army of highly-trained, robot-like spies and assassins. The plan was to catch them young, I mean real young. Some were new-borns, and the oldest was only about five. Anyway, we figured if we trained them up from that kind of age we could create a team of near perfect soldiers.'

Munson took another sip of his coffee and placed the cup down on the table. He reached over to the tray of pastries and grabbed a croissant that had caught his eye. 'I can see where this project went wrong,' he said taking a bite from the croissant. 'I bet you ended up with a bunch of Danny DeVito's instead of Arnold Schwarzenegger's, didn't you?'

'It wasn't quite that bad, but you're on the right lines.'

'And the clown who thought the idea up?'

Pincent gave an embarrassed shrug. 'Like I said, a headstrong idiot.'

'You also said dickhead.'

'Yeah, well, it's back in the days when I was trying to make a name for myself by being forward thinking and innovative. Thing is, back then I thought that just being different meant I was clever. You know what I was like. We all learn, in the end.'

'So what happened with the project?'

'It was disbanded years ago.'

'After how long?'

'Twelve years.'

'Twelve years?' Munson balked. 'It took you twelve years to realise that it was a shit idea?'

'That's what happens when it's your idea Jack.'

'And what made it get disbanded?'

Fonseca interrupted eagerly. 'One of the test cases committed suicide.'

Jack looked at her. She was deadly serious. He turned back to Pincent. 'Only one? You went twelve years before one of them topped themselves? I'm impressed. How many test subjects were there?'

'Five.'

'Five? From the start?'

'Yeah.'

'I think I've figured this out already. One of the average ones committed suicide so the project got disbanded, but in your group of five, you had one that fitted the mould didn't you?'

Pincent nodded and looked away.

'Sorry,' said Munson raising an apologetic hand. 'It's the caffeine kicking in. Carry on. I didn't mean to jump ahead.'

All through the conversation Milena Fonseca had been studying Munson's every move. He had a feeling she was assessing him. She would only know whatever Pincent had told her about him and it looked like she was trying to get a feel for what kind of agent he was. He wondered if she had sussed out yet that he was a drunk, amongst other things. He glanced over at her and smiled. She kept up her stare but didn't reciprocate the smile. Yep, she'd rumbled him. She could probably smell the rum on his breath. Good, he thought. Let her focus on that, she'll maybe miss the important stuff.

Munson popped the last piece of his croissant into his mouth, winked at Fonseca and turned his attention back to Pincent who had just finished pouring himself a coffee.

'There was some, what you might call, dubious experimentation carried out on them,' Pincent continued. 'We'd never get away with it nowadays of course, what with all these human rights laws and stuff.'

24

'And the fact that they were kids.'

'Yeah.'

Munson grinned ever so slightly. 'So, what kind of dubious experimentation?'

'Well, first of all there was all the military training, which, let's face it you can give to anyone if you catch them young enough. But then we tested some mental enhancement drugs on them.'

As he took his last sip off coffee and considered how long to wait before pouring himself another, Munson became aware that both Fonseca and Pincent were staring at him. This was obviously a crucial part of the story.

'So what did the drugs do?' Munson asked.

Pincent carried on. 'Some were designed to increase awareness, heighten senses, that kind of thing, and others were used with the intention of helping the subjects to take orders.'

'Mind control drugs?'

'Yeah.'

Munson couldn't wait any longer. He grabbed the coffee jug and poured himself another drink. 'You know what?' he said. 'I think I've heard enough about the Blackwash thing to work out the rest for myself.' He sniffed his second cup of coffee. It didn't smell as great as the first one, a sure sign that he was now fully awake. 'I suppose the big question is, if one of them committed suicide and you scrapped the whole project, what happened to the other four?'

'Wanna take a guess?'

'I'd guess that three of them are six feet under, but your golden boy was kept on in some other capacity?'

'Close.'

'So tell me. 'Cause I'm dying to know how this has panned out.'

Pincent took a sip of his coffee. 'I should have cleaned the whole thing up back in the day. Instead, I let my emotions get involved and now I'm fucked. That's why I need you. This is the reason I kept you on the payroll.'

'I thought you kept me on the payroll because you liked me.'

'Nah. It was as contingency for the current situation. This is even more "off the record" than your usual assignments.'

'You being blackmailed?'

'No.' Pincent grabbed the largest croissant from the silver tray and took a huge bite out of it, then spoke with his mouth full, almost as if he wanted the words not to come out, but Munson heard them loud and clear anyway.

'You were almost right. Three of them are gone. But the fourth one doesn't work here, or anywhere else for that matter.' He paused for dramatic effect before adding, 'the fourth one got away.'

'Got away? How?'

'It's not important.'

'Yes it is.'

Pincent made a loud gulping sound as he swallowed some of his croissant. 'I let him go,' he said.

'Why?'

'Because I liked him.'

'Good answer.'

'Thanks.'

'So you let him go because you liked him. But now he's resurfaced?'

'Actually he resurfaced a few years ago. He was arrested for murdering some one in a small village.'

Munson feigned a sarcastic look of shock. 'And what? He's now been released from prison and he's coming after *you*, because this time it's personal?'

'Very funny, but I'm afraid it's worse than that.'

'He's coming after *me?*'

'Enough with the wisecracks, already. No more coffee for him Milena. He gets snippy.'

'So I see,' said Fonseca pulling the jug of coffee away from Munson's reach.

'Look,' Pincent went on, 'after he murdered the nun, he should have gone on death row, or at the very least life imprisonment.'

'But?'

'But I pulled some strings and we got him off on an insanity plea. He was sent to a mental institution instead.'

'Why would you do that?'

'I told you. I liked him.'

'A lot by the sounds of it. Good looking was he?'

'Shut up.' Pincent's patience seemed to be wearing thin. 'He was a good kid. Well he *was* back in the day. He'd been orphaned. They all had. But I liked him. He was the best one of all of them. A real natural. Killing came easy to him, and not because he was evil, but because we caught him early and showed him that it was all right to kill.'

Munson blew out his cheeks and checked with Milena Fonseca to see how she felt about the situation. Her face gave away nothing, so he turned back to Pincent.

'And now he's escaped from the asylum?'

Pincent nodded and pushed the remainder of his croissant around the plate. 'You got it. He's been on the loose for almost thirty-six hours.'

Munson nodded, acknowledging Pincent's problem. 'Do you want him found? Or *not* found?'

'I want him to have never existed.'

'Okay. What damage has been done so far?'

Milena Fonseca suddenly sprung into life and butted in. 'In the early hours of this morning a cop in B Movie Hell had his head cut off by a psycho in a yellow mask with a red mohawk on the top of it.'

Munson raised his eyebrows. 'And that's *our* guy?'

'It has to be,' said Pincent.

'But if he's wearing a mask how can we be absolutely sure?'

'We can't,' said Fonseca. 'But even if by some freak chance it's not our guy, it certainly won't hurt to catch him will it?'

'I suppose not.'

Munson eyed up a Danish pastry with a jam filling, only for Milena Fonseca to snap her fingers at him and divert his attention back to her. 'Now here's the thing,' she said. 'The yellow mask is a blessing in disguise. A real Godsend for us. At this point no one knows who's behind the mask except for us.'

'It shouldn't be hard to work out though,' said Munson.

True,' said Pincent, 'but I've bought us some time. Under instruction from me, the asylum hasn't yet reported that our guy has escaped.'

'Our guy?' You've not mentioned *our* guy's name yet,' Munson noted.

'His name is Joey Conrad.'

'Joey Conrad? Hmmm. How many people in the department know about this?'

'Not many.' Pincent stood up and adjusted his tie as if he was looking into an imaginary mirror. 'Jack, these days, you're about the only person I can trust to clean up a mess like this. Milena will go with you and oversee everything.'

'Why? What's she bringing to the table?'

Fonseca cleared her throat. 'I'm the ranking officer here.'

'Really?'

'Yes,' she confirmed. 'Devon's had some problems recently and I've been brought in to oversee his operation. I'm coming with you to make sure this all goes smoothly.'

Munson didn't like the sound of that one bit. 'Devon. That's not gonna work.'

Devon shook his head apologetically. 'We all have our orders Jack. Milena is no fool. Don't underestimate her.'

'Fine. So what's in it for me?'

'After this job, you can retire properly. On a very substantial pension.'

Munson pretended to mull over the proposition for a few seconds even though his mind was already made up. He wanted the action way more than he wanted (or needed) the financial incentive. 'Okay. I'm in.'

'Good,' said Pincent. 'The two of you are going to pose as mid level ranked FBI agents. Milena has sorted out some identification for you, and the B Movie Hell police have been told to expect you. Milena will sort out anything else you need while you're there. If anything dangerous comes up, she'll stay out of it. But if anything happens to you, she can report back to me immediately.'

Munson smiled. 'If anything *happens* to me?'

'Jack, you're the best I have available to me, but be under no illusions, Joey Conrad is a killing machine. If you *do* find him, there's a good chance you'll wind up dead.'

Munson didn't really need to be told the last part. He knew Joey Conrad every bit as well as Pincent did. And just like Pincent had said, *no one* who worked on Operation Blackwash *ever* admitted to it. And that included Munson himself.

Five

Down in The Booty Parlour (a private underground area of The Beaver Palace) the on-duty greeter Clarisse, a veteran of the place, stubbed out her sixth cigarette of the morning. She wasn't paying a great deal of attention to what she was doing, so she winced when out of the corner of her eye, she spotted some of the ash spill over from the overloaded ash-tray onto her desk. Her boss Silvio Mellencamp didn't like to see a loaded ashtray on his greeter's desk. It created an impression that hygiene wasn't important, he said. And hygiene was a major selling point in The Beaver Palace.

But today everything was on hold. A murderer who the local cops had dubbed "The Red Mohawk" had created quite a stir. Everyone was glued to the local news, hoping to learn more. Clarisse was no exception. Her attention flitted between the constant drone of the newsreaders on the small TV on the wall and the vibration of her cell phone when her friends texted her about "updates" from the news. It seemed that all anyone could think or talk about was The Red Mohawk. In a town where nothing ever happened, this was some serious excitement.

No one knew who the masked killer was or where he had come from. Or why he'd killed Pete Neville. Young Mr Neville had been a regular visitor to the whorehouse and he had always been pleasant. He hadn't been particularly skilled in the bedroom but he had always treated the girls with respect, which was more than could be said for a lot of the other customers. With no motive yet established for Pete's grisly murder, it meant that anyone could be next.

Clarisse heard a couple of the girls getting into a scuffle in the hallway. They were always getting into arguments, usually over things like missing tubes of mascara and lube.

'Can you idiots keep the noise down?' she yelled down the corridor at them.

'Sissy's got my vanilla scented lube!' one of the girls shouted back.

'She's wearing my leopard print pants!' another voice screamed. The sound of some face-slapping and the tearing of clothing followed that particular announcement. And someone called someone else a skanky bitch.

'I'm warning you,' Clarisse called out. 'I'll get Mack down here. He'll put that lube to good use on both of you if you don't behave. Now pipe down. I'm trying to watch the news!'

The girls went deadly quiet for a few seconds. Then right on cue, just as Clarisse expected, she heard a slapping sound followed by the rapid pounding of footsteps and finally a door being slammed shut. She sighed and shook her head before turning back to the news reporter.

Work was annoyingly distracting that day. Especially given that only one client had come in. A young man named Kevin had taken advantage of the local outpouring of grief and sympathy at Pete Neville's death to make his first visit to The Beaver Palace. He was an anxious young man with bright ginger hair and matching freckles, and he came from a strict family. His father was the local priest and his mother a charity worker, so visiting a brothel was risky business for him. Not that he needed to worry. Discretion was valued as highly as hygiene in this place.

But Kevin's appearance and the scuffles over vanilla-scented lube and leopard print pants weren't Clarisse's biggest problems. Those irritations had just been the start of what was about to become a very stress filled day, high on drama of all kinds. She should have seen it coming days or even weeks earlier.

Kevin came racing out into the lobby from the first door on the right of the corridor. His sweater was draped over his arm and he was buckling up the belt on his jeans. He was perspiring profusely, his forehead soaked in sweat. Clarisse winced at the sight of a fresh patch of chunky vomit on the front of his white singlet.

'Everything okay Kevin?' she asked. Kevin stopped dead in his tracks and stared over at her as if he hadn't noticed her there before. He looked like he'd seen a ghost. *Or his parents.*

Clarisse frowned. 'What's the matter?'

Kevin pointed at the orange coloured vomit stain on his undershirt and took a deep breath before responding. 'She puked on me!'

Clarisse looked at the sick patch. 'Baby did that?'

'Yeah. I never asked for it. Is that normal?'

'No. Would you like me to wash it out for you?'

Kevin shook his head. 'No. Actually yes, my mom... I wouldn't want to... no wait, actually, I don't know. Can you clean it right now?'

'Sure honey.'

He seemed genuinely distressed. If it really had been his first time then the experience of being vomited on by Baby might well put him off returning. Some diplomacy was required. 'Did you get what you'd paid for?' Clarisse asked.

'No I didn't. I paid for a blowjob but she puked over me almost straight away. This really isn't for me. I shouldn't have come.'

'I'll tell you what,' said Clarisse smiling. 'You take a seat over there for a minute and I'll get Linda to come and sort you out. While you're with her I'll get that undershirt cleaned up for you.'

Kevin didn't look convinced. He seemed to be caught in two minds. Some persuasion was required. Clarisse pointed at a soft comfy red sofa set up against the wall behind him. 'Take a seat there a second while I call Linda. They're talking about that killer on the news.'

He looked over at the sofa and then up at the television. It would take him a while to make a decision, the poor lad. He was totally traumatised and incapable of making even the simplest choice. While he stood distracted by his own inner monologue and the voice of the newsreader, Clarisse picked up the phone and dialled Linda's number.

'Hi Linda,' she said. 'Can you come out here and take a young man off my hands for a while. Poor Kevin here has had a bit of a bad first experience and I think your calming influence is just what he needs.'

'Sure thing, Clarisse.'

Clarisse put the phone down and smiled at Kevin again. 'If you want to give me that undershirt I'll have it dry and looking like new for you in twenty minutes,' she said. 'Linda will keep you entertained in the meantime, no extra charge. You'll like Linda. She's never sick on anyone. And I'll get her to give you a teabag.'

'I don't drink tea.'

'That's not what I meant. Trust me, you'll like it. Here, give me your undershirt.'

Kevin peeled off his undershirt and handed it to her. Then he sat down and spent the next thirty seconds trying to work out what Clarisse meant about the teabag.

At about the moment his facial expression revealed he'd worked out what it was, Linda, a veteran buxom blonde in her early forties appeared and escorted him off down the hall to room six. As soon as the door closed behind them, Clarisse headed off down the hall to Baby's room to find out what had happened.

Baby had been acting strangely for a while. Clarisse, with all her experience should have confronted her before, but Baby was a little different to the others. She was one of the unfortunate girls in the business who wasn't there voluntarily and for that reason Clarisse had always cut her a little slack. Baby was only nineteen and had been groomed into the job from an early age. She had started off as a hairdresser and washer of dirty laundry. Clarisse and the other girls had raised her as best they could, and did their best to prolong her childhood but they all knew that her destiny was inevitable.

The day after her fifteenth birthday Mr Mellencamp put her to work. As was his way, he had sex with her first and then threw her into action so that she could start paying for the roof he had put over her head. She had quickly become popular with a lot of the older guys and nervous first timers because she had a permanent sweet-yet-terrified look on her face. In the case of Kevin Sharp, Clarisse had actually recommended he try Baby because she thought the two of them might get on quite well and Baby deserved the first shot at making him one of her regulars. The innocent young guys often tended to stick with the same girl on every visit. And Kevin looked innocent.

She knocked hard on Baby's door. 'Baby? You okay in there?' she called through the door. There was no response.

She turned the doorknob and walked into the room. The bed in the centre of the room was a little unkempt, but she'd seen it plenty worse over the years. From the bathroom in the far corner she heard the sound of someone retching. The bathroom door was ajar. Through the gap Clarisse could see the soles of Baby's feet. The young girl was naked and on her knees vomiting into the toilet. Her long scraggly dark hair was hanging over the side of the toilet seat. There were remnants of vomit in her hair and it looked in serious need of a wash. Clarisse stepped inside the bathroom and knelt down beside her, scraping her hair away from her face to try and keep it clear of any vomit.

'You okay sweetie?' she asked.

Baby didn't look up. Instead she vomited again. Clarisse rubbed her back in an attempt to comfort her.

'Is this the first day you've been sick?' she asked.

Baby pulled her head out of the toilet and looked up at her. She had tears running down her face. 'Third day running,' she said.

Clarisse nodded in acknowledgment. She paused before adding the next, inevitable question. 'You taken a test?'

'Yes.'

'How long have you known?'

'A while.'

Clarisse rubbed her back once more then stood up. 'I'll get someone in to sort it out for you.'

Baby shook her head. 'Clarisse,' she said with pleading eyes. 'I want to keep it.'

Over the years Clarisse had become familiar with this type of situation. Several girls had gotten pregnant and hoped to keep the child. The best way to deal with it was to keep the girl as calm as possible. 'Fair enough, honey,' she said. 'I'll try and sort something out for you. Stay here and get some rest. I'll be back in a while.'

There was no way in hell the boss would let Baby keep it. They didn't allow pregnant girls at The Beaver Palace. Not any more. It was bad for business. Normal practice would see Baby's unborn child terminated before the end of the day.

Six

Taking a shit in the morning was becoming more of a strain for Hank Jackson as he got older. Award ceremonies were over in less time than his early morning trips to the toilet and they tended to be smoother too. His doctor had been telling him for years that he needed to incorporate more fruit and roughage into his diet. But it was hard to remember to eat fruit, particularly in the evenings because it interfered with his drinking. Hell, Hank couldn't sleep without polishing off a six-pack of Heisler Beer first.

His drinking had gotten worse in tandem with his business going down the shitter. Ever since he'd ended up in debt to Silvio Mellencamp he'd been struggling to stay afloat. The used car business wasn't doing a roaring trade. The wealthy residents of B Movie Hell tended to have brand new cars delivered to their doors, courtesy of a scheme Mellencamp had introduced. And the problem was, no one with the exception of the occasional youngster was interested in a second hand car these days. Hank's lot was full of bashed up old bangers and former stock cars that had seen better days. Shit, half the vehicles were good for nothing other than scrap metal, but he still had to try and sell them. He needed to sell something soon just so he could fix a leak in the roof above the toilet. It was bad enough that he spent half his time sitting on the toilet, but these days he had to do it while wearing a big grey Stetson hat to keep the crap from the septic tank from dripping onto his head. And the hat was making him sweat even more than all the straining.

He'd opened up the car lot, imaginatively titled *Jackson's Motors* at eight a.m. and not had sight of one customer for the first half an hour before his morning newspaper was delivered. As soon as it had arrived he'd headed straight to the en-suite washroom in the corner of his office. He'd been sitting on the can for half an hour trying to force out a particularly stubborn turd when he heard the bell ring above the door of his office. His first customer in three days had picked the worst possible time to show up.

'I'm just in the john. I'll be out in a sec!' he shouted out. After half an hour of straining he'd not dropped even a tiny pebble, but the sudden anxiety of knowing he was now being rushed caused his stomach to loosen slightly, albeit only to release some trapped wind. If the new customer in his office had replied to his announcement that he was taking a shit, he wouldn't have heard it, such was the length and volume of the escaping fart.

'Who's there?' Hank called out, while waving his hand in front of his face and holding his breath.

A deep male voice responded. 'I'm looking for some wheels.'

'By wheels, do you mean wheels? Or a car?' Hank hated it when people used slang. *Wheels!* Honestly, of all the slang terms to use for the word car, it was the one that irritated him the most.

'You got a stock car out front. I want it,' the voice replied.

'Okay, hang on. I'll be right out. Can you just turn on the radio on my desk for a second?'

The person in his office duly obliged and some music filtered in through the toilet door. Hank recognised the song playing. It was *Earth Angel* by Marvin Berry and The Starlighters. Much to Hank's relief, the man in the office turned up the volume. It allowed Hank the opportunity to unleash a loud trumpeting noise from his backside without fear of it being heard by his new customer. He breathed a sigh of relief and wiped some sweat from his brow. Even though he was still desperate for a shit the release of trapped wind eased his discomfort immensely.

He wiped the sweat off his hand and onto his pale green polo shirt, then reached down and grabbed a handful of the cheap white toilet paper from the roll on the floor by his feet. He gave his ass a quick courtesy wipe. He was slightly concerned that he might have "followed through" when he'd broken wind. A quick rummage back and forth with the toilet paper and then a glance back at it confirmed his suspicions. He chucked the dirty paper down the toilet and grabbed another handful. One more decent wipe ought to be enough to make it safe to pull up his pants and hurry out into the office.

He picked up the roll of toilet paper and unravelled three sheets. As he tore them off there was a loud knock on the door. With the door being less than a metre in front of him he was conscious of how close he was to his newest customer.

'Hey, I said I'd be out in a sec. Gimme a minute will ya?' he called out.

The man in the office didn't knock on the door again. Hank couldn't tell what he was up to because the radio was still blaring out real loud. He went for one more quick wipe of his ass. Three or four rubs back and forth were enough to do the trick, he decided. He didn't bother to check the paper for skid marks this time, fearing he might lose his customer if he took any longer. Instead he dropped it straight down the toilet and stood up. He pulled his pants up in a hurry and turned to flush the toilet. He yanked at the handle, giving it a good hard tug to make sure it flushed properly. In sequence with him releasing the handle on the toilet there was a loud crashing noise behind him. The toilet door had been kicked in. Hank turned around, his face frowning with a mixture of anger and shock at the impatience of his new customer.

That's when he saw who he had been speaking to through the door. It was a large man in a bright red jacket and black jeans, wearing a yellow mask over his face. A yellow mask with a vile grin across its face, hollowed out eyes and red stripe of hair on top.

'Shit.'

Seven

Being Chief of Police in B Movie Hell had always been considered a cushy job. The post was traditionally awarded to someone near retirement, so that they could spend their final days attending social functions and opening supermarkets. That was all there was to it, *until today*. Now it was a shitty position that no one wanted, because there was a cop killer in town.

Chief O'Grady walked in to the briefing room and avoided eye contact with all of the other officers. Their voices quieted down to a hush as he approached the podium. By the time he had taken up his place behind it, the silence was deathly. He looked up. There wasn't a single empty seat in the room. It wasn't the world's biggest briefing room anyway, but it had never been so busy that it had officers standing at the back behind the five rows of seats. For the first time since the Christmas party just about every officer on the B Movie Hell police force was in attendance. Usually a briefing would have plenty of absentees. But it wasn't often that they had one the day after a cop killing. Everyone was in their standard blue uniform with the exception of two of the senior detectives in the front row who were wearing plain clothes.

The B Movie Hell police force employed approximately forty officers. This wasn't a town that dealt with a lot of crime, certainly not serious crime, and certainly not murder. And cop killers? They'd never had one before. This was uncharted territory.

'Good morning everyone,' O'Grady started. 'For anyone who hasn't seen it, Lucinda has organised a collection for Pete Neville's family. So far we've got enough for some flowers and a card, but it would be nice if we could come up with something a little more personal, so anyone wishing to donate money or ideas should see Lucinda as soon as possible.'

He took a deep breath as he looked down at the notes he had brought in with him. On top of the notes was a sheet of plastic for the overhead projector. On it was an artist's impression of the killer, pieced together from information provided by Officer Randall Buckwater who was the only witness.

'It's a terrible thing, what happened last night,' he said, looking back up at the audience.

'That's an understatement,' a voice from within the audience mumbled.

O'Grady raised his hands slowly to call for quiet in the hope of quelling any further outbursts before they started. 'I don't know what you're all working on right now, but in case anyone is in any doubt about this, let me make it clear. Catching this killer is now everyone's top priority.'

A few more, mostly approving comments flew up from the audience.

'I've sent Randall home for the morning. He just needs a few hours sleep and then he's itching to help find this killer. He's pretty shaken up, obviously. But he's given our sketch artist a description of Pete's killer.' He glanced down at the picture again. 'The press haven't seen this yet, but they will in about half an hour.'

'So let's see it!' someone shouted out.

'Okay.' O'Grady picked up the sheet of plastic and slipped it onto the projector on the desk to the right of the podium. Before switching it on, he added one final comment. 'Now because the killer was wearing a mask this doesn't have the level of detail we were after, but the mask and clothing are very distinct.'

He reached down and pressed a button on the side of the projector. The internal light switched on and a picture lit up on the whiteboard behind him. A picture of the masked murderer of Pete Neville.

An Irish voice in the audience piped up rather loudly with the phrase "What a cunt." O'Grady ignored it and stepped aside to make sure everyone could get a good look. 'The observant ones among you will have noticed that we've coloured this one in. Colour is important with this character. Note the distinct red leather jacket. No store in town sells these. I'm convinced we're dealing with someone from out of town, but if anyone recognises the jacket, feel free to shout out now.'

There was a moment of absolute silence in the audience as everyone took in the image on the whiteboard.

'Okay,' O'Grady continued. 'Now take a close look at that yellow mask. This is obviously the most outstanding feature. Randall swears that this is exactly how it looked. Says it's imprinted on his mind forever. It's a yellow skull with some blacked out teeth and he swears it was grinning at him. And this red bit on the top, that's a strip of hair, called a Mohican or Mohawk. It's a style that's popular with punk rockers and people who are just generally retarded. Now until we have something better to work with, or someone identifies this freak, we're simply calling him the Red Mohawk, but I guess most of you already know that from watching the news.'

38

One of the two plain clothed officers in the front row raised his hand. It was Benny Stansfield, a veteran detective with a fairly aggressive attitude who wasn't much of one for paperwork and fancied himself as the Dirty Harry of the department. He'd been a thorn in O'Grady's side for years. He worked under the misguided impression that because he wore his own clothes he was somehow more *rock 'n' roll* than everyone else in the department, and therefore normal rules didn't apply to him. What made it more irritating was that he didn't look as cool as he thought. His beige suit was a little too big for him but the freedom it provided allowed him to gesticulate wildly whenever it suited him. He wore the same filthy brown tie every day. It was obvious that he simply threw it over his head each day and never fully tightened or untied it. His brown hair was greasy and just a tad too long for an officer. His don't-give-a-fuck attitude was topped off with a patch of two-day-old stubble on his chin but nowhere else.

'Yes Benny,' said O'Grady, grateful that someone had finally chosen to raise a hand instead of shouting out unprompted.

'Why call him the Red Mohawk?'

O'Grady frowned and pointed at the picture on the whiteboard. 'Because he has a red Mohawk.'

'I get that Chief,' said Benny. 'But why does he have to have a nickname? Surely that just glamorises this scumbag?'

'Well, yes,' said O'Grady defensively. 'But it's a pretty cool nickname, don't you think?'

A few of the officers behind Benny nodded in agreement and the guy sat on Benny's left nudged him and whispered, *"He has got a point."*

'Who came up with the nickname?' Benny asked.

'I did,' said O'Grady. 'You got a problem with it?'

'I don't see the point in it.'

O'Grady resisted the urge to call Benny an asshole, even under his breath. Instead he looked around at all of the faces in the room, making sure he had their full attention. It was time to hit them all with the one piece of good news he'd had that morning. 'Look at it this way Benny,' he said, focussing back on the most outspoken member of his audience. 'Picture the front page of the newspaper, the big headline, it says "Benny Stansfield captures The Red Mohawk, lands ten thousand dollar reward." Got a nice ring to it don't you think?'

Several officers, including Benny visibly sat up in their seats.

'That's right,' O'Grady continued. 'There's a ten thousand dollar reward for anyone who brings in The Red Mohawk.'

'Ten thousand?' said Benny. 'Where did we find ten thousand dollars?'

'Silvio Mellencamp has kindly put up a ten thousand dollar reward for anyone who captures this guy and brings him in alive.'

The mention of the reward had the desired effect. Suddenly everyone looked like they were itching to get out and hunt for the killer without a moment's hesitation.

Benny put up his hand again. 'What happens if I find this Red Mohawk guy and circumstances dictate that I have to shoot him in the face a few times until he's dead? Is there still a reward?' he asked.

O'Grady smiled. It was just the question he had been hoping for. 'If anyone kills The Red Mohawk, Mellencamp's not paying the ten thousand dollars.'

Howls of disapproval rang out from the audience. O'Grady raised his hand to call for quiet before continuing. 'Let me finish,' he said. 'If anyone kills The Red Mohawk, the reward won't be ten thousand dollars. It'll be a *hundred* thousand. Mr Mellencamp was very clear about that.'

In the front row Benny stood up and turned to address his fellow officers. He gesticulated excitedly with his arms like a preacher trying desperately to keep his congregation from falling asleep during the boring parts of a sermon. 'So what the hell are we waiting for?' he yelled. 'Let's get out there and find this bastard!'

As the sound of chairs grating against the floor filled the air, O'Grady called out for calm. 'Wait a second!' he yelled. 'Hold on a goddamn minute. There's one other thing.' He waited for quiet and for everyone to sit back down, or at least stop running for the door, which they duly did. 'The FBI is sending a couple of agents down here to work with us on this. I'm not sure when they're due to arrive, but let's see if we can find this sonofabitch Red Mohawk before they get here.'

'Why the fuck do we need the FBI?' a voice in the audience called out.

'We don't,' said O'Grady. 'Our standard line is that we're going to offer them every possible courtesy. But my off-the-record message to each and every one of you is this; make sure the hundred thousand dollars goes in one of *your* pockets. And don't tell the FBI anything about it. They probably frown on this sort of thing. Let's solve this one on our own and dish out some good old fashioned B Movie justice!'

O'Grady expected some rousing cheers from his audience of officers. Instead he noticed that they were all looking to the door on his left. Standing in the doorway with a face as pale as a ghost with a hangover was his secretary Brenda. She was visibly trembling. In the twenty-five years she'd worked in the department he'd never seen her look so nervous. And her hair was uncharacteristically messy. It was tied back in a ponytail, which wasn't unusual but it looked like she'd been in a fight with a randy cat.

'What is it Brenda?' O'Grady asked.

'Chief,' she said, brushing a few stray hairs out of her eyes. 'Daisy Coltrane has just called. She says she's just found Hank Jackson with his head down the toilet in his office.'

O'Grady tutted. 'What's unusual about that?'

'Well, she also found his hands in the till and his feet under the desk, but so far she says she can't find the rest of him anywhere.'

Eight

Clarisse glanced at the mirror on the wall and checked her appearance one final time. Her black negligee was the right kind of classy, just the way Mellencamp liked it. Her bra and thong were visible underneath it, but to get a good look one would still have to stare. And Mellencamp liked a good stare, even if he'd already seen what was on offer a million times before. She'd teased her blonde hair just how he liked it too, and her large barrel curls wouldn't move even in a gale, thanks to an excessive amount of hairspray. She smacked her dark red lacquered lips to make sure her lipstick was on evenly. That would seal the deal. He liked the dark red lipstick. She took a deep breath and knocked twice on his door.

'Come in,' he yelled through the door.

She took a deep breath, turned the doorknob and let herself in, wondering what state she would find him in. Over the years she'd seen him in just about every compromising position known to man, usually involving him with his pants down. Sometimes he was with one girl, other times he had a whole group of them, and on several occasions he'd been on his own. Clarisse was never flustered or fazed by anything she caught him doing, not these days anyway.

His personal bedroom suite consisted of a huge four-poster bed on one side and a built-in Jacuzzi at the rear. He was usually in one or the other. Judging by the direction his shout of *"Come in"* had originated from she guessed he was in his Jacuzzi on the far side of the room. And she was right. There he was, leaning back, his large hairy torso visible above the bubbling water. He had a broad smile across his face, with his wispy black goatee wrapped around it. His fat bald head was sweating profusely.

'Hi Clarisse,' he beamed. 'What can I do for you?'

'They mentioned you on the news this morning,' she replied.

'Did they? What for?'

'Said you'd offered a reward for the capture of that guy they're calling the Red Mohawk.'

His eyes fluttered briefly. 'Oh *yes*, that's good. Keep going.' He breathed heavily, leaning his head back.

Clarisse saw the back of a young dark haired girl pop up from beneath the water in front of him. 'What's that?' the girl asked.

'I said keep going.' Mellencamp pushed her head back under the water with his left hand.

Clarisse closed the door behind her and walked over to the Jacuzzi, stopping three feet away.

'There's something else you need to know though,' she said.

'Good. *Good.* Go on.'

'One of the girls is pregnant.'

Mellencamp didn't respond for a few moments. He closed his eyes and pulled a face reminiscent of someone who'd taken a swig from a bottle of vinegar. Clarisse recognised the look. He was on the verge of ejaculating, probably into the mouth of Jasmine, the girl beneath the water.

Clarisse watched his expression change a few times until finally his jaw dropped and his eyes slowly opened. A sure sign that he was done. He reached over to his right and felt around until his hand settled on a glass of cognac on the side of the Jacuzzi. He picked it up and took a long sniff of it.

Jasmine resurfaced from under the water and began pushing her hair back from her face and wiping some bubbles away. She turned and caught sight of Clarisse.

'Hi Clarisse,' she said, blinking.

'Hi Jasmine.'

Mellencamp took a sip of cognac and then lurched across the hot bubbling water to the side nearest Clarisse. He leaned over the edge and looked up at her, his lower half still under the water, bubbles dripping down his hairy chest. 'What were you saying?' he asked.

'Can we talk in private?' Clarisse asked.

Mellencamp looked back at Jasmine. 'You're gonna have to go back down,' he said.

Jasmine frowned. 'Huh?'

Mellencamp grinned at her and pointed down at his ass, which was just below the water and rather suspiciously was surrounded by more bubbles than any other part of the Jacuzzi. Jasmine's lip curled into a sneer as she glanced down at it.

'Hurry up,' said Mellencamp. 'Me and Clarisse need to talk in private.'

Jasmine took a deep breath and once more disappeared beneath the water, in the direction of Mellencamp's butt.

Clarisse knew that Jasmine would come back up for air soon enough so she got to the point quickly. 'One of the girls is pregnant,' she repeated.

'Pregnant?' Mellencamp lifted his glass of cognac towards his mouth again. 'Which one?'

'Baby.'

The look on his face made it hard to tell what he was thinking. On the one hand, Clarisse knew for sure that the news of Baby's pregnancy would have angered him, but she also had to take into consideration that he had Jasmine's tongue wiggling around up his butt.

His eyes twitched a few times before he eventually responded. 'How do you know she's pregnant? Who told you?'

'*She did.* After she threw up on a client.'

'She *threw up* on a client? Oh for fucks sake!' His mood visibly darkened, in spite of the rimming. 'Any idea who the father is?'

'She said she doesn't know.'

'You believe that?'

'I believe *she* believes it.'

'Okay, so call the doctor in.'

'She wants to keep it.'

Mellencamp placed his drink back down. At that moment Jasmine resurfaced from the water behind him. He threw her a stern glare, which resulted in her taking a deep breath and disappearing back down behind him in a hurry. He looked back up at Clarisse. 'I don't give *a fuck* what Baby wants,' he growled. 'She can't keep it. Call Bob and get him in to sort it out this afternoon.'

Clarisse grimaced. 'Bad news,' she said. 'Doctor Bob is on vacation. He and Julie have gone out of town for a while. They won't be back for a fortnight.'

'Well can someone else do it?'

'Only the hospital in Lewisville.'

Mellencamp scowled, then juddered momentarily as Jasmine no doubt hit a sensitive spot beneath the bubbles. 'Not for Baby,' he said. 'She can't go to the hospital.'

'Well there's one guy who works at the hospital who also runs a private practice on the side. His name is Dr Chandler. He won't do house calls outside of Lewisville but he is discreet. At the right price.'

'So what, Baby would have to go to Lewisville?'

'Yeah. If you're that desperate to get it done now then it'll have to be done out of town.'

Mellencamp sighed. 'Fucking hell.'

Clarisse shrugged apologetically. 'She's going to be out of action for a while either way. I think the sooner we get it done the better. The longer we leave it, the more determined she'll be to keep it.'

Jasmine resurfaced once more. She wiped some bubbles away from her nose and looked at Mellencamp with pleading eyes, hoping not to have to go down again. He reached over and stroked her face, then leant back and kissed her on the cheek before waving her away.

As she climbed out of the bath his eyes lingered on her naked ass as he mulled over what to do about the current situation. Eventually he turned back to Clarisse.

'Fine,' he said. 'But tell her she's going to hospital for some scans or something. Let her think we're allowing her to keep the baby. But get Arnold to take her. Tell him to make sure the doctor understands what needs to be done, you know, in case this Chandler fella thinks it's immoral or something. Arnold will make him understand what he's got to do.'

'Arnold? Are you sure you don't want one of the other guys to do it?'

'Positive. Arnold's a ruthless cunt. If the doctor needs a little gentle persuasion, Arnold will do it with pleasure.'

'I know that, but Baby and Arnold don't get on, remember?'

Mellencamp picked up his drink and took another sip. 'You said she wants to keep the baby. And I know what a pain in the ass she can be when she wants something, so get Arnold to take her.'

Clarisse couldn't believe what she was hearing. 'You haven't forgotten what he did to her last year, have you?'

Mellencamp stood up and moved back to his original spot at the back of the Jacuzzi, carrying his glass of cognac with him. He sat back down and leant back against the side. 'With Arnold,' he said. 'Baby will know that if she tries to do anything stupid like run away again, he'll make her wish she hadn't. So *get Arnold to take her.*'

Nine

Jack Munson and Milena Fonseca caught a two-hour flight to a naval airbase thirty miles from Grimwald's Mental Asylum. The guys at the base were expecting them and a few of them already knew Munson. He was handed the keys to a brand new Mercedes Benz and within five minutes of landing they were on the road and headed to the asylum. Munson had insisted on driving even though he knew that Fonseca was concerned that he had been drinking. So he was pleased when she didn't protest.

They hadn't had much chance to discuss anything on the plane. Munson had deliberately created a fuss about wanting the plane's flight attendant to bring him a bacon sandwich and then complained when he'd been given ketchup instead of brown sauce. By the time they landed he had downed three more cups of coffee. With the caffeine and food in his belly he felt like he was sober enough to deal with Fonseca. And his mood had lightened a little. So by the time they were cruising down a quiet country lane that led to Grimwald's he was finally ready to indulge in some getting-to-know-you banter.

'You want to ask me something don't you?' he said.

'I've been asking you questions for twenty minutes,' Fonseca replied. 'You've just been ignoring me.'

'I was kind of zoned out, not deliberately being rude.'

Fonseca sighed, but chose not to argue. 'Pincent never told me the full story of why you were placed on indefinite leave,' she said bluntly.

Munson didn't take his eyes off the road. And for an inappropriately long time he considered not answering her. Eventually though, when she had almost given up hope of getting a reply from him he responded to her question with one of his own.

'How did you end up as Pincent's boss?'

'He had some problems.'

'Like what?'

'Family stuff.'

'Devon doesn't have a family.'

'That's his problem.'

Munson knew what she meant. 'You got any family?' he asked.

'Yes, but I don't discuss them.'

'That's a good way to be in this business. A spouse and kids will get you in trouble, make you a target.'

'I know,' said Fonseca defensively. 'This isn't my first day on the job.'

'So Pincent's family problem. Has he ever talked to you about it?'

'No, but that's because I don't like to talk about other people's families any more than I like to talk about my own. But if you mean do I know about wife and kids being murdered, then yes I do. And from what I can see he's never gotten over it or fully accepted it.'

'Hardly surprising though is it? I mean it's a hard thing to deal with. It ripped him apart back in the day. He's not been the same since,' said Munson remembering how distraught his friend had been upon discovering that he had lost his entire family in one afternoon. 'I think he copes with it very well though. The agency should cut him a little slack.'

'These days Pincent is the only one in the department who gets cut any slack at all,' said Fonseca with a touch of bitterness creeping into her voice.

'What do you mean by that?'

'The reason I got promoted above him is because he was caught using government resources for his own personal agendas. Quite how he didn't get fired I'll never know. Anyone else would have been out the door in a flash.'

Munson took his eye off the road for a moment and glanced across at Fonseca for the first time since they had left the airport. 'What was he doing?' he asked.

'It would be unprofessional of me to say.'

'How so?' Munson asked, concentrating on the road ahead once more.

'You wouldn't want me discussing your personal problems with everyone else would you?'

'I couldn't give a shit. Come on, what was Devon doing that he shouldn't?

'Sorry buddy, but it's classified,' said Fonseca with a cursory smile. 'But seeing as you couldn't give a shit what people say about you, how about you tell me why you got sent out to pasture? Your file says nothing about it. In fact, your file doesn't say much about anything.'

'You know why that is?'

'No. That's why I'm asking.'

'It's classified.'

Fonseca tried a different approach. 'You know there's a lot of rumours going around the department about what it was that made you start drinking.'

'I said I don't want to talk about it.'

'I know, but rumours have a habit of generating into something completely over the top. I'd just like to hear your side of the story.'

Munson breathed in hard through his nostrils. 'Give it up,' he growled.

'Fair enough,' said Fonseca, lightening her tone a little. 'But just know this. Pincent's days in the department are numbered. After you and I clean up this latest mess of his, he's history. He knows it too. But you, if you want any more jobs like this tossed your way, you're going to have to be more open than this, because you'll be reporting in to me.'

'I won't be reporting in to anyone. I'll be going straight back to my retirement once this job is done,' said Munson.

'That's probably for the best,' said Fonseca staring out of her side window. 'They don't have guys like you in the department any more. None that I've seen anyway.'

'That's why they called me The Ghost. If there is anyone like me in the department these days, you'd never see them. They'd be a ghost.'

'I would know about them though. I can assure you.'

'And I can assure you, you wouldn't. Do you know what was special about my appearance in Pincent's office today?'

'No, what?'

'It's the first time I ever showed up there as myself. On every other occasion I've been into that building I've been in disguise as either a cleaner, a bearded hostage negotiator, an accountant, you name it. Guys like me are kept at a safe distance from people like you.'

Fonseca looked surprised. The look quickly changed to one of scorn however. 'Bullshit,' she sneered. 'You would never have got into the building without my authorisation today.'

'That's because I'm history Milena. There will be other guys now, doing all the dirty jobs I used to do. And you will never know who they are.'

'Trust me. I'll know. Times have changed since your jolly boys club Jack. There are no secrets any more. Not at my pay grade.'

'Oh but there are. At your pay grade there are some things that you *can't* know about.'

'I'm high enough to know everything.'

'That's where you're mistaken sweetheart. You're now *too high* to know everything. When you got promoted above Pincent it put you at a level where you cannot know everything. Because if you knew half the shit that was going on beneath you, you'd be fired and charged with treason. Guys like me and Pincent protect you from that. You coming along on this mission is just about the dumbest thing you could have done. You're going to see shit that will stick to you for the rest of your career. And you won't be able to report it because you're already in too deep.'

Fonseca smiled. 'You have no idea what you're talking about. Like I said, times have changed. Modern day agents don't make bad jokes and inappropriate wisecracks for starters.'

'I bet they do when you're not around.'

Fonseca's cell phone rang and Munson was appalled to discover that her ring tone was *As Long As You Love Me* by The Backstreet Boys. She took the call and spoke in hushed tones for the next five minutes to someone who Munson assumed was her boyfriend, or husband. She wore no rings on her fingers that might indicate she was in a relationship. In fact, Fonseca wore no jewellery of any kind. Just smart but plain black clothes. She wasn't giving much away at all, apart from the fact that she was a fan of The Backstreet Boys.

She ended the call abruptly when up ahead on the left of the road the formidable sight of Grimwald's Mental Asylum came into view. It was a hulking grey stone building set in the middle of a huge country estate. It was like looking at a medieval castle. Those walls would be hiding a million horrible stories, involving a vast number of insane individuals.

'This is the place,' said Munson. 'The former home of Joey Conrad. You sure you want to go through with this? Because it's not too late for you to get a cab home you know?'

'Oh I'm ready,' said Fonseca. 'You just wait. I'm full of surprises.'

Ten

The Alaska Roadside Diner wasn't especially busy. It wasn't in Alaska either, much to the bemusement of anyone who arrived there from out of town. It was in B Movie Hell and it was the second most successful roadside Diner after the local McDowell's. There were a few folks eating in the booths by the windows and a couple of loners eating breakfast at the counter. In spite of the lack of numbers, The Alaska was unusually noisy because everyone in there was talking, mostly about the murder of Pete Neville.

The waitress, Candy, a curvy blonde forty-something in a pink and white uniform that was two sizes too small, took a food order from a couple of guys in one of the window booths and made her way around the counter to the cooking area out back. The boss, Reg was flipping burgers while watching the news on a small square portable television. It was a TV that he'd hung on the wall himself a few years earlier. Reg wasn't much of a handy man so the TV was tilted ever so slightly to one side. It annoyed Candy and even though it probably annoyed Reg, he was too stubborn to ever admit it, so it remained there at a slight angle. The lop-sidedness of it made the scrolling bar at the bottom of the news channel look as if the words were going to spill out of the bottom corner of the screen. Reg was staring at (and attempting to read) the words as they scrolled across. His foot-high chef's hat was sliding off his head ever so slowly as he leaned further to read the scrolling bar. Candy crept up behind him and straightened it for him to prevent it from sliding off completely.

Reg was a balding red-faced fifty-year old with a belly that provided customers with the evidence that he enjoyed his own burgers. He covered his baldness underneath his beloved chef hat and overcompensated further by cultivating a thick bushy brown moustache underneath his nose. He had a thick growth of chest hair too which was protruding over the top of the white string undershirt he was wearing. And by ten o'clock every morning his baggy blue jogging bottoms had formed a sweat patch right up the butt crack. To look at him one would never know that he used to be a fine sportsman and a very accomplished marksman on the rifle range. These days he was an unhealthy sweaty blob. Candy reminded him of it constantly but he didn't appear to give a shit.

She squeezed past him and pulled a handful of post-it notes with details of food orders on them out from the pouch on the front of her pink apron. She stuck them slap bang in the middle of the TV screen that Reg was staring at, covering as much of it as she could. It was a guaranteed way to grab his attention. And to annoy him. Reg worked faster when he was agitated about something.

'Got a real strange guy out there,' she said. 'Table six, cheeseburger, fries and a coke.'

'What's strange about that?' Reg asked, peeling the post-it notes off the television.

'He's talking to himself.'

'Lots of people do that. I talk to myself all the time when you're not around.'

'I know, I hear you all the time.'

'So what's the big deal?'

'This guy asked his imaginary friend if he wanted anything to eat.'

Reg took his eyes off the television and glanced over at her. 'Okay so he's a bit nuts. As long as he pays for his food and his friend's imaginary milkshake who cares?'

'Well, if other customers pick up on it, they might leave.'

Reg looked back up at the news and began sticking the post-it notes up on the wall above the grill without paying much attention to what he was doing. 'Personally,' he said. 'I think most people would rather be in here with a fruitloop who talks to himself than out on the streets. According to the news there's been another murder this morning.'

Candy looked up at the television. 'Anyone we know?' she asked.

'They haven't given a name out, but apparently it's someone who works at Hank Jackson's used car lot.'

'The only person who works there is Hank Jackson though, isn't it?'

'Yep.'

'So Hank is dead?'

Reg flipped over a burger on the griddle with his rusty silver spatula. 'You should be a detective,' he said.

'Oh God, my friend Patty dated him for a while. She said he had terrible flatulence, but apart from that he was nice a guy.'

'Well he probably still is, but from what they're saying on the news, he's a nice guy with no head. Or hands. Or feet.'

Candy felt her stomach turn. She feared she might throw up for a second and put her hand to her mouth just in case. 'You are kidding right?' she gasped.

'Nope.'

'Seriously? They cut off his hands and feet as well as his head?'

'*They?*'

'You know what I mean. The killer.'

'Yep. An eyewitness saw the masked fella drive off in one of the cars from the lot.'

'That's shocking. He killed him just for a car?'

Reg shrugged and flipped another burger over on the griddle. It made a loud sizzling noise and a puff of smoke blew up in his face. He coughed as he waved his hand in front of his face to clear the air. 'Knowing Hank Jackson like I do,' he spluttered, 'I should imagine he did something stupid like pull a gun on the guy.'

'Does he own a gun?'

'I dunno. He might do.'

Candy felt the reality of the murders more now that there had been a second. This was no freak occurrence. Someone was actively beheading innocent people around town. Everyone had a reason to be scared. 'I don't think I'm going to sleep tonight,' she said.

'Someone will get him soon,' said Reg.

'How can you know that?'

'Benny called and said that Silvio Mellencamp is offering a reward for anyone who catches this guy, dead or alive. There's plenty of folks who'll want a piece of that money.'

'Well I know what *I'd* do if I saw the killer,' said Candy. 'I'd start running and I wouldn't look back. Hank Jackson should have run too, or called the police.'

'Be hard to call the cops while you're having your head cut off I suppose,' Reg suggested.

'You're not funny.'

'I don't care.'

Candy looked up at the television again. 'Do the cops have any idea about the identity of the killer yet?' she asked.

'They showed a mocked up picture of him just now,' said Reg. 'The mask he wears is fuckin' horrible. It's this big yellow rubber thing with a red stripe of hair down the middle of it.'

'Does he have any other distinguishing features?'

Reg lowered his head and peered quizzically at her over a pair of imaginary spectacles. 'The mask wouldn't be enough for you to recognise him?' he said.

'Don't be a dick,' Candy snapped. 'I mean if he's not wearing the mask how would you know it's him?'

Reg turned back to the TV. 'The car he stole is a yellow stock car with a red stripe down the middle. If you *can't* spot a guy in a yellow and red mask driving around in a yellow and red car you deserve to get your head cut off. This guy is just asking to get caught.'

Candy cast her mind back to the last time she had driven past Hank Jackson's car lot. It was a few weeks earlier when she was looking for a car for her son to learn to drive in. 'I think I remember seeing that car,' she said. 'My son wanted it. He thought it looked cool. I thought it was a death trap. Now I suppose it really is.'

Reg didn't hear her, or he was taking no notice. He pointed up at the TV again. 'There he is,' he said. 'That's the guy.'

Candy looked back up at the TV. The mocked up image of the killer was on the screen with the caption – RED MOHAWK: DO NOT APPROACH THIS MAN.

She stared hard at the picture on the screen for a few seconds, taking the image in. She recognised the clothes the killer was wearing.

Black jeans and a shiny red leather jacket.

Her jaw dropped and she steadied herself by pressing a hand down hard on Reg's shoulder.

'That's the guy in the diner who's talking to himself,' she said.

Eleven

Baby had a quick shower and threw on a pair of light blue jeans and a grey sweatshirt. As she tied her hair back into a ponytail she thought about the plan she had spent the last few days formulating. So far it was going well. Doctor Bob, the guy who normally carried out abortions had gone on vacation to Fiji for two weeks. This was the window of opportunity she had been waiting for.

When Kevin Sharp had showed up that morning, she knew she had found an unwitting accomplice for her plan. While he waited nervously on the bed for her, she had nipped into the bathroom and poured a small amount of syrup of ipecac down her throat. Quite a few of the girls at The Beaver Palace used the stuff regularly to help keep their weight down. Baby had used it to make herself vomit over Kevin Sharp, thereby alerting Clarisse to the situation. And it had worked perfectly. Clarisse had automatically assumed that Baby was pregnant and not bothered to watch her take a test, which was normal practice if a girl claimed to be knocked up.

Several months earlier one of the other girls had fallen pregnant and foolishly declared that she wanted to keep the baby. Dr Bob was called and the girl's abortion was carried out the same morning before word of her protest spread. Baby had correctly surmised that she would receive the same treatment. But with Dr Bob out of town, Baby was being taken on a hastily arranged road trip to Lewisville. This would provide her with a rare opportunity to escape from The Beaver Palace and B Movie Hell all together. If she blew this opportunity, she might never get another.

The first road bump in her plan came when she discovered that Arnold had been chosen to drive her there. He had beaten her black and blue less than a year earlier after she had refused to play a particularly dangerous sex game with him. The two of them had not spoken since. Clarisse had seen to it that Arnold was not allowed anywhere near Baby from that moment on. So the fact he had been chosen to drive her to Lewisville indicated that if she did try to make a break for it, the punishment could be quite severe.

She had barely finished tying up the laces on her sneakers when Clarisse popped her head around the door and told her it was time to go. One of the younger male security guards marched her out to the front of the palace.

Arnold was waiting for her in a black Mercedes Benz E-class. The engine was running and the front passenger door was open. Baby

54

climbed in and closed the door without looking at Arnold. The road ahead would be long and probably quiet.

The two of them didn't speak for the first ten minutes of the journey. Baby made a point of either staring straight ahead or out of the side window. The Mercedes was one of approximately twenty that belonged to Silvio Mellencamp. It had dark tinted windows like all of his cars (apart from the convertibles). No one on the outside world would know that she was inside.

Her heart was pounding hard in her chest as she tried to figure out a way to manipulate Arnold into letting her out of the car. She also had to pick the right time, a time when an escape route presented itself. She wished she knew B Movie Hell better, but her trips out of The Beaver Palace had been far too infrequent for her to ever establish her whereabouts.

'Have we got enough gas to get where we're going?' she asked.

Arnold ignored her. In her head she counted to ten, then tried again.

'Are you hungry?' she asked.

He continued to ignore her and stared straight ahead down the highway. He had one giant shovel-sized hand on the steering wheel. His forearms were huge too. The tight black T-shirt he was wearing barely covered half of his huge biceps. His face was worn and leathery from the effects of working outdoors for much of his life. He was one of Mellencamp's henchmen, sometimes working as muscle for hire, other times carrying out jobs in the gardens of the estate. His hair was thick and brown, hanging down by his shoulders. On the surface of it, he looked like a charming ladies man, but as Baby knew only too well he was actually a vicious woman hating bully.

Her inquiry about whether he was hungry had obviously weighed on his mind though, because almost a minute after she had asked the question, he suddenly answered.

'There's a diner up ahead. We can get some food there.'

'Great,' Baby replied. 'I could use the bathroom too.'

For the first time in the journey he took his eye off the road and glanced across at her. 'Don't go getting any ideas,' he said. 'If you're thinking of running off again, I can assure you, you'll wish you hadn't.'

'Why would I want to run off? We're going to the hospital, right?'

'Yeah. But just know this, if you *do* decide to be an idiot and try to run off, you'll put me in a position where I have to hit a pregnant woman, and I don't want to have to do that. But if you make me –

'I won't. I promise.'

'Right.'

Arnold turned his attention back to the road ahead. To further cement that the conversation was over, he reached down and turned on the car stereo. The two of them sat listening to a song on the radio and ignored each other for a few minutes. As the song drew to a close and the disc jockey began talking over the last few bars, Baby spotted the diner up ahead on the right. She pointed out to it.

'Is this where we're stopping?' she asked.

'Yeah. The Alaska Roadside Diner,' said Arnold, slowing the car down.

There were five cars, a white Fed Ex van and a red pickup truck parked out in front of the diner. Arnold pulled into a space between the red pickup and a yellow stock car with a red stripe that ran from the front of its hood up to the windscreen and then across the roof and along the trunk. He glanced across at it and muttered something about it being *"a cunt's car"*.

The deejay on the radio announced that there was a newsflash coming up. Arnold didn't wait to hear it. Instead he switched the engine off, killing the radio at the same time. He opened his door and climbed out. He didn't close the door, but leaned back in and looked at Baby. A strong breeze outside blew his greasy hair across his face. 'What are you waiting for?' he asked.

'I didn't want to jump straight out,' she replied. 'In case you thought I was going to run off, you know, like you said earlier?'

'Just get out of the fucking car.'

He didn't sound in the mood for any more backchat so she opened the door and climbed out. She surveyed the area around them. There was nothing to see but the never-ending highway that stretched all the way to the horizon and a wide-open expanse of grassy fields on the other side of the road. Arnold was staring at her like he knew exactly what she was thinking. His eyes were daring her to make a run for it. This definitely wasn't the right time. She would have to be patient and pick a moment when he was distracted or vulnerable. She desperately hoped that such a moment would come.

Arnold slammed her door shut for her and grabbed a hold of her left arm. He marched her up to the diner's entrance. His grip on her arm was tight, almost tight enough to leave a red mark. To any onlookers though, it could easily appear that they were a couple and he was maybe just a tad possessive. As Arnold pushed open the glass door at the entrance, Baby took one last glance back at the road and the cars in the parking lot hoping that it might provide her with some inspiration.

The red pickup truck might offer an escape route she decided. If only she could find a way of hiding in the back of it.

Arnold hauled her through the door into the diner. Baby hoped she might see some cops having lunch, or maybe someone who looked like they would help her out if she created an argument with Arnold. There were two young men both wearing light blue "all-in-one" mechanic's overalls. She recognised them as regular visitors to The Beaver Palace. They were sitting at a table on the far side of the diner. These two guys were known as the *Friday night* types. The kind of guys that would finish work, drink themselves senseless in a local bar and then if they didn't strike lucky with any local girls, they headed to The Beaver Palace. One of them, the larger of the two, who she knew only as Skidmark, had been extremely rough with her on his last visit. The memory of his open hand being thrust into her face flashed through her mind and she looked away hoping not to make eye contact with him, or his buddy Termite.

Sitting in a booth by the window on his own was a guy she didn't recognise. He was in his early twenties and was wearing a really cool shiny red leather jacket. His face was chiselled and unshaven and he had wavy brown hair. He was staring down at the menu on the table, but as she looked over at him he glanced up. He stared right at her, his gaze suggesting he didn't welcome her staring back at him. His eyes were dark and pierced right through her. She looked away, embarrassed, and scanned the rest of the room. Everyone else in the diner either smiled or nodded in acknowledgment at Arnold. Everyone in B Movie Hell seemed to know him well and therefore probably knew not to cross him. The only customer who didn't acknowledge him was the guy in the red jacket.

Arnold yanked hard at her arm and pulled her towards the counter with him. He grabbed a stool and pulled it out.

'We're sitting up here,' he said, gesturing for her to sit on the stool.

She hopped up onto it. Arnold grabbed another stool from further down the counter and dragged it over, then sat himself on it right next to her. He pressed his hand into her back forcing her to face straight ahead and not look at any of the other customers. There was no sign of any waiter or waitress behind the counter so Arnold shouted loudly in the direction of the kitchen out back.

'YO CANDY! ANY CHANCE OF SOME SERVICE?'

There was a delay before a woman's voice shouted back from the kitchen area. 'Be right with you Arnie!'

Baby leant across and prodded Arnold in the arm, knowing that he hated to be prodded. It was time to provoke him into an argument in public. 'Arnold,' she said coyly.

'What?'

'I want to keep the baby.'

Arnold took a deep breath through his nostrils and picked up a menu from the counter. The look on his face, and a slight twitch underneath his eye gave a good indication of his anger at her for mentioning her pregnancy out loud in a public place.

'Shut up,' he said quietly but firmly.

'But –

Before Baby could antagonise him further a waitress bounded out of the kitchen area and headed over to them. She was a buxom forty-something lady in a pink apron with big curly blonde hair. A plastic badge on her left breast had the name Candy on it in black lettering. She smiled politely at Baby. But, when Baby smiled back Candy jerked her neck in the direction of the booths by the window. When Baby didn't react, she threw a glance in the same direction and then stared back at her wide-eyed. Baby frowned, so Candy repeated the actions again, all the while maintaining a fake smile. Baby looked over at the booths. Candy seemed to be trying to draw attention to the guy in the shiny red jacket who was sitting on his own. He was staring right back at Baby like he hadn't taken his eyes off her from before. His stare was still menacing and unpleasant so she blinked and diverted her eyes back towards Candy, who by now had stopped jerking her neck and glancing at the booths, but was still maintaining her blatantly fake smile. Arnold missed the whole incident because he was studying the menu closely, running his finger down the list of different burgers available.

Candy shook her head, sighed and turned her attention to Arnold. 'Hi Arnold,' she said, 'What can I get for you?'

Arnold stopped running his finger down the menu when he spotted what he wanted. 'Here,' he said. 'I'll have the Double Boobie burger, with no salad, large fries and a black coffee.'

He put the menu down on the counter and glanced up at Candy to see if she had taken down the order. Candy did the same thing she had done to Baby. She jerked her neck subtly in the direction of the guy in the corner booth and threw a glance his way. It was wasted on Arnold.

'Did you get that?' he snapped. 'Double Boobie burger--

Candy took a step back away from the counter. Her nostrils flared and her bottom lip trembled. The blood seemed to drain from her face in a matter of milliseconds. Her pen and notepad slipped from her hands and fell to the floor as she began edging slowly back towards the kitchen area. She was staring at the booth in the corner. Baby turned her neck slowly to see what had gotten Candy so flustered. What she saw made her blood turn cold.

The man in the red jacket had slipped a rubber mask over his head. It was a yellow mask with two large eyeholes and a red strip of hair along the top of it. He slid out from the booth and stood up. Suddenly nothing else in the world seemed to be moving. For the first time since arriving in the diner Baby became aware of the music blaring out of a Wurlitzer jukebox in the far corner by the washrooms. Gogol Bordello was singing a song called *Start Wearing Purple.*

As the masked man took his first steps towards her, it finally dawned on Baby that she was staring at the vicious killer the police had dubbed The Red Mohawk. He stood well over six feet tall. In his right hand he was holding a shiny silver meat cleaver by his side. The sun coming through the window glinted off the sharp edge of it. Baby watched in stunned bewilderment as this hulking figure of a man walked towards her and Arnold. He grew bigger with every step he took, blocking out more of the light coming in through the windows with each passing moment. He stopped directly behind the unsuspecting figure of Arnold and lifted the blade slowly up from his side.

Arnold still hadn't seen him. And by this point he was the only person in the diner who hadn't. It took the wielding of the blade above Arnold's head to spark the rest of the diner's customers into life. Everyone seemed to scream out at once, all warning Arnold of what was to come.

He turned to see what the fuss was all about, but it was already too late. As he laid eyes on the horrific masked figure looming over him, the silver meat cleaver in the masked man's hand made a swooshing sound as it crashed down onto the counter.

Although the world continued spinning, everything in the diner had begun to move in slow motion. A momentary silence that seemed to last an eternity finally came to an end when Arnold let out an almighty scream of agony. And everything and everyone went batshit crazy. The diner erupted like everyone in it had been thrown from a rollercoaster.

Baby's eyes bulged in terror. Her plans to escape from Arnold had vanished. Her thoughts were now only of escape from the masked man with the meat cleaver. Should she run straight away, or wait a second and hope not to draw attention to herself? And why the hell was she even thinking about it when she should already be running? The blade had come down on Arnold's left hand. It sliced off all of his fingers and the top of his thumb.

The other customers leapt up from their seats and began rushing for the exits. Candy screamed and raced out back. Arnold made a choking sound as he lifted his severed hand up and stared wide eyed at it, disbelieving of what he was seeing. What remained of his hand shook as if the weight of it were too much, which was ridiculous. Life drained out of him, as blood gushed from the holes where his fingers used to be. His face had gone pale and his eyes were wide and glassy. And then, as if he'd finally realised that most of his hand had just been chopped off, he screamed wildly.

The two Friday night guys from the window booth rushed to Arnold's aid. Skidmark dived bravely onto the masked man's back, throwing his arms around him and attempting to drag him away from Arnold. The masked man lowered his head, pressed his chin into his chest momentarily and then smashed it back into Skidmark's face. Even with all the screaming, thundering of fleeing footsteps and Gogol Bordello singing *Start Wearing Purple*, Baby still heard the sound of Skidmark's nose breaking. He slid off the masked man's back and staggered back, his nose like a bloody spout. The masked killer turned and with one swift swing of his already bloodied meat cleaver, sliced open Skidmark's stomach from one side to the other. Blood spilled out through the ten-inch long gash and Skidmark doubled over, his hands instinctively grabbing his belly and trying to hold his guts in. He crumpled to the floor as his attacker nonchalantly flicked some blood off the blade and squared up to Termite. Skidmark's buddy froze in horror at the ruthless attack that had been carried out on his friend.

The look on Termite's face soon changed from terrified to bewildered when The Red Mohawk gently tossed his meat cleaver over to him. It took the young mechanic by surprise but he managed to catch it by its handle. He stared at the blood on the blade and then looked back up just in time to see the Red Mohawk slam his right fist into his face. From her seat at the bar, Baby got a clear view of the whites of Termite's eyes as his pupils slid upwards. He fell backwards and the meat cleaver slid from his hand, joining him in a race to hit the floor.

Throughout all of this, Arnold had kept staring at his mangled hand and screaming. The masked murderer reached down and picked up his meat cleaver and turned back to face Baby and Arnold. He took two steps towards them then reached out and grabbed a handful of the thick hair on top of Arnold's head, which only caused Arnold to scream even more. He yanked it hard and hauled Arnold back off his stool.

Arnold landed with a thud on the floor on his backside. He held up his bloody stump of a hand in defence. The Red Mohawk yanked hard on his hair with his clenched fist and dragged him back across the floor of the diner.

Arnold's eyes rolled around in in his head, unable to focus on anything as he was dragged past the dead bodies of Skidmark and Termite. He yelled out again, only this time he made more than just agonised screams. 'BABY!!!' he bellowed. 'HELP ME!!!'

Even if she had wanted to help him, she couldn't have. There was nothing she could do to stop the psycho with the meat cleaver from dragging him towards the Men's washroom on the far side of the diner. Arnold kicked and screamed with every last ounce of strength he could muster, but it was to no avail. His attacker kicked the door of the washroom open with the heel of his right boot and backed into it, dragging Arnold through with him, screaming and crying like a hysterical chimp.

As the door swung shut behind them and Arnold's agonised screams became muffled, Baby realised she was the only person left in the diner. She heard the sound of car engines starting up outside as other customers fled. And then she heard Gogol Bordello again.

Start wearing purple!

Baby often felt like the lyrics from her favourite songs were speaking to her, offering her important life advice, but *start wearing purple?* That was not helpful in the current situation. She needed to think for herself. She knew this was the opportunity she had been waiting for, her big chance to escape to the real world. It hadn't panned out anything like how she had imagined it would, but when God answers your prayers and gives you an opportunity to grab the gift you want most above all else in the world, you've got to take it, no matter how ugly the wrapping paper is.

Baby had no desire to hang around and become the next victim of the Red Mohawk. It didn't sound like it was going to take long for him to finish slicing up Arnold in the washroom. So without waiting for a second invitation she jumped off her stool and ran out through the front door and into the parking lot.

Twelve

'Well this looks like a fun place,' said Munson, staring up at the front of Grimwald's Mental Asylum. He had to tilt his head right back to see all the way to the top. The building almost disappeared into the clouds above. 'No wonder everyone in here is mental. Look at the place, it's creepy and depressing.'

For the first time that day it looked like Fonseca agreed with him. She too was staring up at the front of the building, ogling the huge grey exterior. Every now and again at unpredictable intervals an unsightly gargoyle of some kind would be protruding out of the brickwork. And on even more infrequent occasions, there was a narrow window.

'It's definitely a shithole,' Fonseca mumbled, half to herself.

The large arched front doors they were standing outside were made of thick oak wood and painted black, adding to the unwelcoming appearance of the place.

They waited for almost a minute after Munson had rattled the large stone door knocker before the doors opened and a man in his mid-twenties greeted them. He wore a light blue tunic and matching trousers. He had curly ginger hair, possibly permed. It was hard to tell without staring inappropriately. He greeted them with a smile as they approached the doors.

'Good afternoon. Can I help you?' he asked.

'Yes,' Fonseca replied. 'I'm Milena Fonseca and this is Jack Munson. You should be expecting us.'

'Yes, of course.' He outstretched a hand. 'Pleased to meet you. My name is Justin.' Fonseca shook his hand. His handshake was very limp.

'Nice to meet you Justin,' she said courteously. 'We've come to see….'

Justin interrupted her. 'About Joey Conrad?'

'Yes, that's right.'

'Good. If you'd both like to step inside, I'll take you to his room.'

Fonseca stepped through the open door into the asylum. Munson followed behind and shook Justin's hand, attempting to crush it for his own amusement. 'Are you Conrad's doctor?' he asked.

Justin winced at the aggressiveness of the handshake. 'No, I'm just a nurse,' he said pulling his hand away. 'His doctor is indisposed at the moment.'

'Who is the doctor?'

'Doctor Carter.'

'And when will he be free?' Munson asked.

Justin paused, then smiled. '*She* will be free in about half an hour, but seeing as time is of the essence she asked me to show you to Joey Conrad's room and assist you in any way you like until she becomes available.'

'Fair enough,' said Munson.

The reception hall inside the building was almost as depressing as the outside. Everything was grey. Grey floor, grey walls, grey ceiling. All it needed was a Morrissey song playing in the background.

'Do you need us to sign in?' Fonseca asked, looking around for some kind of reception desk. The hall was empty with the exception of a small table by a large grey steel door opposite them. The table had a vase on it containing some almost dead flowers.

'No. There's no need to sign in today,' said Justin. 'This way please.' He walked towards the steel door.

'Why don't we need to sign in?' asked Fonseca, standing her ground.

Justin stopped and turned around. 'It was my understanding that your visit here was off the record,' he said. 'You might not want to leave traces of your visit here for others to find at a later date. Correct?'

'That is correct,' said Munson.

Fonseca glanced at Munson. She didn't look convinced. He whispered in her ear. 'We can always sign in on the way out if you still feel strongly about it.'

'I think we should,' she whispered back.

'I bet you ten bucks you change your mind.'

'You're on.'

For the first time the two of them shared a smile, the kind that suggested they both thought they would win the bet rather than any indication that they were warming to each other.

Justin walked ahead and swiped a card through a reader by the steel door. As soon as he heard a loud click he pulled it open. 'This way please,' he said holding the door open for them. Fonseca made her way through first. Munson hung back and tried to drink in everything he was seeing around the place, which wasn't much.

Justin led the way through a maze of dull grey corridors, chuntering away the whole time about various patients who had stayed in each of the rooms they passed. The guy seemed to have a boring anecdote for just about every area of the asylum. It made Munson long for a swig of rum from the bottle he'd stashed in his jacket pocket.

'How exactly did Joey Conrad escape?' he asked bluntly, interrupting one of Justin's pointless tales. The nurse stopped talking in mid-sentence and turned around. He looked somewhat offended by the interruption. Munson took the brief pause as an opportunity to take an extensive look around at the hard stone walls and high ceilings to see if there were any air vents or trapdoors that might be utilised in an escape attempt.

Justin took a moment to respond to the question as if he had more than one possible answer and was inwardly debating which was the best one to give. Eventually he settled on one that sounded surprisingly genuine. 'Our security is crap,' he said.

'I can see that,' said Munson, exchanging a glance with Fonseca who seemed to be in agreement.

Justin offered no further explanation, possibly because he was miffed by Munson interrupting him. Instead he hurried on along the corridor until he eventually took a right turn and led the way up a stone staircase. At the top of the stairs they went through another door and arrived in a corridor that was much darker than all of the others they had seen.

'It's the last door on the left,' Justin said. 'This way. Sorry it's a bit dark, but some of the lights are out up here.'

'No shit,' said Munson.

Justin pulled a large set of keys from his trouser pocket as he led the two investigators along the corridor. He stopped at the last door on the left and flicked through his keys until he found the right one. He unlocked the door and pushed it open.

'There you go,' he said, stepping back out of the way.

Munson walked in first to get a good look. Fonseca followed. There wasn't much to see. It was a very basic single bedroom, more like a prison cell than a living quarters. In the corner was an open door that led into a washroom the size of a cupboard, which consisted of a very standard toilet and a small washbasin. The walls were painted pale blue, as was the floor and the ceiling. Where every other part of the building had been plain grey stone, finally they had found an area with a lick of paint.

'Not exactly five star is it?' Fonseca observed out loud.

'It's not supposed to be,' said Justin poking his head around the door.

Munson absorbed the characteristics of the room in a matter of seconds. There was no visible way of escaping. No windows, no air vents, no grill in the floor. Nothing. And it smelled really bad. He took a second stab at getting some information from Justin. 'So, seriously, how did Joey Conrad escape from this place? If this was really his room then he sure had a long way to travel to get out of the building.'

Justin nodded in agreement. 'Well yeah, but from what we can tell he just walked right out the front door.'

'Walked right out the front door?' Munson repeated aloud.

'Yeah.'

'Walked? Literally just walked out the front door?'

Justin shrugged. 'I guess. I mean I didn't see it. I wasn't on duty when it happened. Maybe he waltzed out. Or moonwalked. Your guess is as good as mine.'

Maybe it was Justin's attitude, or maybe it was just because the air in Joey Conrad's room was a little stale, or maybe it was because Munson was desperate for a swig of rum, but whatever the reason was, he'd decided he didn't like Justin much. The guy was irritating.

'Okay,' said Munson. 'So Joey Conrad moonwalked out of here the other night. Explain to me how no one noticed him and nothing he did set off an alarm.'

'Like I said before, our security is crap.'

Munson took a long hard look at Justin, studying his face to try to gauge if he had something to hide. It didn't look that way. He was probably just a smartass. 'Fine. So the security is crap. Can you elaborate on that for me please?' he probed, challenging the nurse to back up his claim. 'Is it lack of numbers? Poor training? What? Why is security so crap?'

Justin took a deep breath and let out a sigh before replying. 'The asylum doesn't pay well and consequently we have some of the most inept security guards you will ever encounter. It's not usually a problem, because for all their faults they're usually slightly cleverer than the patients.'

'But not in this case?'

'Well, I'm no doctor or psychiatrist, Mr Munson but I'd say this, Joey Conrad, although very strange and occasionally very violent, he's no dribbling idiot.'

'Did you speak to him much?'

'All the time.'

'And?'

'And nothing. He never replied. I don't think he liked me.'

'That's a surprise,' said Munson under his breath.

Fonseca picked her moment to intervene. 'Mind if we have a look through his things?' she asked.

'Be my guest.'

Fonseca walked over to a small chest of drawers beside the bed and pulled open the top drawer. Munson continued to interrogate Justin. 'Did he have any hobbies or anything that set him apart from the others?'

'I don't think so,' Justin replied. He pointed to a portable television that was nailed to the wall in the corner of the room. 'I think he likes movies though. He's one of those who's got his own television and a DVD player. And as far as I know he can operate them just fine on his own.'

There was a shelf on the wall next to the television. It had a row of DVD's stacked upright on it. Munson walked over to get a closer look at them. He ran his finger along the spines of the cases reading the titles as he went. 'That's a pretty odd selection of films for a grown man isn't it?' he commented when he came to the end of the stack.

'Hospital policy,' Justin replied. 'We don't let them have anything unsuitable, like violent or sexy stuff.'

Behind them, Fonseca asked a question. 'Is this his only book?' Munson looked around. She was pointing at a thick red hardback book she had pulled out of the drawer on the bedside table.

'What is it?' Munson asked.

Fonseca pulled a pair of black-rimmed spectacles out of her breast pocket. She slipped them on and opened the book. 'It's the bible,' she said.

'Oh. Boring.'

'As far as I know that is his only book,' said Justin. 'He's not much of a reader.'

Munson turned back to take a closer look at the DVD's. They were all family films. He picked one out and read the back cover. 'This is enough to drive anyone crazy,' he commented.

Fonseca looked up. 'What is it?' she asked.

'High School Musical. He seriously watches this?'

Justin shrugged. 'I don't even know where they get the DVD's from.'

'How do you mean?'

'DVD's, cigarettes, all that kind of stuff. Someone smuggles it in for the patients.'

'And nobody confiscates any of it?' Munson asked, failing to mask his disgust at the apparent lack of discipline in the asylum.

'Like I said, security is pretty slack round here.'

'Actually, you said crap.'

'Crap, slack, there are many ways to describe it. Thing is, if a patient wants to watch High School Musical, it ain't hurting nobody.'

Munson opened the DVD case and looked inside. 'What if it's not High School Musical?' he said holding it up so that Fonseca could see it.

Fonseca peered over her glasses at him. 'What's that?'

'Last action Hero.'

Justin frowned. 'What's wrong with Last Action Hero?'

'It's a terrible film.'

Munson closed the DVD case and put it back. He picked out the next DVD along. It was a copy of *The Incredible Journey*. He flipped it open and took a peek at what was inside, then replaced it and picked up another. He checked inside all six of the DVD's on the shelf. None of them contained the correct disc.

'Anything interesting there?' asked Fonseca.

'Yeah. As well as Last Action Hero, he's got Three Amigos and Galaxy Quest.'

'Any significance to that?' she asked.

'Ever seen any of those films?'

'I think I saw Last Action Hero once, years ago.'

'Shit isn't it?'

'Actually I quite liked it.'

Munson resisted the urge to continue arguing about the quality of the film. 'Well all three of these films have the same plot.'

Fonseca looked puzzled. 'How so?'

'Galaxy Quest. Basically the cast of a Star Trek type show end up in outer space for real, playing the parts of their characters trying to defeat aliens and shit. In Three Amigos, three actors from a TV western end up in the Wild West taking on a real gang of Mexican bandits. And The Last Action Hero was some character that came out of a movie and into the real world.'

Fonseca still looked confused. 'How is this relevant?'

'Relevant?' said Munson. 'To what?'

'To the Joey Conrad case?'

'Oh. It's not. I'm just trying to show you that I know a lot about movies.'

'Why?'

'Because I know a lot about movies.' He noticed that Fonseca now looked completely bewildered, and not amused. 'Also, it might give us some insight into the mental state of Joey Conrad.'

'How?'

'I don't know yet.'

'So it *is* just about showing me that you know a lot about movies?'

'Mostly, yeah. Hey, I've been out of the office for a long time. I miss the banter.'

'Fine. Are we done?' asked Fonseca.

'Actually no,' said Munson. 'There are six DVD's here. I've only told you about three of them.'

'Seriously? You're still going with this?'

'The other three are more interesting,' said Munson.

'They'd better be.'

He pointed at the last three DVD's on the shelf. They were cases for *The Goonies*, *The Wizard of Oz* and *Finding Nemo*. 'Inside these three he's got the films *Halloween*, *The Terminator* and *The Texas Chainsaw Massacre*.'

Justin's cheeks burned red. 'I had no idea he had those,' he said.

Munson ignored him and nodded at the book Fonseca was holding. 'Is that really The Bible? Or is it just a bible cover wrapped around a book about the Manson family?'

Fonseca shook her head. 'Nah,' it's just a bible,' she said, flicking through a few pages to make sure.

Munson slapped Justin gently on the back. 'How long did you say Dr Carter was going to be?'

'About half an hour I think,' Justin replied.

'Go and get her now.'

'She's kind of busy.'

Munson raised his voice a notch. 'Go and get her now so that Agent Fonseca and I can talk about you behind your back.'

Justin swallowed hard and blushed a little more. 'I'll see if I can find her.'

'Don't *see* if you can find her,' said Munson. 'Go and *get* her. *Now!*'

Justin turned on his heels and hurried out of the room. Munson looked at Fonseca. 'I'm no shrink,' he said. 'But Joey Conrad is running around B Movie Hell in a mask slicing people up with a meat cleaver. I'd say some of these films have had an influence on him, wouldn't you?'

'I guess so. I'm not much of a movie fan though in case you hadn't guessed. I'm more into books myself. And I think he was influenced by this one.'

Munson looked at the book in Fonseca's hand. 'The Bible? How so?'

Fonseca turned the book around and held it open for Munson to see. 'There's one passage underlined here,' she said. 'It's a meaningful one.'

68

Munson put the DVD's down on the shelf, walked over to her and grabbed the book out of her hand. Halfway down one of the pages was a passage underlined in red. It was Jeremiah 31:15

Thus says the Lord: "A voice is heard in Ramah, lamentation and bitter weeping. Rachel is weeping for her children; she refuses to be comforted for her children, because they are no more."

When he'd finished reading it he frowned at Fonseca. 'Okay, that means nothing to me,' he said.

'Lucky for you I know a lot about books,' said Fonseca, *'especially this one*. The passage he has underlined could be very significant.'

'Go on.'

'Some people believe that it's a prophecy.'

'About what?'

'The slaughter of the innocents.'

Thirteen

Candy backed through the strip PVC curtain and into the kitchen, put her head down and ran for her life. She didn't get far. After two blindly taken strides her head crashed into Reg's chest. She looked up, her heart racing. Even the sight of her boss made her jump with fright. Reg for his part looked confused. But much to her relief he was carrying his hunting rifle in his right hand. And he'd removed his ridiculously oversized chef's hat.

'What the fuck is all that noise about?' he asked.

'He's gone crazy!'

'Who?'

'Who do you think? The guy I was telling you about, the one in the red jacket. He put the mask on and started killing people. We gotta get out of here!'

Candy attempted to run around Reg to head for the back door. He grabbed a hold of her arm and stopped her in her tracks.

'Is he still out there?'

'He's chopping people up with a meat cleaver. He cut Arnold's hand off!'

'Big Arnold?'

'Yeah.'

Over the sound of the jukebox they both heard a loud scream. It was high pitched, but not enough to be feminine.

'What the fuck was that?' Reg asked.

'Arnold I think. The guy dragged him into the men's room.'

'What for?'

'How should I know?'

'Fuck it,' Reg grumbled softly. He took a deep breath and made a tentative step towards the dining area.

'Did you call the cops?' Candy asked.

'No, I went and grabbed my rifle. I wanted to see the guy for myself first.'

Reg poked his head through the PVC strip curtain and took a look around the dining area.

'Is he still there?' Candy asked.

Reg reeled his neck in and turned to face her. 'There's a girl just run out through the front door,' he said. 'Was she with Arnold?'

'Was she wearing jeans and a grey sweatshirt?'

'Yeah.'

Candy nodded. 'Then yeah, she was with him.'

Reg frowned. '*Shit*. And you think the guy in the mask is still in the washroom with Arnold?'

'With what's *left* of him. Come on let's get the hell out of here before he comes back out!'

'Fuck that,' said Reg. 'You call the cops. I'll deal with this fucker.'

'Shhh!' Candy grabbed a hold of Reg's vest and yanked him back away from the strip curtain. 'I think I heard the door. He's coming back out,' she whispered.

Positioning herself to the side of the curtain where she hoped she couldn't be seen, she peered through it and watched the masked killer walk back out of the washroom. He stepped over the dead bodies of Skidmark and Termite. Then he stopped and stared out of the windows at the front of the diner. The girl who had come in with Arnold was running across the highway towards the open field on the other side. He watched her for a while, but after a few moments he seemed to get the sense that he was being watched and he turned his head towards the kitchen area. Candy didn't need to tug at Reg's undershirt this time. Like her he jumped back out of sight so he couldn't be seen through the curtain.

'What are you going to do?' Candy whispered.

The Gogol Bordello song playing on the jukebox came to an abrupt end, leaving them in silence for the first time since the carnage had begun. Candy whispered again, even quieter than before. 'What are you going to do?'

Reg snapped open his rifle as quietly as he could. He reached into a pocket on his sweatpants and pulled out a cartridge to load into it, his finger trembling with nerves.

'Are you gonna shoot him?'

'No I'm gonna *throw* the rifle at him,' Reg whispered back sarcastically.

'I was only asking.'

Reg snapped his rifle shut. 'Is he still there?'

Candy stuck her neck out to see if the masked killer was still visible through a small gap in the curtain strips. There was no sign of him. She heard the sound of the front door gently closing. Hoping that it was a sign the killer had left she took a few tentative steps towards the curtain. 'I think he's gone,' she whispered, beckoning Reg to follow her.

With no new song coming on the jukebox there was nothing to be heard from the dining area at all. As Candy edged closer to the strip curtain she heard the sound of a car engine starting up outside. She poked her head right through the curtain. Through the window at the front of the diner she saw the yellow stock car with the red stripe had started up. The masked killer was sat behind the steering wheel.

'He's going!' she whispered, much louder this time. 'Quick! Now's your chance.'

Reg barged past her and out into the dining area. 'Call Chief O'Grady,' he ordered. 'Now!'

Candy turned and dashed over to the phone on the wall in the far corner of the kitchen. She picked up the receiver and dialled 9-1-1, all the while straining her neck to see if she could make out what was happening through the gaps in the curtain. Reg had vanished and judging by the sounds of the screeching tyres, the Red Mohawk was reversing onto the highway to make his getaway. She barely noticed the dialling tone kick in on the phone, but she definitely heard a noise from outside. A loud crack. It made her jump. She recognised the sound. It meant that Reg had fired off a shot from his rifle. It echoed loudly even though it came from outside.

Through the sound of the echo she caught the end of a greeting on the other end of the phone. 'What service do you require?'

'Police please.'

'Connecting you now.'

The line went quiet again. Outside Reg fired off another shot from his rifle. This time as well as a loud echo, Candy heard him cursing at something.

A woman's voice spoke out on the other end of the phone. 'B Movie Hell Police, can I help you?'

'Hi yes, this is…..'

Before Candy could finish her sentence she heard a police siren outside. She took a few steps back towards the kitchen area, stretching the telephone cord as far as it would go. A police car, with its siren blaring and blue and red lights flashing, raced past the front of the diner. It was followed by the sound of another gunshot blaring out from Reg's rifle. Candy put the phone back to her ear.

'Hi, sorry about that,' she said. 'I'm calling about a murder at the Alaska Roadside Diner, but a police car has just flown past. I think you guys are already on it.'

'Is that Candy?'

Candy recognised the other woman's voice. 'Yeah, Lucinda, hi. We just had that masked madman in here. He killed at least three people…. I think.'

'Stay calm Candy. We've got a few cars headed your way right now. And at least one car is already in pursuit of the suspect. He won't get far. We'll get him this time.'

'Thanks Luce.'

'Gotta go. My switchboard is lighting up.'

The line went dead. Candy replaced the receiver on the wall and turned around just in time to see Reg walk back into the kitchen holding his rifle. Smoke was drifting gently out of the barrel.

'Any luck?' she asked him.

Reg shook his head.

'Did you miss him completely?'

'Who?'

'The Red Mohawk.'

'Oh him. No, he was half a mile down the road by the time I got out there. I did manage to hit the girl though. Got her in the arm I think. It knocked her down but she got back up and carried on running. After that she was too far away for me to get a clean shot.'

Candy reeled back in shock. 'You shot *the girl?*'

'Yeah.'

'Why?'

'Did you see the birthmark on her face?'

'No. What birthmark?'

'Never mind. Just hand me the phone. I gotta make a call.'

Fourteen

'Okay, so religion ain't exactly my thing,' Munson admitted. 'Tell me, what the fuck is the slaughter of the innocents?'

Fonseca could have revelled in knowing something that Munson didn't, but she was gracious enough not to, even after he had inflicted all his tedious film knowledge on her. Besides, gloating about something she had learned about in Sunday School when she was about eight years old wasn't her style. She showed him the page from the bible that had the underlined passage on it.

'You've heard of King Herod, right?' she said.

'Yeah, I've heard of him, but that's about as far as my knowledge of him goes.'

'Well he was this King a few thousand years ago,' Fonseca said, as if she were explaining the story to a child. 'And when he was told that the son of God had just been born he sent out soldiers to murder all the boys under the age of two years old?'

'Where the hell was this?' Munson asked.

'Bethlehem. Or Jerusalem. I can't remember exactly. It's not that important.'

'It's not?'

Fonseca pulled a phone out from inside her slim black jacket. She used it to take a quick photo of the underlined passage in the bible, and then turned back to Munson. 'To cut a long story short, King Herod was told that a boy had been born in Bethlehem.'

'Or Jerusalem.'

'Do you want to hear this story or not?'

'Go on.'

'Herod was warned that this boy was to become the King of the Jews and would eventually overthrow him. So he sent his men into Bethlehem and ordered them to slaughter all of the boys under the age of two years old.'

'That's stupid.'

'Which part?'

'All of it. It makes no sense. What kind of idiot would order the slaughter of a load of innocent kids?'

'A King, a president, a prime minister….'

'Do you ever get tired of being smug?' Munson interrupted.

'No. Do you?'

'Never. So what does it mean? Are you saying Joey Conrad is intending on killing a bunch of innocent kids?'

'Well at this point we don't even know for sure that it was *him* who underlined it.'

'True,' Munson agreed. 'But let's assume it was him, just for convenience sake. After all, we've not got a lot else to go on here. What would possibly make him want to kill young boys?'

Fonseca shut the book and placed it back in the top drawer of the bedside table. She closed the drawer. 'I think that's a question for his psychiatrist when she gets here,' she said. 'Joey Conrad might not be intending to kill young boys. So far he's only slaughtered an innocent police officer.'

'So *far*,' said Munson thinking hard. 'But this King Herod fella, you say he was only trying to kill the baby Jesus, right?'

'So the bible says.'

'And why did he want to kill Jesus again? I'm struggling with that part. What possible harm could a baby do to a King?'

'Well nothing,' said Fonseca. 'As a baby, Jesus obviously couldn't hurt Herod, or defend himself. But Herod feared he would be a threat when he was a grown man. Far easier to kill him as a baby.'

Munson sniggered.

'What's so funny?' Fonseca asked.

'It's just that it sounds like a rip off of the Terminator if you ask….'

The words had barely fallen out of his mouth before he realised what he had said. Fonseca realised it too.

'What were those films again?' she asked.

'Halloween, Texas Chainsaw Massacre and The Terminator.'

Munson walked back to the DVD's he had been flicking through earlier. Without even picking one up he suddenly spun back around and faced Fonseca, his eyes showing signs of life. Something was going through that hung-over brain of his and it was working fast.

'What is it?' Fonseca asked.

'He killed that cop last night with a meat cleaver, didn't he?'

'Yes. Why?'

'Texas Chainsaw Massacre. The killer's weapon of choice was a meat cleaver.'

'Really, because even though I've never seen it I would have thought his weapon of choice was a chainsaw.'

'Sure, to the uninitiated. But anyone who's seen the film a few times would know that he uses a meat cleaver more often than not, because he's chopping up his victims like meat because he's a cannibal.'

'What's your point?'

'I was just thinking that maybe he's re-enacting parts of these films. He's wearing a mask, that's an obvious one. He's used a meat cleaver, which is slightly less obvious.'

'Maybe more of a tribute,' Fonseca suggested.

'They all wore masks, technically anyway,' Munson pondered aloud. 'I mean the Halloween killer and the Texas Chainsaw guy, they definitely wore masks. And the Terminator was a cyborg with a human face.'

'So the mask is a tribute, and the meat cleaver is a tribute? What are you getting at? I don't see how this is gonna help us catch him?'

'Well the Terminator and the Halloween killer were both hunting for a young woman. The Halloween guy, Michael Myers, turned up in a town called Haddonfield. He was looking for his long lost sister or something. But the Terminator showed up in Los Angeles I think, and he was trying to kill a woman before she gave birth to the saviour of mankind.'

Munson looked like he'd talked himself into a corner and had no idea where his theory was taking him.

'You're clutching at straws,' said Fonseca.

They were interrupted by a woman's voice. 'Actually he might be on to something there.'

Fonseca spun round to see who had spoken. Standing behind her at the entrance to the cell was a lady in her mid thirties. She was wearing a long white coat over a blue tunic. Her long brown hair was scraped back into a ponytail. Her face was pale and narrow, highlighted only by her bright red lipstick. She smiled at them.

'Hi, I'm Dr Carter,' she said. 'We need to talk. There are a few things about Joey Conrad that you should know about.'

Fifteen

Baby raced out into the parking lot. She had no idea what the best direction was to run. She contemplated her earlier plan of hiding in the back of the pickup truck. That was now far too risky and just plain stupid. Her number one priority was to get as far away from the diner as possible. Running along the highway was one option, but if the masked killer had a car it wasn't necessarily the smartest thing to do. She chose instead to run across the road to the open field on the other side.

She couldn't remember the last time she'd sprinted anywhere. But as she rushed across the road she was galloping for all she was worth. Unfortunately she didn't have much in the way of grace as a runner. Her arms and legs flailed around wildly, hindering her progress and tiring her out. In the diner's parking lot all of the other vehicles were pulling away and speeding off down the highway, with the exception of the yellow car with the red stripe and the red pickup truck. The pickup truck may have belonged to Skidmark or Termite. As for the yellow and red stock car, well that was almost certainly the car of the killer.

The field stretched on for as far as she could see. Its tall grass swayed gently in the wind, oblivious to the urgency of everyone and everything around it. As Baby charged through it she could feel it brushing harshly against her ankles. It was almost knee high and made running that little bit more strenuous. Its length also hid just how uneven the ground underfoot was. With every stride she took she felt her feet landing awkwardly, twisting one way or the other. An ankle sprain or a fall was highly likely, but it was a risk she had to take.

She was barely thirty metres into the field when she heard the first gunshot. It rang out loud from a fair distance behind her. She didn't dare look back but she hoped that someone had shot the masked madman.

A gust of wind blew hard in her face as she was attempting to take a deep breath. Oddly the wind seemed to knock the air out of her lungs rather than fill them. She was already slowing down, losing energy and momentum with every stride. She only covered another twenty metres before the second gunshot rang out. It was followed by the sound of a police siren. There seemed to be all kinds of chaos going on behind her, but she had the horrible sensation that if she turned around to take a look she would see the skull-faced psychopath chasing after her. If he was anything like the masked killer in most horror movies he'd be walking really slowly but still catching up with her. She promised herself that if she tripped over she'd do the sensible thing and get straight back up, unlike most of the characters in Slasher movies, who inexplicably start crawling along the ground instead of getting back up and running.

As her breathing became heavier and her legs weaker she feared she wouldn't be able to carry on for much longer. But she was determined to keep going for as long as her stamina would allow.

SNAP!

She didn't know exactly what the sound was but she suddenly felt like someone had hit her across the arm with a hot metal poker. Whatever it was it spun her around. She stumbled and lost her footing completely, turning over on her ankle.

For a short but sickening few seconds all she saw was an endless repetition of

Grass,
Blue sky,
Grass,
Blue sky,
Grass.
THUD
Grass.

She landed face first in the stuff. Fortunately the grass was high enough to hide her from the road. For a few seconds she lay still, stunned by the fall and unsure what caused it. She rolled onto her side, most of her body staying concealed beneath the long grass. Her heart was pounding, and she was still breathing heavily. And she was dizzy from all the flashes of blue sky and grass.

But most of all her arm hurt. Just above the elbow. It felt like a wild animal had taken a bite out of it and now a parasite was sucking away at the blood. She rolled onto her back and stared up into the clear blue sky. The sun was shining brightly. But now her hearing wasn't working quite as well as before. She could still catch the sound of the police siren and maybe even the echo of the gunfire and the wail of screeching tyres. But everything had become blurred and the noises were melding together. But then right *out of the blue* a man's voice spoke clearly and confidently to her.

'*Get up! Run!*' he said. She recognised the voice. In her mind's eye she saw the face of the man who had spoken. He looked serious. He *was* serious. '*Do as you're told,*' he said.

She took a few deep breaths and pressed down on the ground with her good arm to steady herself as she climbed back to her feet. She was all alone in the middle of the field. There was no man in sight. A second bout of major dizziness came over her as she stood up. Her head felt like it was covered in candyfloss, sticky and cloudy. She grabbed at her injured arm in the hopes of brushing away whatever it was that seemed to be causing the pain. The palm of her hand touched on something wet but warm on her sleeve. She looked at her palm and saw that it was covered in blood. *Her blood.* A stream of it was oozing out of a gash in her right arm, just above the elbow. It looked like someone had ripped the sleeve on her sweatshirt open with a rusty knife.

The sight of the blood panicked her. How had it happened? She took a quick look back at the diner. There was no sign of the Red Mohawk but that didn't mean he wasn't around somewhere, maybe hiding in the long grass.

The diner seemed a long way off in the distance now. The yellow car with the red stripe was gone. In its place standing and staring at her was an old guy in a white undershirt with a sweaty bald head. It was hard to focus on him, but Baby thought she recognised him as a customer from The Beaver Palace. He was brandishing a long rifle and it looked like he was reloading it. She touched the blood on her arm again. Had this man fired his rifle at her?

Fuck it. He must have done.

She heard a man's voice again. *'Run Baby run.'*

That was good advice. She turned her back on the old guy with the rifle. Summoning every last ounce of strength she had she carried on running as far into the fields as she could.

She heard no more gunfire. In fact she heard nothing over the sound of her own breathing which had become increasingly loud. Eventually when she could run no more she stopped to catch her breath. The highway and the diner had become a small blot on the horizon behind her. No one seemed to be pursuing her any more. Even so, she had to keep on moving because her arm was pumping out blood, not profusely, but enough for her to feel the constant throb of it. She pressed her sleeve hard against it in the hope of slowing down the bleeding. The sleeve already had a dark patch of blood licked into it and it was spreading.

The further she walked the weaker her legs became. Her knees began to ache and her feet felt heavy. Just when it felt like she could go no further she spotted a small cottage up ahead on the horizon. Mustering up all the energy she had left she carried on towards it, her walk becoming more of a stagger with every step she took.

By the time she reached the cottage the feeling of dizziness had turned to nausea. She tried to take deep breaths and blinked desperately in order to stop herself from passing out. If she could just get to the cottage and sit down for a few minutes she was sure she would be fine. A drink of water wouldn't go amiss either.

The cottage was old and run down. The walls were made of rickety white panelled wood and it had a thatched roof that had seen better days. Around its perimeter was a shaky wooden white picket fence. Halfway along the fence was an open gate. She staggered over to it and rested her left hand on one of the wooden panels, inadvertently smearing some blood onto the fence. She didn't dare to use her other hand because her arm was too weak from the bullet wound.

There were several small square windows along the side of the cottage, some with net curtains behind them that she couldn't see through. At the far end there was a narrow red door. The paintwork on the door was chipped in several places, showing signs of age.

She staggered up to the door. Before she could knock on it, it opened inwards. A man's face peered around the door's edge. He was in his early forties. His face was complicated. None of his features were quite where they ought to be. He had big cheeks and thick sideburns. His hair was scruffy and covered his ears. And he looked at her through a pair of narrow green eyes, doused with suspicion.

'What do you want?' he asked, his mouth moving out of synch with his words.

Baby struggled to get an answer out, barely managing to make herself heard as she said, 'I think I've been shot.'

The man looked at her arm. She held up her bloodied left hand.

'Oh dear,' he said. 'You need medical attention.'

He opened his door wide and stepped out. Baby blinked a few times to be sure her eyes weren't playing tricks on her. The man was wearing a blue outfit and a red cape. He was dressed as Superman, although thankfully he was wearing red shorts instead of speedos. He was only slightly taller than Baby, standing at little over five and a half feet. He hurried behind her, slipped an arm around her back and grabbed her gently by the wrist.

'Here, you look unsteady on your feet,' he said.

'I feel like I'm going to faint.'

'Don't worry. Supergirl's got you now. Let's get you inside.'

'Don't you mean Superman?'

He didn't answer. Not that it mattered too much. Baby felt relieved just to have found someone so welcoming and compassionate. He had taken great care not to squeeze her injured arm too tightly, and for that she was grateful. He led her through the open doorway. 'I'll put some tea on for you,' he said. 'Then let's get this injury tended to.'

'Thank you,' said Baby. 'That's very kind of you.'

She stepped into a kitchen with a dusty red tiled floor that was cold underfoot. There was a large wooden table in the centre of the room with nothing on it but a brown teapot on a large wicker coaster. There were two large wooden chairs, one on either side of the table.

'Sit yourself down,' the man said. 'I'll put the kettle on. A cup of sugary tea will sort you out.'

'I don't take sugar.'

'Maybe not sweetheart, but you've lost a lot of blood. You'll have to make an exception this one time. The sugar will do you good. It'll keep you awake and restore some red blood cells.'

'Oh, okay.'

He helped her over to the nearest chair, pulled it out with his free hand and saw to it that she collapsed down onto it and not the floor. She was relieved to finally be sitting down. Being in the care of someone who seemed to know what he was doing calmed her down a little. She managed to get her breath back and her head began to clear. Much of the anxiety she had felt when she first saw the blood on her arm was subsiding.

'You can call me Litgo,' she heard the man say. 'I'm not really Supergirl.'

'Okay.'

Behind her she heard him close the front door. Then she heard him slide a deadbolt across, securing it shut. She looked over her shoulder and saw him slipping a thick rusty metal key into the lock. He twisted it and another bolt clicked into place. He tucked the key back in a pocket on his red shorts and turned around to face her.

He smiled broadly and for the first time she noticed that he was missing his front teeth. The sight of his gappy smile shocked her a little and she began to feel light headed again.

'I think I'm going to faint,' she said, aware that she was slurring.

'That's okay Baby,' he said approaching her, his features blurring out of focus as he got nearer. 'You're in safe hands now.'

As everything around her darkened and blurred again she knew she was about to blackout. Litgo reached out and grabbed her shoulders to prevent her from sliding off the chair.

As she drifted into a state of unconsciousness she managed to ask him one last question. 'How do you know my name?'

Sixteen

Dr Carter led Fonseca and Munson into the Asylum's staff room.

'I'm sorry if this isn't exactly The Ritz,' she said apologetically, gesturing around the room.

She wasn't kidding either. Munson checked out the selection of battered old sofas that were strung out around the perimeter of the room. In the centre of it all was a white wooden kitchen table with a few plastic chairs around it. Munson had better furniture in his own apartment. Even his cockroaches would turn their noses up at this stuff.

'Not at all,' he said politely. 'This is fine, really.'

'All of the furniture is either second hand or was donated by a charity,' Dr Carter added. 'Can I fix either of you a coffee?'

At the far end of the room was a small kitchenette. On a sideboard was a microwave, a kettle and a half full jug of filter coffee.

'Black, two sugars,' said Munson.

'White, no sugar for me please,' said Fonseca.

Dr Carter gestured to the white table in the middle of the room. 'Please take a seat.'

While Munson and Fonseca took up seats on opposite sides of the table, Carter rummaged around in a cupboard above the jug of filter coffee and pulled out a couple of mugs, one red and one blue and a jar of powdered milk. The mugs were covered in cracks and brown stains. There was a distinct whiff of burnt coffee in the air.

'How long has that coffee been brewing?' Munson asked.

Dr Carter shrugged, but offered no verbal response. She poured a spoonful of powdered milk into the red mug. As she lifted the coffee jug off the hotplate, Munson could see the stuff was far from fresh. The contents at the bottom were much darker and thicker than the stuff at the top.

'Are you having one yourself?' he asked.

'No. I can't stand the stuff,' Carter replied.

Munson glanced across at Fonseca and saw that she too had seen the state of the coffee and was well aware that one of them was about to luck out and get the gritty, shitty stuff from the bottom.

Both of them craned their necks to see which mug got the good stuff. The red mug had the powdered milk so it was obviously for Fonseca. Dr Carter held the jug over the blue mug. She was about to pour the contents in when Fonseca called out to her.

'Has Joey Conrad ever been violent?' she asked.

Dr Carter turned around, swinging the rancid jug of coffee with her. 'Yes. He beheaded someone last night. That's why you're here isn't it?'

'Of course it is,' said Fonseca. 'Mine's the red mug is it?'

'Yes.'

Dr Carter turned back to the coffee mugs and poured the first drink into Fonseca's red mug. Fonseca winked at Munson who mouthed the word "Bitch" in return, then smiled to show he was only kidding.

Carter finished pouring the coffee, and brought the two mugs over to them. She placed them down on the table in front of the two agents and sat herself down at the head of the table.

'Has he been violent before?' asked Munson, flicking at something that was floating at the top of his coffee. 'I mean, like recently?'

'Yes.'

'Can you tell us about it?'

'Are you aware yet that he's killed again this morning?' Dr Carter asked.

Munson and Fonseca shared a concerned look. It was news to both of them. 'Who? What's happened this morning?' Munson asked.

'He's killed a car salesman and stolen a car. He's still in B Movie Hell.'

Fonseca leant forward in her chair. 'How long ago did this happen?'

'An hour ago maybe. It came on the news just before you arrived. It's why I wasn't here to greet you. I was getting up to speed with the latest information.'

'Just one person dead?' Munson asked.

'That's what they're saying on the news.'

'Cause of death?'

'Same as the cop last night. Head hacked off with a meat cleaver. Feet and hands too apparently.'

Fonseca grimaced. 'Have you any idea where he got this meat cleaver? Or the mask and clothes he's wearing?'

'I'd guess he's stopped off at a butcher's and a party store.'

'Is there definitely no way he could have got the stuff here?'

'No.'

Munson scratched his chin. 'And you said he's stolen a car?'

'That's what they're saying on the news.'

'But they haven't worked out his real identity yet?'

'No.'

'And you haven't told anyone?'

Dr Carter shook her head. 'We're under strict instructions not to say a word to anyone.'

'Good,' said Munson looking over at Fonseca. 'You know I can't be here any longer. I'm going to have to move faster than this, especially if he's got a car now.'

'I wouldn't worry too much about that,' said Dr Carter.

'Why not?'

'There's only one road in and out of B Movie Hell. It's across a bridge a hundred feet above Lake Flaccid. The local police have a roadblock stopping anyone from getting in or out without them approving it first.'

'That's brave of them,' said Munson. 'Most people would probably be glad to see the back of a serial killer. Keeping him in town is an admirable thing to do.'

'It's a close knit community,' said Dr Carter. 'From what I know of the place they'll want to find Joey Conrad and dish out their own form of justice before you get your hands on him.'

Munson took in the information. A community that was willing to deal with a serial killer rather than hand him over to the government. That could be problematic. He needed to get to Joey Conrad before the locals discovered his identity.

Fonseca continued quizzing Dr Carter. 'Did you know about the videos in Conrad's room?' she asked.

'I knew he had some DVD's yes, but I wasn't aware that he had the horror films you were talking about before.'

'How does he get hold of the films? Who supplies them?'

'I don't know exactly,' said Carter. 'It's one of those things we turn a blind eye to. And to be honest, we've encouraged him to watch films because he's shown a great deal of interest in a drama class we have here. In fact a lot of the patients have responded to it.'

Fonseca shook her head. 'If you're turning a blind eye to the DVD's, then how can you be sure that the same person smuggling them in didn't get him the mask and meat cleaver too?'

'That's unlikely. We'd spot stuff like that.'

Munson butted in. 'A drama class you say? Doing what?'

'Doing drama,' Dr Carter replied. For a moment it looked like she would keep her response brief and sarcastic, but eventually she continued. 'A lot of the patients here have multiple personality disorders. Joey Conrad is one of them. The drama class allows them to show off these personalities without fear of being judged or analysed.'

'Great,' said Munson under his breath. 'A bunch of nutjobs re-enacting One Flew Over The Cuckoos Nest. Nothing mental about that.'

'What personalities does Conrad have?' Fonseca asked.

Dr Carter took a deep breath. 'He takes on the personality of characters he's seen in films. He's a kind of film nut. Knows a lot of trivia. He can quote and re-enact entire scenes from most of his favourite films.'

'So it's entirely possible that now he's wearing a mask and beheading people, he's pretending to be a character from one of the horror movies we found in his room.'

'I guess so.'

'Like the Last Action Hero,' Munson snapped.

'What?' asked Fonseca.

'Last Action Hero.'

'What's that supposed to mean?'

'He's out of your theatre now. He's out in the real world, playing the part of a fictional character.' He looked at Fonseca. 'I didn't want to mention this upstairs because it was little more than a hunch, but those Last Action Hero and Galaxy Quest movies got me thinking.'

Dr Carter looked at Munson quizzically. 'I'm not following.'

Fonseca understood immediately. 'I know what you're getting at,' she said.

'Well I don't,' said Dr Carter.

Munson spelled it out for her. 'Last Action Hero, a fictional character from a movie comes out into the real world. Now if Joey Conrad thinks he's say, the killer from the movie Halloween, he could go round B Movie Hell terrorising and murdering the locals.'

Dr Carter didn't look convinced. 'Wasn't the Halloween killer trying to kill Jamie Lee Curtis?'

Munson took a swig of his coffee. It was as foul as it looked. 'Yeah, she was his sister, or something.'

Fonseca had been about to take a sip of her own coffee but saw the look on Munson's face and wisely put her own mug back down. 'Do you think he might be looking for a relative?' she asked.

'He has no relatives,' said Dr Carter. 'I thought you'd know that.'

'No long lost aunts or uncles?'

'Definitely not.'

'Okay,' said Munson. 'That rules out the plot of Halloween then. But the mask could still mean he's pretending to be the guy from Halloween or the one from the Texas Chainsaw Massacre? Or both.'

'Both?' said Fonseca and Dr Carter at the same time.

'Well they both wore masks, and probably both killed with a meat cleaver at some point.'

'And what was the Terminator known for? Did he use a meat cleaver or wear a mask?' Fonseca asked.

Munson shrugged. 'Technically he wore a mask, but the Terminator's main thing really was that he was trying to kill a woman named Sarah Connor.'

He was about to take another sip of coffee when he remembered how rancid it was. He stopped short with the mug a few inches from his mouth. Fonseca took up the questioning.

'Dr Carter, are you aware of the slaughter of the innocents?' she asked.

Dr Carter nodded. 'Of course. That's when King Herod ordered his men to execute all the boys in Bethlehem under the age of two.'

'That's right,' said Munson, acting as if he'd known the story for more than five minutes. 'He was trying to kill Jesus, the son of God.'

He noticed Fonseca raising her eyebrows at him, no doubt amused by his sudden claim to be knowledgeable about the subject. Before he could delve any further into the matter, Justin the nurse poked his head around the door.

'Have you guys seen the news?' he asked.

'What is it now?' asked Dr Carter.

'The Red Mohawk has just killed three more people at the Alaska Roadside Diner in B Movie Hell. The cops are after him in a high speed pursuit. This is gonna get huge about now.'

Munson stood up from his seat at the table. 'Milena I've got to go.'

'What are you going to do?'

'I'm going to head into B Movie Hell and make Joey Conrad disappear before it's too late. When you're finished here, call me.'

86

Seventeen

The first police squad car to respond to the report of the disturbance at The Alaska Roadside diner was a black and white Plymouth Fury designed for high-speed chases. It arrived at the crime scene just as the yellow and red stock car pulled away with its tyres screeching and a ball of dirt and smoke in its wake. Without hesitation the lone officer in the Plymouth flicked on the siren and the flashing blue and red lights, radioed for backup and floored the accelerator. There was no way he was letting the psychotic masked killer get away this time.

Up ahead, the Red Mohawk checked his rear view mirror. Beneath the hideous mask that covered his face, he allowed himself a sly grin. These motherfucking police scumbags were playing right into his hands. He pressed his boot down on the accelerator of the yellow Chevrolet he had stolen from Hank Jackson an hour earlier. The car was a piece of shit, with a fucked up, clapped out old engine under the hood. He knew that when he chose it. But engine size and speed weren't priorities. Hell, he wanted, no *needed*, the cops to stay in pursuit of him. If he outran them or threw them off his tail, he wouldn't be able to kill the sons of bitches.

There was one car in pursuit. One was not enough.

He needed…. no actually *fuck it, he wanted* at least three police cars on his tail. These incompetent redneck B Movie Hell fuckwits could surely manage to get three cop cars in pursuit of him. It's not like he was hard to spot.

Well, it took them the best part of five minutes, by which time the Red Mohawk was losing patience. The first squad car on his tail was irritating him in the extreme with its shitty never-ending siren. The asshole let everyone know he was in pursuit with his flashing blue lights, but the Red Mohawk was certain that the gutless asshole had no intention whatsoever of catching up with him. Not on his own.

It took a swift turn onto a second deserted road that led to *Who-the-fuck-knows-where*, before the second and third squad cars made their appearance. Thanks to the dumbass bastards on the police frequency that the Red Mohawk had tuned his car radio into, he knew that two further Plymouth Furys were waiting behind a giant billboard, ready to join in the chase the second he drove past it.

Now it wasn't wasted on the violent killer that these two patrol cars could have formed a roadblock, albeit a flimsy one, but they had chosen not to. Reason? They didn't want to confront him any more than the loser who'd been on his tail since the diner. So now he had the three squad cars on his tail, just as he planned. It was time to take them down. None of them wanted to be at the front of the chasing pack. None of them wanted to pull up level with him. But *all* of them were probably hoping to God that he crashed his car and killed himself.

The Red Mohawk had no further need to listen to the police frequency on the radio. Some driving music was required in order to soundtrack what was to follow. Any music would do. He turned the dial on the radio. The first tune to hit the airwaves was *The Star Spangled Banner* by Enrico Pallazzo. Not the most appropriate killing tune, but murderous nonetheless.

He took one more glance in the rear view mirror. The three pursuing vehicles were chasing in single file, all keeping their distance. Just enough distance for him to pull some *fucked up shit* on them.

'Get ready for this, muthafuckers,' he muttered to himself.

He reached down and grabbed the handbrake, yanking it up hard. The front wheels locked and his car spun around viciously. It turned a full one hundred and eighty degrees before he dropped the handbrake and slammed the gear into reverse in one quick move. As he'd expected, the cops panicked and slammed their brakes on. The car furthest back almost crashed into the trunk of the one in the middle. The crash was avoided but the poor sucker who had previously been at the rear had to swerve around the fucker in front of him, which meant he reluctantly found himself second in line for what was to come.

From the Red Mohawk's point of view, things were going perfectly. He'd shown them he was unpredictable and foolhardy. As he pressed his foot down hard on the accelerator and began reversing at high speed down the highway with the cops pursuing him in an extremely passive aggressive manner, he prepared to give them surprise number two.

He wound down the electric window on the driver side of his car and reached over to the passenger seat where he had a sports bag full of good shit. He pulled out his weapon of choice. An Uzi 9mm. Already loaded and ready to use.

He pointed the Uzi out of the window at the first cop car. It was twenty-feet away, keeping up the façade that it couldn't quite catch up with him. As he took aim he saw the facial expression of the driver change. No more steely-eyed *I'm-coming-to-get-you* bullshit. This was now one wide-eyed motherfucker.

The Uzi fired off a shitload of rounds in a matter of seconds. It was hard to control the aim, but with an Uzi, who the fuck cares? The job was done in emphatic fashion.

One of the front tyres burst on the first cop car, the front grill took a few shots too, but more importantly, the windscreen took the majority of the bullets. One side of it, the driver's side, turned crimson too. The driver had taken at least a couple of shots in the head. Before the Red Mohawk even had a chance to turn the Uzi on the second car, things began to take shape. The lead car ground to a halt almost as soon as the driver's head hit the steering wheel. The driver of the second car tried to avoid a full on crash into the rear of it but succeeded only in catching the rear corner. It flew up over the top of the front car and flipped over in mid air. Further back, car number three attempted an emergency stop but skidded and crashed "side on" into the back of the front car. Half a second later the middle car landed upside down on the highway with an almighty bang. Its roof crumpled as if it was made from tin foil.

The Red Mohawk, eased his stock car to a crawl then stopped in the middle of the road. He opened the car door. Over the warbling of Enrico Pallazzo singing about *"the rocket's red glare"* he heard the sound of cops dying and the distant muttering of the police radio frequency asking them if they were okay.

He climbed out of the car, his Uzi primed and ready to use. The nearest squad car was on its side. The driver was already dead. A few yards further back was the second car, the one that had flipped over onto its roof. Its wheels were still spinning round at quite a high speed. This was the one with the police radio still working. A female voice was inquiring about their current situation. The Red Mohawk opened fire on the car, peppering it with rounds as he walked towards it. Bullet holes rattled through the crumpled remains of the vehicle.

No chance of any survivors there. Even the radio died a sudden death. He ceased fire and turned his attentions on the third car. It was still upright but the hood had been crushed. It was half its normal length, courtesy of it bashing into the trunk of the front car. Inside it two cops were slumped forwards in the front seats, both their faces were bloodied. Neither of them was conscious but the Red Mohawk took no chances. He aimed the Uzi at the pair of them and opened fire again. The two cops bodies juddered erratically as if they were body-popping. The fuckers were dead now. For sure.

With the Uzi raging hot in his hand the Mohawk eased off the trigger and ceased firing. He looked around and listened intently to the highway. Someone was still alive. Somewhere. Some fucker was moving.

He noticed that on the far side of the final squad car the back door was open. He strode around the car, Uzi raised, looking for any sign of a survivor. It didn't take long to spot one.

Crawling on his hands and knees into the desert wasteland at the side of the highway, leaving a trail of blood behind him was an overweight balding man with a serious case of builders crack. His baggy blue jeans were hanging around below his buttocks, dragging his underpants down too. His white sweatshirt was covered in dirt and traces of blood. He had obviously been seriously injured in the pile up and was in no fit state to walk or run from the scene. He looked back and saw the sight of the masked killer behind him, Uzi in hand, primed and ready. The man whimpered but said nothing. He continued his fruitless attempt to crawl into the desert, hoping maybe he would be spared.

He didn't stop crawling until the dark cold shadow of the Red Mohawk loomed over him, shielding him from the afternoon sun.

The man rolled over onto his back. He was a pathetic, disgusting mess. A feeble excuse for a human being. His life, not worth a jot, no doubt wasted on booze, junk food and bad television. He raised a hand to shield himself from a glint of sunlight reflecting in his eyes from over the shoulder of the Mohawk.

'Please,' he pleaded. 'I'm not a cop.'

The Red Mohawk raised his Uzi and pointed it at the man's head, then asked, 'So what are you?'

'I'm not a cop,' the man repeated. 'I'm just a guy. I was in for a ride along. I'm just a local nobody.'

'A local?'

'Yeah.'

'Wrong answer.'

The Red Mohawk had heard all he needed to hear. He opened fire on the guy's face. Bullets punctured holes through his skull. His blood and brains sprayed out all over the road.

Eighteen

Baby could feel someone's hand stroking some strands of her hair across her forehead. Her hair felt damp and clammy, her brow sticky with sweat. She opened her eyes. She was lying on her back on a sofa looking up at the faces of two men. Their features were blurred. She blinked a few times and tried to rub her eyes. That was when she remembered the gunshot wound in her arm. She winced as a stinging sensation raced through her.

'It's okay Baby, you're safe now,' said one of the men.

She used her left hand to rub her eyes and pinched the bridge of her nose. Her vision cleared and she noticed that her bloodied hand had been washed clean. She focussed on one of the men. It was Litgo, the odd fellow in the Superman costume who had let her into his home.

'How long have I been asleep?' she asked.

'About half an hour,' Litgo replied.

She couldn't really see the other man so she twisted her head around to get a better look at him. He had shaggy brown hair that hung in front of his eyes because he was leaning over her. She soon recognised him. It was Benny Stansfield, a senior cop who paid regular visits to The Beaver Palace. He smiled at her.

'You're gonna be fine Baby,' Benny said. His voice was calm and reassuring, a character trait she associated with him from their previous meetings.

'I think I've been shot,' she said.

'Yes you have. But there's no need to panic. You got quite lucky because the bullet only really grazed your arm. It passed right through so you've got no shrapnel or debris in there that could cause an infection.'

'Wow, *lucky me*,' said Baby with a hint of sarcasm. She'd taken offence to the suggestion that she'd been lucky.

'Benny smiled. 'Take it easy there, tiger,' he said. 'You've had quite a morning. But I promise you, you're safe now. You've got nothing to worry about.'

She looked back over at Litgo. His smile was still very unsettling due to his lack of front teeth. For the first time she noticed something else about him that she'd somehow missed before. He had a pair of fake breasts underneath his Superman outfit. Well, she assumed they were fake. Either that or he was in the middle of a sex change operation. She remembered him referring to himself as Supergirl earlier. It made sense now. He was wearing a Supergirl outfit, not a

Superman one. That's why he had the red shorts instead of the tight red underpants over his blue tights. What a weirdo.

Benny was much more approachable. She remembered having sex with him at The Beaver Palace once a few months earlier. He had been quite pleasant and a considerate client.

'Did you catch the guy in the mask?' she asked.

'We've got a bunch of guys on the tail of that lunatic right now,' said Benny with a warm smile. 'He won't get far. His five minutes of fun terrorising this town are about to come to an end.'

'Good.' Baby rolled her legs off the sofa and sat upright. 'I felt like he was after me. He stared right at me in the diner just before he started killing people.'

'That's interesting,' said Benny. 'Because I was wondering if maybe you knew him? He killed your friend Arnold, and from what I've been told, Arnold was his first victim. Have you any idea why that was? Did you or Arnold do anything to rile him up?'

'No. He just walked up to Arnold with a meat cleaver and attacked him.'

'So was he already in the diner when you arrived?'

'Yes. He was sitting near the jukebox. Like I said, he stared right at me. I turned away and that's when he put the mask on and came towards us.'

'You saw him without the mask on?'

Baby nodded. 'Uh huh.'

'Can you give me a description of what he looked like?'

'He was just a normal looking guy with dark hair and a creepy stare.'

'That's good, Baby. We'll get you to look at some mugshots down at the station later and see if you can identify him, if you feel up to it that is?'

'I do feel a bit better,' said Baby. 'But my arm feels really heavy and numb.'

'See,' said Litgo grinning. 'That sugary tea I gave you has worked a treat. And I bandaged up your arm nice and tight to stop the bleeding.'

Baby looked at her arm. Her right sleeve had been ripped off just below the shoulder. But sure enough the wound was wrapped tightly in white bandage, although a trickle of blood had seeped through it. She remembered thinking that Litgo was a touch creepy when she first met him, particularly when, just before she had passed out, he had called her by her name.

'How did you know my name?' she asked him again.

Litgo glanced at Benny before answering. 'I got a call from the folks who work at the diner. They said you were heading my way.'

'Oh. How did *they* know my name?'

Benny reached out and grabbed her by the hand. 'Someone there recognised you,' he said. 'You're lucky so many people in town care about you. You're a popular young lady. Now come on, see if you can get up. Then we can get you out of here.'

Baby stood up slowly. Her legs and in particular her knees felt stiff from all the running she'd done earlier. She wasn't used to that kind of exercise. 'Where are we going?' she asked.

'I'm taking you back to The Beaver Palace,' said Benny.

'Shouldn't we go to the police station first? Or hospital?'

'Sure. We can go anywhere you want. Come on, my car is just outside. But we need to hurry.'

'Why?'

'Because I said so.'

Nineteen

Milena Fonseca and Dr Carter had been watching the news on a small portable television on the wall of the asylum's staff room ever since Jack Munson had dashed off in the direction of B Movie Hell. The latest news flash was even more alarming than the last. Things in B Movie Hell seemed to be getting worse by the minute. More cops were dead, killed in a high-speed pursuit of The Red Mohawk. And another civilian, some poor sucker on a ride-along with the cops, had been murdered too for good measure. Three police cars were wrecked too. But the manner of the latest slaughter was deeply concerning.

'Where the hell did he get a gun?' Fonseca asked aloud, hoping for an answer from herself more than she was expecting one from Dr Carter. 'From what they're saying here it sounds like he had a *machine gun*. Where would he get automatic weapons around here?'

Dr Carter didn't answer the question. 'You're not drinking your coffee,' she said, nodding at the rapidly cooling red mug of filth on the table in front of Fonseca.

'It's a tad strong for my liking,' Fonseca replied. 'Can you think of anywhere around here where he could get a gun? I mean he only escaped yesterday, right? And already he's got a mask, a meat cleaver and a very powerful firearm. Yet no one seems to be reporting them as stolen. He steals a car and its reported in minutes because he murders the car salesman. But the gun, the clothes, the mask and the meat cleaver, nothing. Not a peep. Where did he get them?'

'Have your read his file?' Dr Carter asked.

'Every word of it.'

'Well then you shouldn't be too surprised by how resourceful he is. When they brought him here it was clear he was very well trained in all aspects of military stuff. He's highly intelligent, resourceful and motivated, he just doesn't have a grasp on reality. The file explains most of it in my opinion.'

'It doesn't explain how he got a machine gun.'

Dr Carter shrugged. 'Maybe he found it at the car lot when he stole the car?'

'That's unlikely, don't you think?'

'I don't know. What I do know is that your agency trained him up to be a combination of James Bond, Jason Bourne, Rambo, Freddy Krueger and God knows who else. He's a man for any given situation. He was supposed to be the ultimate soldier. A man who could do kung fu, work undercover, infiltrate enemy fortresses, fly fighter planes, disguise himself as anything from a bartender to a female wrestler. And I should think they taught him how to acquire weapons at short notice. Your people trained him, so don't be sitting there asking me how he managed to get his hands on all this stuff. You should know better than I do.'

Fonseca leant back and raised her hands defensively. 'Woah, steady on. This nonsense happened before my time.'

'Of course. But you should still know more about it than me.'

'You'd think so, but someone seems to have covered a lot of it up. You know much more about Joey Conrad than I do.'

'So it would seem, Agent Fonseca. But I really can't tell you how he acquires weapons or how he does kung fu. What I can tell you about is his mental state and his erratic behaviour.'

'Kung fu,' said Fonseca, glancing back up at the news on the portable television. 'Does that mean you've seen him do kung fu in here?'

'No. But I'm sure he could.'

'Has he ever been violent in here?'

'Just once.'

'What happened?'

'A few weeks ago he beat up another patient.'

'Any particular reason?'

'Neither of them were willing to talk about it.'

'Any idea what triggered the fight?'

'No. I didn't even give it much thought at the time. But now that Conrad has escaped I think I can guess what it might have been about.'

'Really? What?'

'The guy he beat up is called Dominic Touretto. A couple of months ago Touretto escaped from here. He was on the run for about a week before we got him back. He was picked up by the cops in B Movie Hell. Anyway, I guess it's possible Conrad wanted to know how Touretto escaped so he could do the same thing. Maybe he was trying to beat the information out of him.'

'And how did Touretto escape?'

'We can't work it out. We think he just climbed over the wall, but we're not sure. No one escaped from this place for years. Now we have two escaped patients in two months. Not very good is it?'

Fonseca finally felt like she was getting somewhere. 'Why didn't I know about this before?' she asked.

'Why would you know?'

'Hang on.' Fonseca reached into her pocket and pulled her cell phone out. She flicked through a few menus, accessing the confidential files she had on all of the inmates at Grimwald's. 'There's nothing about this in Touretto's file,' she said, eyeing Dr Carter suspiciously.

'About his escape?'

'No. About his altercation with Joey Conrad.'

Dr Carter looked offended. 'Well it wasn't a fight worth putting on record. It was the kind of incident that is best sorted out with a handshake. We can't make official documents of every fight that goes on in this place. We'd never get anything done.'

Fonseca looked around at the state of the staff room and figured that they didn't get much done anyway. 'So you think Conrad wanted to know how Touretto escaped, in order to plan his own escape?'

'Like I said, I didn't at the time. But it makes perfect sense now.'

'Yes it does. Can you take me to see Touretto please?'

'I can, but be on your guard, he's very unpredictable.'

'In what way?'

'In every way.'

Twenty

Munson was eager to get into B Movie Hell as soon as he could. It hadn't taken him too long to shake off Milena Fonseca. Whatever it was that Devon Pincent wanted him to do in B Movie Hell, he was pretty sure it would need to be done without Fonseca seeing it and reporting back to headquarters. He'd grown tired of playing dumb and making daft wisecracks to give Fonseca the impression he wasn't a competent agent. And he'd made a big deal about Joey Conrad's potential links to movies in the hope she would hang around at the asylum for a while trying to follow up on the theory. He'd bought himself some time. He hoped it would be enough.

The highway was deserted, so Munson took the opportunity to call Pincent on his cell phone. After an irritating wait to be put through by the switchboard operator at headquarters he heard Pincent's voice on the other end of the line.

'Devon Pincent. How can I help you?'

'Devon, it's Jack. I'm heading into B Movie Hell and I'm on my own. What's going on?'

For a few seconds Pincent didn't respond. When he did, he lowered his voice, practically to a mumble. 'Sorry Jack but if this is a personal call, you'll have to contact me at home. In fact I'm heading home now. Why don't you call me there in about an hour?'

'At home?'

'Yeah. You've got my number, right?'

'Umm, yeah.'

'Okay. Bye.'

Pincent hung up.

Charming.

Munson tossed his cell phone onto the passenger seat. What the fuck was going on? Whatever it was, it was serious enough and "off the record" enough that Pincent couldn't talk about it on the company phones.

Up ahead he saw the bridge that led to B Movie Hell. It was a beast of a bridge for such a hick town. A good fifty feet below it was a very wide lake. A police car was parked across the entrance to the bridge, preventing him from driving onto it. One police officer was sitting in the driver seat of the car. Another officer was outside adjusting the population figure at the bottom of a road sign that read –

WELCOME TO B MOVIE HELL
POPULATION 366_

Munson pulled up short of the bridge. The officer who was adjusting the population sign stopped what he was doing. He walked over to the front of Munson's car, holding a hand up to warn him not to move.

Munson wound down his window and held out his FBI badge. 'Hi, I'm Jack Munson FBI, you should be expecting me.'

The officer came around to the window and took a look at the FBI badge. 'Okay, wait here a second,' he said.

He walked back to the police car that was obstructing the road and spoke with the officer sitting at the wheel. A brief conversation ended with both officers eyeing Munson suspiciously before the driver reversed a few metres, leaving the way clear for Munson to proceed onto the bridge. They waved him through. Munson didn't hang around. He gave them a grateful wave back and cruised onto the bridge.

Once he was over the bridge he drove for another five miles down the highway until he saw The Alaska Roadside Diner. There were two police squad cars parked outside it. He steered his Mercedes off the road and parked up next to one of them, facing the large window at the front of the diner. He had a perfect view of all that was going on inside. Three cops were standing by the diner's counter. They were in deep discussion with a buxom blonde in a pink waitress outfit. Munson killed the engine and reached into his jacket pocket. His fingers settled on his concealed bottle of rum. He pulled it out and took a swig from it. It tasted good. He savoured the taste for a few moments before slipping the bottle back into his jacket. He sighed heavily and climbed out of the car. In the distance he heard the sound of police sirens blaring. Joey Conrad was still wreaking havoc somewhere.

He walked past the front window and up to the diner's entrance, feeling invigorated by the taste of the rum. The three cops and the waitress spotted him. They stopped talking and turned to look at him. They had been so engrossed in whatever they were discussing that they hadn't even noticed him pull up outside.

Munson pushed the door open and walked in confidently.

'Afternoon all,' he said gruffly.

The oldest of the three police officers walked towards him, no doubt intent on stopping him from walking in on their crime scene. He was a fifty-something, overweight, donut-eater in an oversized blue Stetson. One of the younger officers trailed along behind him, looking over his shoulder.

98

'Are you the FBI guy?' the older officer asked.

Munson pulled out his ID badge and held it up. 'Jack Munson, at your service,' he said with a cursory smile.

The officer peered closely at the ID badge. Munson afforded him less than two seconds before he slipped it back into his jacket.

'Can one of you bring me up to speed on what's happened here please?' he asked, walking around the two officers impeding his path towards the other one and the waitress. He propped an elbow against the counter and crossed one ankle over the other. He hoped that his blasé attitude would confuse and unnerve them.

The cop at the counter was in his late twenties with shoulder length blond hair. He pointed at the older cop Munson had just walked past. 'Randall is the ranking officer here and the only one who has seen the killer in the flesh. You should ask him.'

Munson turned round to see the tubby officer in the Stetson had followed him back to the counter and was now standing very close to him. Close enough that he might get a whiff of the rum on Munson's breath.

'Is that true? You've seen the killer?' Munson asked while trying not to exhale too heavily.

'I was there when he showed up last night' said Randall. 'He cut off my partner's head with a meat cleaver.'

Munson reached out and shook his hand. 'Then you must be Randall Buckwater,' he said. 'I've read the file. Were you really singing *On the Wings of Love* as you drove away from the crime scene?'

Randall closed his eyes. "Shit. Did they really put that in the file?'

'I'm afraid so.'

'I knew I shouldn't have mentioned it.'

Munson had Randall right where he wanted him. The officer was embarrassed and looked like he was inwardly beating himself up about the singing incident. It was the perfect time to start asking awkward questions. Munson had already noticed a trail of blood that led from an overturned stool by the counter to the men's washroom. 'Did someone get dragged into the men's room?' he asked.

'Uh, yeah,' Randall replied. 'Body's already gone to the morgue though.' He nodded to the two other officers. 'You guys had better be on your way. Got to start notifying the families of the victims before the press identify them on TV.'

'Yes sir.'

The two younger officers mumbled among themselves as they headed out to one of the cars parked out front. It left Munson with just Randall and the waitress to question. The waitress looked quite shaken.

'Pity I didn't get here earlier,' said Munson. 'Can you please recap for me what happened. Either of you?'

'This is Candy,' said Randall pointing at the waitress who was still standing behind the counter. 'She came out from the kitchen and saw the Red Mohawk guy slice off the first victim's hand with a meat cleaver. Then he sliced up two other guys who tried to restrain him.'

'I only saw what he did to Arnold,' said Candy. 'Then I ran into the kitchen and hid.'

'Right,' said Randall, seemingly keen to do the talking himself where possible. 'At that point everyone else ran out. Skidmark and Termite were killed just over there where that pool of blood is.' He pointed at a puddle of blood in the middle of the floor. 'We found the body of Arnold in the washroom. His head had been hacked off as well as his fingers, which ties up with what Candy saw. Lot of blood everywhere as you'd expect.'

'Skidmark and Termite?'

'Yeah.'

'What are their real names?'

'Skidmark Armstrong and Termite Smith.'

'Oh.' Munson turned his attention to Candy the waitress. 'Any idea why he dragged this Arnold guy into the washroom?'

'No idea,' Randall replied on her behalf.

'I wasn't asking you.' Munson pointed at Candy and asked again. 'Any idea why he dragged Arnold into the washroom?'

She shook her head.

'She's in shock you know,' said Randall. 'Cut her some slack.'

Munson ignored him. 'Did you see the killer leave the washroom?' he asked her.

To Munson's irritation, Randall answered for her again.

'As soon as the killer heard the first cops arriving on the scene he fled in a stolen car. Two or three squad cars were on his tail straight away.'

'Yeah. And they're already dead. I just heard it on the radio.'

'Well three or four more are out looking for him now.'

Munson disregarded Randall's latest piece of information and leaned across the counter to try and invade Candy's personal space. She was the person most likely to babble and reveal something that might be of use.

'Candy. What can you tell me about the victims here? You knew them, right?'

'Skidmark and Termite are mechanics from the local garage. They come in for lunch all the time.'

'*Were* mechanics.'

'Huh?'

'They *were* mechanics,' said Munson facetiously. 'What about Arnold, the guy he dragged into the washroom? Who was he?'

Randall butted in again. 'His full name was Arnold Bailey. A very well-known local guy.'

'Well-known. What for?'

'He was a handyman, worked at Mellencamp's.'

'Mellencamp's?'

'The Beaver Palace.'

'The whorehouse?'

'Gentleman's Club.'

'Of course.' Munson once again reverted to Candy. 'And did Arnold the handyman from the Gentleman's Club do anything to provoke the killer?'

'Nothing,' said Candy. 'The whole thing just happened out of nowhere.'

'Uh huh. Was Arnold here on his own?'

Candy nodded. 'Yes.'

Munson took another look around at the floor and at the number of dirty plates, mugs and glasses dotted around on the tables and the counter. It looked like the place had been busy before the murdering had started. 'Okay. So everyone else got away. And the Red Mohawk, he chopped Arnold up in the washroom. Then what? You say he fled at the sound of the sirens. Did he just walk out to his car? Or did he do anything else?'

'Straight out to the car,' said Candy.

Munson stared out at the parking lot. As he did, something caught his eye. The two cops who had left the diner had driven off in the police car he had parked up next to. But instead of driving down the highway they were attempting to drive the car across a grassy field on the other side of the road.

'What the fuck are they doing?' he asked.

Randall shrugged. 'Cam must be driving. He's got no sense of direction.'

Behind Randall the door to the men's washroom opened and another police officer walked out. The sound of a toilet flushing inside the washroom filtered out. The officer was in his early twenties with black greasy hair. He was mopping his brow with a handkerchief. He saw the others staring out through the window at the police car driving across the field.

'They going after the girl?' he asked.

Munson caught sight of Randall and Candy both throwing evil looks at the guy.

'What girl?' Munson asked.

The officer stared at him, looking surprised, as if he hadn't noticed him before. 'Who's this guy?' he asked.

'I'm Agent Jack Munson from the FBI. What girl?'

Twenty One

Litgo sat down in his favourite armchair in his front lounge. He picked up the phone from the coffee table by his side and dialled the number for The Beaver Palace. His heart was beating fast and his palms were sweating. He felt tense and nervous, as if he were a teenager on a first date all over again. As the dialling tone kicked in he had a flashback to the time when as a sixteen-year-old he'd picked up the phone to ask Clarisse Foster for a date. As terrifying experiences went this was up there with the Clarisse Foster incident, which hadn't gone well. He shuddered as he remembered the awful rejection and the teasing at school that followed. He hadn't asked a woman out on the phone since, but he remembered the feeling of the sweaty palms and the desire to hang up before it was too late.

'Hello Beaver Palace,' said a female voice on the other end of the line.

'Hi, can I speak to Mr Mellencamp please?'

'Who's calling?'

'My name is Litgo.'

'Litgo? Not Litgo Montenari from the cottage in the Dyersville field?'

'That's right.'

'Hi Litgo. It's Clarisse. Remember me? We went to school together?'

'Clarisse Foster?'

'Yeah. Remember you called me up and asked me out once?'

Litgo felt his butt cheeks tighten. All the old teenage angst came rushing back. 'No,' he replied defensively, while twiddling with his long red cape.

'Really?'

'Can I speak to Mr Mellencamp please?'

'How come you don't ever come up to The Beaver Palace?' Clarisse asked. 'You'd like it here. There's lots of girls to choose from. Are you still single?'

'Uh, yes.'

'Still cross-dressing?'

'I need to speak to Mr Mellencamp. It's important.'

'We have lots of great outfits here you could try on. You really should drop by one day.'

'Yes, that sounds nice, but I really need to speak to Mr Mellencamp.'

'Okay. What's it about? He's a very busy man.'

'I found Baby, the girl who went missing this morning after the murders at the diner.'

'Wow, really?' said Clarisse. 'Is she okay?'

'Yes. She's fine. I mean, she's been shot in the arm, but I bandaged it up and I think she's gonna be okay.'

'Wow. Good for you Litgo. Mr Mellencamp will be really pleased to hear that. We were all so worried when we heard Arnold was killed. We thought Baby might have been killed too.'

'Well she's fine. Benny Stansfield is bringing her back to you right now.'

'That's great. I'll put you through so you can tell Mr Mellencamp yourself.'

'Thank you.'

Litgo waited anxiously to be put through to Mellencamp and took some deep breaths, hoping desperately that he wouldn't stammer when he finally got through. His palms were sweating quite profusely by now (and his ass cheeks were warming up). Speaking to his teenage crush Clarisse Foster again, after all the years he'd spent avoiding her had made him even more anxious. Mind you, his conversation with her had actually gone quite well, all things considered. She'd even suggested he drop by The Beaver Palace too, a place that he'd never been to as a paying client. He was probably the only guy in town who had never been up there, but now that he knew Clarisse was working there, he was considering changing that. He was surprised that she knew about his cross-dressing though. He'd enjoyed wearing ladies clothes ever since he was a teenager. In fact, he'd probably started it not long after the rejection from Clarisse.

His maudlin thoughts were interrupted by the sound of Silvio Mellencamp's voice. 'Hi Litgo, how are you?'

'Umm, I'm good thanks. How are you Mr Mellencamp?'

'I've been better. There's a bloody serial killer going round town chopping people up and it's making my asshole itch. Everyone is asking me my fucking opinion about it and I haven't even got out of my fucking dressing gown yet.'

'Oh.'

'I don't even know why I'm telling you this,' said Mellencamp, obviously realising that he was ranting pointlessly. 'Anyway, Clarisse tells me you've got some good news for me. What is it?'

'I found Baby.'

'You did?'

104

'Yeah. She'd been shot in the arm. I fixed her up and called Benny Stansfield to come collect her. He's just picked her up and he's bringing her back to you now.'

'Excellent news! So I'm guessing the reason you're calling to tell me this is because you want a reward of some sort?'

'Oh no,' said Litgo defensively. 'I just wanted to let you know. I thought you might be worried about Baby.'

'Well you're right. I *was* worried about Baby, and you've now put my mind at ease Litgo, so I owe you a big favour. What would you like?'

'Oh nothing really.'

'Bullshit,' Mellencamp guffawed on the other end of the line. 'I know you Litgo. You're a good guy but you don't have a girlfriend and you've never been up to The Beaver Palace, which is a shame because cross-dressing is positively encouraged up here you know. You'd like it.'

'Umm, I've just been busy.'

'Ha ha ha! What nonsense. I'll tell you what. You can come up here any night this week for one whole night and have sex with as many of the girls as you like. All free of charge. How's that sound?'

Litgo felt his eyes light up and his jaw drop. 'Seriously?'

'Damn straight. In fact I'll tell you what. You can bring your Wonder Woman costume and your Supergirl costume if you want. I'll get the girls to dress up as Iron Man and Thor and some crazy shit like that. And Judy would make a great Incredible Hulk. You'll have the time of your life and I guarantee you, afterwards you'll be up here all the time.'

Litgo swallowed hard. 'Could I spend the night with Clarisse Foster?' he asked.

'If you want to,' said Mellencamp sounding confused. 'But there's a lot of younger girls here you know. Baby for instance. She owes you at least a hand job for fixing up the bullet wound in her arm.'

'I think I'd like to try Clarisse first,' said Litgo.

'Fine. Whatever. Why don't you come on up tonight? We'll have a dress up party. You'll love it.'

'Okay. Thanks Mr Mellencamp.'

'You can call me Silvio. Bye.'

Mellencamp ended the call before Litgo could respond with a goodbye of his own. Litgo placed the receiver down on his phone and took a deep breath. This was turning out to be a great day indeed. His lifelong dream to get it on with Clarisse Foster might finally be about to happen. He could feel a rock hard boner coming on just thinking about it. The bulge in his shorts wasn't a great look for Supergirl, but hey, no one was watching. This called for a drink.

He stood up and headed out to the kitchen to grab a bottle of his favourite cider. In his fridge he had a stash of *Randy Panda* cider. He picked one out and cranked the lid off with his teeth. On top of the fridge he had a pocket radio. Normally the radio only got used when he was doing the washing up. But this was a special occasion. He switched it on and smiled to himself. This was a significant moment in his life, and it would be good to hear a song that would remind him of the moment whenever he heard it again in the years to come. He fiddled with the tuner knob and prayed he would find a good tune.

It took a few seconds before he found one, but it was one he recognised in an instant. *Human* by The Killers.

That'll do!

Litgo began wiggling his hips, staring at his bottle of cider as if it were a dancing partner. He enjoyed a good dance while wearing his Supergirl outfit, the cape was great for swinging around, as long as he didn't trip on it. While wiggling his hips he boogied back a few steps, then forward a few, performing some kind of strange hybrid of the Charleston and the Macarena. After a good twenty seconds of boogying he spun around and took his first sip from the bottle of cider. He stared out of the kitchen window and shuddered as he realised he had an audience. Standing at the window and staring in was a man in a yellow rubber skull mask, grinning insanely back at him.

The Red Mohawk had come for Litgo.

Twenty Two

Milena Fonseca followed Dr Carter up to the third floor. Halfway down a long corridor Dr Carter stopped outside one of the doors and pulled a set of keys out of a pocket on her long white coat.

'This is Dominic Touretto's room,' she said. 'Just be on your guard because he really is a mixed bag. He's placid ninety-nine per cent of the time, but if he's off his game he can be a bit of a handful, particularly with women. He's a real fantasist. Don't be surprised if he makes a few lewd comments.'

'I can handle a lewd comment,' Fonseca replied.

'I'm sure you can. But make sure you ignore them. Don't let him engage you in any off topic sexual innuendos.'

'Understood.'

Carter unlocked the door and pushed it open. Before walking in, she called out. 'Dominic, it's Dr Carter. Are you decent?'

'I might be.'

Dr Carter looked at Fonseca and rolled her eyes. 'That's the best we can hope for,' she said. She peered around the door and then stepped inside.

'Hi Dominic, how are you today?' she asked, waving Fonseca in.

Fonseca followed her in to get a look at Touretto. He was lying on his back on a single bed by the far wall. He was a short fellow, barely over five-feet-six tall. He had brown hair swept up into a quiff, probably to make himself look taller. He was wearing a black T-shirt and a pair of dark blue sweatpants. His eyes lit up at the sight of Fonseca and he shifted swiftly into a seated position on the edge of the bed.

His room was almost identical to Joey Conrad's. He had a television and DVD player with a shelf of family orientated DVD's. Unlike Conrad he also had a decent collection of books on a shelf below.

'Who's she?' he asked, nodding at Fonseca.

'This is Milena Fonseca,' Dr Carter replied. 'She's with the FBI and she's investigating the escape of Joey Conrad. She'd like to ask you some questions, if you that's okay with you?'

'Questions? About what?'

Fonseca stepped forward and offered her hand. 'Questions about Joey Conrad,' she said.

Dr Carter grabbed her wrist and gently pulled her arm away from Touretto. 'No contact with the patient, please,' she said softly. 'For your own safety.'

'Joey Conrad is mental,' said Touretto.

Dr Carter sighed. 'Dominic, what have I told you about calling people mental?'

'Sorry.'

Fonseca noticed that he had a slight discolouration around his left eye, like the last remains of a bruise.

'What happened to your eye?' she asked.

Touretto reached up and touched the bruise by his eye. Dr Carter replied on his behalf.

'Joey Conrad hit him.'

'Why did he hit you?' Fonseca asked, careful to make it look like she knew nothing about the assault and was merely showing concern for his well-being, a ploy that she hoped would coax more information out of him.

'Because he's a cunt.'

'Pardon me?'

'He's a cunt.'

Dr Carter once more interjected. 'Dominic, what have I told you about calling people cunts?'

'Sorry.'

Fonseca repeated her question. 'So why did Joey Conrad hit you?'

'Because he's a motherfucker.'

'Dominic!' Dr Carter snapped.

'A cocksucker.'

'Dominic!' Dr Carter's voice lowered a touch and took on a far more authoritative tone. Touretto looked down at his feet and mumbled a barely audible apology.

'So,' said Fonseca. 'Why did he hit you? Did he have a reason?'

Touretto nodded. 'Yeah.'

'What was it?'

Touretto glanced over at Dr Carter. 'I can't tell you in front of Dr Carter,' he said.

'Why not?'

'Because she's a slut and a whore.'

Fonseca sensed there was much more to Dominic Touretto than first appeared. She had taken a brief look at his confidential files on her cell phone while Dr Carter was leading her up to his room. She hadn't delved deep enough to establish his character though, only the crimes he had committed.

'This is normal behaviour for him,' said Dr Carter. She seemed unfazed by it, or at least she did a very good job of appearing to be desensitised to the unpleasant remarks.

'Would you mind if I talked to Dominic in private for a moment?' Fonseca asked.

Dr Carter looked surprised. 'Excuse me?'

'I'd like to speak with him privately, please.'

Dr Carter shook her head. 'What? No. Absolutely not. That's out of the question.'

'I just need to speak to him on my own. Only for a couple of minutes.'

'I'm sorry,' said Carter. 'I can't let you do that. It's against hospital rules.'

'Hospital rules,' Touretto repeated childishly.

Fonseca edged closer to Dr Carter and whispered in her ear. 'Let me speak with him in private or I'll have you thrown in jail.'

Dr Carter reeled back at the suggestion, her face revealing that she was shocked by the sudden threat that came totally out of left field. 'You don't have the authority to do that. Don't make pathetic threats you can't back up.'

Fonseca smiled and fixed a confident stare on her. 'You know nothing about what authority I have.'

'I'm no fool Agent Fonseca. I know my rights. You can't throw me in jail for doing my job. The FBI doesn't have the power. I know enough about the FBI just from watching TV to know that.'

'Well here's the thing,' said Fonseca. 'I'm not really FBI. I'm about a hundred pay grades up from that. You know nothing about me, and I'll bet my last dollar you don't really know a damn thing about the FBI either. I, on the other hand know everything about you, Dr Carter, Dr Linda Carter, named after Wonder Woman because your father appeared as an extra in the seventies TV show of the same name. Linda Joan Carter, attended Bengville High School, passed your Psychology exam with a score of eighty-six percent, exactly the same score as your friend Julian Brockman who sat on your left during the exam. Attended Rockwell University and achieved an honours degree, awarded to you by the Dean, Cameron Vosselberg whom you dated for sixteen months, until you unceremoniously dumped him one month after receiving your degree…'

'I'll wait outside,' said Dr Carter. 'You've got two minutes. Not a second more.'

'I'll take as long as I fucking like,' said Fonseca firmly, pointing to the door.

Dr Carter blushed a bright red colour. She was visibly flustered but had wisely decided not to hang around. Hardly surprising, really. She knew that Fonseca hadn't even got down to the really dubious elements of her past.

As soon as Dr Carter was outside, Fonseca closed the door firmly behind her and turned her attentions back to Dominic Touretto. He was sitting on his bed looking rather sheepish as if he knew what was coming next. Fonseca pulled her cell phone from her pocket. She flicked through a few menus until she found some files on Touretto. Her researcher at headquarters had messaged through a bullet point summary of facts about Touretto. Very interesting facts. There was also a brief message to advise that something else was coming soon. Fonseca smiled broadly then put the phone back in her pocket.

'Were you impressed by how I dealt with Dr Carter?' she asked.

Touretto nodded. 'Dr Carter smells. You dealt with her real good.'

Fonseca stood motionless, establishing dominance over him by standing tall in front of him, trying to make him feel uneasy. He fidgeted uncomfortably, for the most part avoiding eye contact.

'So you're Dominic Touretto,' she said.

'Dominic Touretto,' he repeated in the same childish voice he had used when repeating Dr Carter previously.

'And you're a comedian. Am I right?'

He looked up at her and finally made eye contact. For the first time she saw signs of life in his eyes. He wasn't playing dumb any more. She'd grabbed his attention, albeit fleetingly. As if realising he'd revealed too much with his body language he quickly switched back to the confused, shifty, uncomfortable persona from before.

'You enjoy taking the mickey out of authority, don't you Dominic?' she continued.

'Authority. Yes. Yes.'

'Fun isn't it? Especially when the authority is oblivious to what you're doing. But the big laugh comes when the penny drops and they realise you've been winding them up, doesn't it?'

He threw her another confused look. It was obvious he was concerned about where her interrogation was heading.

'Yeah. Fun,' he said, warily.

Fonseca leaned back against the wall and pulled her cell phone from her pocket again. Her update from HQ had arrived. She flicked through a few menus before she continued.

'You've been in here for almost three years now,' she said.

'Three years. Yes.'

Fonseca found what she was looking for on her phone and readied herself to wipe the smug look from his face. 'Dominic Englebert Touretto,' she said. 'Arrested for the murder of an eighteen year old prostitute, correct?'

'If you say so.'

'You pleaded insanity and convinced a jury that you didn't do the murder, and that in fact your alter ego *Roy* was responsible.'

'Roy. Yes.'

'Split personality huh? And your alter ego was called Roy?'

Touretto swallowed hard, but said nothing. He looked down at his feet.

'Roy,' Fonseca repeated. 'I would have seen the joke straightaway. But the jury didn't. And neither did the judge or the prosecution. I bet you couldn't believe your luck?'

Touretto took a deep breath but kept his gaze fixed on his feet.

'You've seen the film Primal Fear, correct?' said Fonseca.

'Never heard of it.'

'Funny,' Fonseca went on. 'Because according to my files you re-enacted scenes from it in court. In the film, Ed Norton plays the part of a guy on trial for murder. He convinces the judge and jury, even his own lawyer, that he has an alter ego called Roy who committed the murder on his behalf. And he gets let off and sent to a mental institution because the jury believe that he's insane and has a split personality, when in actual fact he was a cold, calculated killer.'

Touretto said nothing and continued to avoid eye contact.

'It wasn't until after the case was closed that someone spotted what you'd done, and by then it was too late to call a mistrial.'

'I don't know what you're talking about.'

'Yes you do. You were convinced you were going to prison because the evidence against you was so clear. So for fun you decided to joke around in court, playing the part of Ed Norton's character from Primal Fear. You never expected to get away with it, but then it turned out that no one on the jury or the prosecution had seen the film. They really believed you were insane. And then, *fuck me*, you actually got away with it. And you ended up in here instead of in prison. I bet you couldn't believe your luck.'

'That's not true.' There was a sudden clarity to Touretto's voice that had been absent before.

'Yes it is. You, you're of sound mind. So how about you stop pretending to be mental?'

'We don't use that word around here.'

Fonseca smiled. 'I could easily pull some strings and have you retried. So how about you stop pretending to be crazy and answer my questions.'

She allowed him to sweat over the thought of a retrial for a few seconds before hitting him with her interrogation.

'So, Dominic, or should I call you Roy?' she said slipping her phone back in her pocket. 'Why the fuck did Joey Conrad hit you?'

Touretto swallowed hard. He looked up at her with the same crestfallen look Dr Carter had shown a minute earlier when she was outed as a college cheat. 'It's in *Gone with the Wind,*' he said.

'Pardon me?'

He pointed at the books on his shelf below the DVD's. '*Gone with the Wind,* page eighty-two.'

Fonseca wasn't entirely sure what to make of what he'd said. If it was a prank she hadn't figured it out. She walked over to the bookshelf, keeping an eye on Touretto the whole time. She pulled out *Gone with the Wind* and flicked through the pages until she reached page eighty two. A small photograph slipped out of the pages and fell to the floor. She bent down to pick it up.

'Please don't confiscate it,' Touretto said, his eyes revealing a sudden desperation.

Fonseca held the photo up in front of her face to get a closer look. It was a photo of a girl in black lingerie. She was a pretty young thing, probably in her late teens with a lovely head of dark hair. She also had an unfortunately placed blue birthmark on her face. 'Why am I looking at this?' she asked.

'Joey Conrad wanted it.'

'This is why he hit you?'

'He wanted it for himself.'

'Why?'

Touretto blushed and raised his eyebrows. 'Why do you think?'

'Same thing as you use it for I suppose,' said Fonseca, shuddering at the visual image of Touretto masturbating over the picture.

'I actually met her though,' he said. 'Wanted to keep the photo as a souvenir.'

Fonseca looked at the photo again, studying the girl a little closer. 'She's a friend of yours?'

'Not exactly.'

'Did Joey Conrad ever meet her?'

'Couldn't have done,' said Touretto. 'Unless he's been sneaking out to B Movie Hell at night.'

'What do you mean?'

'She lives in B Movie Hell.'

'You met this girl in B Movie Hell?'

'Yeah.'

'When you escaped recently?'

'Uh huh. She worked in a whorehouse called The Beaver Palace. She let me have the photo as a souvenir, seeing as I was from out of town.'

Fonseca pulled her cell phone from her pocket again and used it to take a picture of the photo of the girl. 'What's her name?' she asked.

'Baby,' Touretto replied.

'Her real name?'

'I don't know. She was just called Baby, honest.'

'What about a surname?'

'I didn't ask for it. Not sure the girls there even have surnames.'

'And did you brag to Joey Conrad about having sex with her?'

'I might have mentioned it.'

'So you did?'

'Yeah.'

'And do you think he broke out so he could go to B Movie Hell and have sex with her too?'

'Probably. He was jealous as hell, I could tell. I wouldn't give him the photo. That's why he hit me.'

'And yet you managed to keep the photo. That's impressive,' said Fonseca, curious as to how he'd managed it.

'I'm very good at hiding that photo. My room has been mysteriously trashed several times since my fight with Conrad. Someone wants that photo real bad, and I'm not just talking about Joey Conrad. I've had to hide that picture up my asshole on more than one occasion.'

Fonseca glanced down at the picture in her hand. It was a little brown around the edges. 'This has been up your bum?' she said, resisting the urge to sniff it for confirmation.

'You're not going to take it are you?'

'Not today. Not as long as you continue to co-operate.' She stuck the photo back inside *Gone With The Wind* on page eighty-two. 'I have a picture of it on my phone. That will do me for now.'

'Please don't tell Dr Carter about it, she'll confiscate it without a seconds thought. And I'd hate to forget how beautiful Baby was. Best night of my life since I got sent here, I can tell you.'

'Did you hurt her?'

Touretto looked at his feet again. 'I got what I paid for. Everything was consensual.'

Fonseca closed the copy of *Gone with the Wind* and replaced it back on the shelf. 'So Joey Conrad didn't know this girl then? You're sure of that?'

'Yeah, there's no way he could have known her. Like I said, he's never been out of this place until he escaped. And I'm sure Dr Carter will confirm for you that he's never had any visitors either. The guy's got no family and he sure as hell ain't got no friends.'

The door to Touretto's room opened and Dr Carter stepped in tentatively. 'That's your two minutes,' she said.

'Get the fuck out!' Fonseca snapped at her. Carter looked shocked but wisely stepped back out of sight and shut the door behind her. Fonseca turned back to Touretto. 'Anything else you can tell me about Joey Conrad?'

'Yeah.'

'What?'

'He thinks he's a million different people. He likes pretending to be characters from movies. He loves his movies.'

'Do you know who supplies him with his DVD's and other things?'

'Let me show you,' said Touretto. He stood up from the bed and pulled his T-shirt over his head, revealing a very muscular torso underneath.

'What are you doing?' Fonseca asked, confused.

Touretto pulled his sweatpants down, revealing that he was wearing no underwear. Fonseca caught a glimpse of his penis which was semi erect. It took her by surprise and she looked away.

'Can you put your clothes back on please?' she said.

'You're not quite so observant as I first thought,' said Touretto grinning and proudly pushing his hips forward to make sure his penis was in her eyeline.

'What do you mean?'

'You pissed off Dr Carter.'

'So?'

'So she just *locked you in*. It's time to introduce you to my alter ego…. *Roy.*'

Twenty Three

'What girl?' Munson repeated.

The officer who had walked out of the men's washroom stood open mouthed, unsure how to answer. His cheeks turned a crimson colour. He looked at Randall.

'Don't look at him!' Munson snapped. 'What girl?'

'Umm.'

'What's your name son?'

'Gary.'

'Gary. What girl? Look at me.'

Munson fixed Gary with a firm stare. The young officer crumbled, just as he expected. 'Umm, there was a girl running across the field,' he mumbled.

Munson turned away from him, freeing him from his vocal stare. He turned his attentions to Candy and Randall to see how they were reacting to the mention of the girl. If the guy from the washroom knew about her then surely they did too.

'Oh right, the girl, yeah,' said Candy slapping her forehead. 'There was a girl in here who ran out across the field when the Red Mohawk appeared.'

'Why didn't you mention this before?'

'I forgot.'

Munson pointed at Randall. 'Your buddies are driving across the field to get that girl. Why?'

'They're probably just checking to see if she got away safely. I'm sure she did. The Red Mohawk drove off down the highway, didn't he Candy?'

'That's right,' Candy agreed. 'The girl will be fine. The Red Mohawk wasn't after her, I don't think.'

Munson nodded as he listened to them concoct the story. Something didn't fit quite right here. Everyone he had encountered in the diner was acting like they had something to hide. And it possibly had something to do with a mystery girl.

'Do you know who this girl was?' he asked. 'I'd like to question her. After all, she's a witness to the killing, isn't she?'

Candy stared up at the ceiling and scratched her chin. 'You know what?' she said. 'I didn't really get a good look at her. She hadn't been in here long before the killer struck. I hadn't even taken an order from her.'

'Uh huh. And where was she sitting?'

'Huh?'

'Where was she sitting? In one of the booths? Or at the counter?'

'Ummm.'

Randall intervened. 'I'd imagine it's hard to remember all these tiny details, right Candy? I mean, I guess you must be in shock.'

'Yes, I am, I think,' said Candy nodding. 'I'm in shock. I don't remember where the girl was. I only really remember seeing her running across the road into the field. Everyone else drove off. She obviously didn't have a car.'

Munson again looked around, studying all three of them to see if they were exchanging sly looks with each other. Out of the corner of his eye he saw a white Fed Ex van pull into the parking lot. The others hadn't noticed it yet. The arrival of another party could offer Randall, Candy and Gary the distraction they needed to stall and work out their stories. He needed answers quickly. Candy was his best bet. The waitress was a bag of nerves. 'But you already told Randall and, excuse me,' he turned his attention to the officer by the washroom. 'What was your name again?'

'Gary.'

'Your full name.'

'Gary Machin.'

'Well, *Gary Machin*, seeing as Candy is in shock and can't seem to remember *shit*, how about you fill me in on what she told you about the girl before she went into shock and forgot everything, and you went for a dump?'

Gary looked to Randall for guidance.

'I told you, don't look at him,' Munson snapped. 'Tell me about the girl.'

'Umm, she ran into the field. That's it, right Randall?'

'That's right,' said Randall.

Munson eyeballed Gary in an attempt to unnerve him into revealing more information, if there was any. The uneasy silence was interrupted by the sound of the bell above the door at the entrance chiming. Everyone spun round to see who had entered the diner. A young man in a blue denim jacket and matching skinny jeans stared back at them with an embarrassed and apologetic look on his face.

'Who are you?' Randall asked.

'Sorry, but I left my wallet here earlier,' the man replied. 'You know, when the masked guy pulled out the meat cleaver. I kind of ran out without thinking. Left my food and my wallet behind. Wasn't really thinking what I was doing.'

'I've got your wallet,' said Candy stepping forward. She reached into the pouch on the front of her apron and pulled out a brown leather wallet. 'Here you go,' she said, holding it out over the counter.

'What's your name son?' Munson asked as the man walked up to the counter and accepted the wallet from Candy.

'Luke.'

'You from round here Luke?'

'Not really. I work for Fed Ex in Lewisville. I deliver parcels round here sometimes. That's my van outside.'

Munson quickstepped over to him and peered over his shoulder at the Fed Ex van outside, pretending as if he hadn't noticed it before. 'Let me walk you out to your vehicle,' he said, placing an arm around Luke's shoulder. 'I'd like to ask you a few things.'

Behind them Randall cleared his throat. 'You know what? He should come with us to the police station for questioning. He could be a vital witness.'

'You can have him when I'm finished with him,' said Munson. 'Stay here and look after Candy. She's in shock.'

Munson guided Luke out to the parking lot. Once they were out of earshot of the diner, he released his grip on Luke's shoulder. He pulled out his ID badge and flashed it at him. 'I'm Jack Munson, FBI. I want you to tell me exactly what you saw when you were in the diner earlier.'

'Okay,' said Luke. The mention of the FBI seemed to have put him on edge. He glanced back into the diner at the watching audience inside.

'Don't look at them,' said Munson. 'Look at me. What happened when the Red Mohawk killed Arnold Bailey?'

'Which one was Arnold Bailey?'

'The guy with no head or fingers.'

'Is that the guy he dragged into the washroom?'

'That's right. Arnold Bailey. Did he do anything to provoke an attack?'

Luke shook his head. 'I don't think so. This Arnold Bailey guy, he looked like he was ready for an argument with his girlfriend. She said something that pissed him off. But then the psycho fella put on a mask and walked up behind him with a fucking great big blade in his hand. He never saw it coming.'

'What girlfriend?'

'Huh?'

'You said Arnold was having an argument with his girlfriend. What happened to her? What were they arguing about?'

'It wasn't an argument as such. I was sitting at a booth near them. His girlfriend, well, I think she was his girlfriend, anyway, she kinda tugged at his arm and said something about wanting to keep her baby.'

'Her baby? What baby?'

'I don't know. I guess she was pregnant, or something.'

'Did she look pregnant?'

'No. But, y'know, I'm no expert. She definitely said she wanted to keep her baby though. But this guy, Arnold, he gave her a filthy look and she shut right up. And then like I said, the guy in the mask came over and chopped his fingers off with this big fucking meat cleaver. Two guys on a table near me got up to try and restrain him but he turned on them. I stayed put. Once the masked guy had killed the two other fellas he went back to Arnold and dragged him off towards the men's room by his hair. That's when I got up and ran the fuck out.'

'What about the girl? What did she do?'

'I don't know.'

'Did she scream? Did she run away? What?'

Luke shrugged. 'Fuck knows man. I didn't hang about. People were going crazy, *everyone* was screaming and running for the exit. It was all a bit mad. Every man for himself, know what I mean?'

'Yeah. So you didn't see what happened to the girl?'

'Sorry, no.'

'That's fine. I'm hearing that she ran over the road into that field over there. Know where she might be headed?'

Luke looked over at the field. 'There's nothing out there. Just one farmhouse. A weird transvestite farmer called Litgo lives there. I've delivered some strange parcels to him in the past. Other than that, it's just fields and swampland.'

'How do you get to Litgo's?'

'I drive. Why?'

'No. I mean what roads do you take? Would you drive across that field to get to him?'

Luke looked puzzled. 'Drive across the field? No. Hell, that would wreck the suspension on my van. There's a dirt track a mile down the road that leads to Litgo's. It ain't perfect. It's a bit bumpy and stuff but it's safer than driving across the field.'

'So why would anyone drive across the field? Munson asked, recalling the sight of the police squad car racing across it earlier.

'Shortcut I guess,' said Luke. 'You'd have to be in one helluva hurry though.'

118

Munson looked out across the field. The police car that had driven out that way had long since vanished over the horizon.

'There's a dirt track a mile down the road, you say?'

'Yeah.'

'Is it signposted?'

'Yeah. You can't miss it. But if you're planning on paying Litgo a visit, watch your step. He's kind of paranoid. Because of his isolated location he's been burgled quite a few times, so these days he leaves little traps around to catch out intruders.'

Munson smirked. 'Like what? Landmines?'

'No one knows, but the last guy who tried to rob him ended up in hospital for a week after something strange happened to him at that place.'

'I'm not planning on robbing him, so I'll take my chances,' said Munson. 'But thanks for the heads up.'

Twenty Four

Benny was relieved that Baby hadn't had much to say since he'd picked her up from Litgo's place. She seemed dazed and quite shaken, which was hardly surprising considering what kind of day she'd had. She'd seen Arnold murdered, been shot in the arm by Reg the chef from the diner and had then lost consciousness in a house owned by a man dressed as Supergirl.

'How you feeling?' Benny asked. 'You okay? You look tired.'

'I am tired. And my arm is still throbbing.'

'You should close your eyes and try to sleep. That will help.'

'Are you sure?'

'Yeah. Trust me. When you've been shot, the best thing to do is sleep. That's what any doctor worth his salt will tell you.'

'Really?'

'Uh huh. Try it. You'll feel better, I promise.'

Baby didn't look convinced but she was timid by nature so she closed her eyes and tried to sleep.

Perfect.

She was still under the misapprehension that Benny was driving her to the hospital. Now that he'd convinced her to close her eyes he could drive her back to The Beaver Palace without her realising and becoming hysterical.

Benny turned down the volume on the radio a few notches. He didn't want anything noisy disturbing his passenger. Unfortunately within a minute of her closing her eyes his cell phone started ringing in his pocket. Keeping one hand on the steering wheel he fiddled around in his pocket until he managed to haul it out. The call was from Reg at the diner. He answered it just before it went to voicemail.

'Hey Reg,' he said, keeping his voice down. 'What's up?'

'Did you get the girl from Litgo's place yet?'

'Yeah. Didn't he tell you?'

'I tried calling him but he's not answering.'

'You know what he's like. He's probably tied himself up in Wonder Woman's golden lasso again, or drunk some of that poison he leaves lying around for burglars.'

Reg laughed politely for a moment before his voice took on a more serious tone. 'Thing is there's something else you need to know.'

'What's that?'

'An FBI agent dropped by the diner just now. He knows there was a girl with Arnold and that she ran off in the direction of Litgo's place. Candy thinks he's going out to Litgo's to see if he can find her. That's why I need to get hold of Litgo so I can warn him.'

'Damn. I heard someone from the FBI was coming to town. We can't have this asshole talking to Litgo. Litgo's no good in a pressure situation like that. He'll crack. You'd better keep trying to call him because he could seriously fuck this up.'

'It's already fucked up,' Reg snapped. 'This fucking Red Mohawk freak has brought a whole load of trouble to town with him. We'd better warn Mellencamp about it.'

'Let me do that. I'm on my way to see him now. Thanks for the heads up Reg.'

'No problem. Speak to you later.'

Benny hung up the phone and pondered the predicament. The last thing he needed was the FBI in B Movie Hell, questioning people like Litgo. If Litgo slipped up and blabbed about Baby then the next person the FBI would come looking for would be Benny.

'Bad news?' Baby asked.

Benny had forgotten about her for a minute and was annoyed to see that she wasn't trying to sleep. 'No, nothing too bad.' He smiled disingenuously at her.

'Where are we going?' she asked.

'What's that?'

'Where are we going?'

'Oh. I'm taking you home.' He stared ahead at the road, but out of the corner of his eye he could see her face drop. The last place this girl would have wanted to go was back to The Beaver Palace. But it was for her own good.

'Home?' said Baby, the disappointment evident in her voice.

'Yeah. You know, The Beaver Palace.'

'But my arm. I need to go to the hospital.'

'I'm taking you there afterwards. I've got to make sure Mr Mellencamp can see that you're safe first. He's been very worried about you, especially after what happened to Arnold.'

'Please,' her voice reeked of desperation. 'Please don't take me back there.'

'Baby,' he said calmly. 'It's for your own good.'

'Who was that on the phone?'

'No one.'

'It was Reg wasn't it?'

Benny could feel himself becoming irritated by Baby's constant questioning. 'Yes. It was Reg.'

'I think it was him who shot me in the arm.'

Benny took a deep breath. 'Baby, if I was you I'd concentrate on working out how you're going to apologise to Mr Mellencamp for all the trouble you've caused today. If it wasn't for you Arnold would still be alive. Mr Mellencamp is pretty upset about that. So instead of worrying about who shot you in the arm, maybe you should start worrying about where the next bullet's going to hit you.'

Twenty Five

Dominic Touretto had no idea what he'd gotten himself into. Fonseca wasn't just a great deal stronger than any of the other women that he had sexually assaulted, she also had a mastery of martial arts at her disposal.

She hadn't had any need to use her fighting skills for some time, but the old instincts were still there. As the naked figure of Touretto lunged towards her, she twisted around, backed into him, stamped the heel of her right shoe down onto his foot and positioned herself ready to throw him over her shoulder.

Touretto yelled out in pain as the heel of her shoe crushed his toes. He wrapped his right arm around her neck and pressed his body up against her back. It was a predictable move and exactly what she was hoping he would do. As she felt his semi-erect penis press into her back she made her move. She leant forward, grabbed Touretto under his armpit and threw him over her shoulder. He crashed onto the floor in front of her. A loud slapping sound echoed around the room, similar to the sound of someone belly flopping into a swimming pool from the high board. The impact of his back on the floor knocked the stuffing out of him instantly. He lay dazed on the ground, staring up at the ceiling. His eyes blinked furiously as he tried to make sense of what had just happened to him.

Fonseca knelt down behind him and grabbed his head, lifting it up from the floor. She wrapped an arm around his throat and squeezed hard, closing off his windpipe. He struggled for a while, but to no avail. Fonseca was too strong for him. The lack of oxygen to his brain coupled with the dizziness he felt from hitting the ground moments earlier made his attempts to free himself futile. When he was on the verge of losing consciousness Fonseca eased her grip on him and lowered his head back onto the floor. She twisted him over onto his front. He let out a tired groan and attempted to climb back to his knees.

Fonseca spotted a stick of roll-on deodorant on the bedside table. She reached over and grabbed it. She flicked the lid off, all the while pressing her knee into the back of her helpless opponent. She grabbed a clump of his hair and pulled his head back. He was now in exactly the position she wanted him. To his great surprise and horror she rammed the lubricated end of the deodorant stick right up his asshole.

It woke him up from his dazed state in an instant. His body tensed and he let out a croaking noise from his throat. Fonseca pressed the deodorant in as far it would go.

'How does that feel?' she yelled in his ear. 'Huh? How the fuck does that make you feel *you sick fuck?*'

Touretto yelled out in pain. 'Ow! Fuck. FUCK. *FUCK!* Not good. I give in. I'm sorry. *Aaaaaagh!'*

Fonseca pulled the deodorant stick halfway out of his ass, then rammed it back in twice as hard as before. Touretto screamed out in pain again. Fonseca let go of the deodorant and grabbed a hold of his scrotum. She squeezed it tightly and dug her fingernails in hard. His screams became even more high-pitched.

'If you don't want me to rip your balls off you'd better fucking behave,' she said, speaking calmly and clearly into his ear.

'I'm sorry. *I'm sorry,*' he squealed.

'Now tell me something. If the door is locked, what's the best way for me to get out of here?'

'You can't.'

She squeezed his balls hard. 'That's not what I wanted to hear. When you need attention in this place, how do you get it? How can we get Dr Carter to come back and unlock the door before I slice your junk off?'

'That's not the real Dr Carter,' Touretto groaned.

'What?'

'The patients took over the asylum a few days ago. That woman who was just in here wasn't the real Dr Carter. She's a patient here. A group of patients overpowered the doctors and nurses last week. It's how Joey Conrad escaped. This asylum is being run by the inmates.'

Milena Fonseca let go of his balls and stood back. 'Don't move,' she said. 'You make one tiny movement and I'll kick that deodorant so far up your ass you'll be using it as a breath mint.'

The pathetic naked figure of Dominic Touretto remained on all fours, his ass up in the air with the bottom end of a deodorant stick poking out. He had managed to maintain his erection throughout the vicious assault Fonseca had inflicted upon him. In fact, if anything it was bigger and harder than it had been before she'd rammed the deodorant up his butt. It caught her eye and distracted her momentarily before she continued questioning him.

'You're telling me that this asylum is being run by the patients?'

'Ever since last Tuesday.'

'So, where are the real doctors?'

'They're all dead. Joey Conrad killed them all.'

Fonseca wasn't sure what to make of the revelations. If she was to stand any chance of getting out of this asylum she was going to have to make some phone calls. She was thankful that she still had her phone with her. She fumbled around in her pocket for it.

'If the patients have taken over, then how come you're still in your room?' she asked. 'Why aren't *you* pretending to be a doctor as well?'

'I didn't want to get in trouble. Pretending to be a doctor's not my thing. I'm not crazy you know.'

Even though he had been warned not to move, Touretto reached back with one hand and began massaging his balls. Fonseca had squeezed them pretty hard and they were probably hurting like hell.

She kept one eye on him as she flicked through the menus on her phone. It was essential that she called Jack Munson right away. He would need to know about this, and fast. But before she had a chance to dial his number she heard a clicking sound. Someone opened the door behind her.

Twenty Six

Silvio Mellencamp's day had been full of ups and downs and a damn sight more stress than he was used to. He hadn't even had time to get properly dressed. He had a lot of things on his mind as he sat behind his desk in his favourite gold-coloured silk dressing gown.

The desk was an exact replica of Bill Clinton's White House desk and provided enough discreet legroom underneath it to fit two of the girls from The Beaver Palace at the same time. Unfortunately for Mellencamp, he'd had to deal with one phone call after another while keeping up to date with the criminal goings on in B Movie Hell so he'd had no time to get any girls under the desk. And now much to his irritation he had another unwanted visitor.

The scruffy blond-haired young man who had taken up a seat opposite him had a broad smile on his face. His name was Cedric Trautman. Clarisse had showed him into see Mellencamp because he claimed to have "big news". He had paid a visit to one of the girls downstairs first and by the look on his face he'd had a good time.

'What can I do for you, son?' Mellencamp asked. He took a puff on a big fat Cuban cigar and tapped the ash into a large ashtray on his desk.

'I'm looking for a job and I heard that you might have an opening.'

Mellencamp glanced over at his personal bodyguard Mack who was standing by the door. Mack shrugged apologetically. It had been a crazy day and he obviously hadn't had time to properly vet all the visitors.

'I was told you had some big news for me,' said Mellencamp, leaning back in his chair and taking a large swig of cognac from a brandy glass that was always half filled. 'You looking for a job had better not be the big news.'

'It's sort of about your friend Arnold,' said Cedric.

Mellencamp took another puff on his cigar and blew the smoke across the desk at Cedric. 'Arnold's dead,' he said.

Cedric coughed and attempted to wave some of the smoke out of his face. 'I heard on the news that Arnold was chopped up by the Red Mohawk,' he said.

'That's old news.'

'Yes I know, and it's tragic an' everything, but I thought if I turned up here real early today and showed a bit of initiative, you might consider taking me on as his replacement?'

'A replacement? Ha! You know Arnold did about a hundred different things here! You're just a kid. How old are you?'

'Nineteen, sir.'

'Nineteen and you think you can replace Arnold, one of my oldest and most trusted friends?'

'Not just like that, sir. I'm willing to work my way up from the bottom, but I figured you must be a man short now, and well, it's always been my ambition to be a henchman for a local Crime Lord in B Movie Hell.'

'*Crime Lord?* Who the fuck are you calling a Crime Lord?' Mellencamp scoffed.

'Um, well you do run a brothel. And I've heard that sometimes when people screw you around you have them whacked.'

Mellencamp took another puff on his cigar and looked over at Mack again. Mack as ever, simply shrugged.

'Whacked,' Mellencamp muttered. 'I think you've been watching too much television. And besides, the correct term round these parts is clipped.'

'Clipped? Okay. I'll remember that. I'm good at remembering stuff.'

'You're good at remembering stuff. Well that's just epic,' said Mellencamp sarcastically. 'And I'm a Crime Lord, huh?' He took another puff on his cigar. 'I guess I kinda like that. And, you know what? I like the fact that you've got balls. It takes a lot of balls to come in here on the day my buddy Arnold gets killed and offer to take his place.'

'Thank you, sir. My father always told me to show a bit of initiative, to be the first in line and all that.'

'That's good advice,' said Mellencamp. 'But before I agree to make you one of my trusted henchmen, tell me, what skills do you have?'

'Skills?'

'Yeah, you know, special talents.' Mellencamp pointed at Mack. 'Take a look at Mack over there. What do you think his special talent is?'

Cedric peered over his shoulder at Mack who stared back at him without revealing any emotion. Mack was six-feet-eight inches tall and almost as wide. He had a shaved head the size of a beach ball. His biceps were huge too. His hands were clasped in front of his waist and they were the size of a couple of shovel heads. Mack had the biggest hands in town and when those babies were clenched into fists, they could break through walls.

After staring at Mack for a few seconds, Cedric turned back to face Mellencamp who blew another puff of smoke into his face with impeccable timing.

'At a guess, I'd say Mack's special talent is that he's good at lifting things,' Cedric stated confidently.

Mellencamp frowned. 'Well d'uh. Of course he's good at lifting things. Look at the size of him. The guy's a fucking giant. That's an obvious one. There's nothing special about lifting stuff. *But* there is a story behind Mack and how he came to be here. You see Mack used to live in Arkansas but he had to leave because the cops were after him for murder. He was muscle for hire. He killed so many people he earned himself the nickname *The Slasher*.'

'The Slasher?'

'That's right, The Slasher. Now guess why?'

Cedric waved away some more smoke that was coming his way. 'I suppose with a name like The Slasher he must be good with a knife. So I guess his special talent is slicing people up with knives, right?'

'Wrong! He strangles people. Those hands of his can squeeze the life out of a man in a matter of seconds. I guarantee you when he slides his hands around someone's throat, that someone is gonna be dead within ten seconds. It's a sight to behold.'

Cedric looked back at Mack then turned back to Mellencamp. His brow was furrowed into a confused frown. 'I don't get it,' he said. 'Why would a strangler be called The Slasher?'

'Because he pisses on all of his victims.'

'I beg your pardon.'

'Mack urinates on all of his victims. That's his calling card. Once they're dead he whips out his Johnson and takes *a slash* on the corpse.'

'But why?'

'To get himself the nickname The Slasher. Keep up.'

'And that's a special talent? Pissing on dead people? Okay, umm, so I guess I could take a shit on some dead people if you wanted? That could be my special talent.'

Mellencamp pondered the suggestion. 'The Shitter?' he said out loud, puffing on his cigar some more. 'No, I don't think I like the name. The Stain, that might work. You could be called The Stain. Or the *Shit Stain*. You look like a shit stain.'

'Seriously?' said Cedric. 'You actually want me to shit on people?'

Mellencamp laughed. 'Nah, I'm just messing with ya. Pissing on people is Mack's thing. You can come up with your own trademark

128

later if you want, but for now I just want to know what skills you have that you think I might need. Why should I hire you to be one of my henchmen? What are your attributes?'

'Well, I'm hardworking sir. I'm honest. I don't steal and I know when to keep my mouth shut.'

'Knowing when to keep your mouth shut is a minimum requirement, boy.'

'Good. Because, you know, I've known about Baby for a long time and I've never said anything to anyone about it. And obviously if you give me a job I'll continue to keep quiet about it.'

Mellencamp had been about to take another puff on his cigar, but held off, holding it an inch short of his mouth as he took on board what Cedric had just said.

'You've known about Baby for a long time?' he muttered, glancing over at Mack momentarily.

'Yes. You know, I know who she really is and stuff, but obviously I've never told anyone, and I never will….' He was smiling at Mellencamp but the smile slowly faded as he took on board the look of displeasure on the other man's face. He swallowed hard, then he added, '….even if I don't get the job.'

'That's good to know,' said Mellencamp. He looked back over at Mack and nodded at him.

Cedric shifted uneasily in his seat, clearly sensing that he might have spoken out of turn. Mack snuck up on him from behind and with one swift tug from his giant hands he yanked Cedric's chair out from under him. Cedric fell back and landed on his ass. His head hit the floor and he found himself staring up at the ceiling. *And up at Mack.*

Mack reached down and grabbed him by his hair. He hauled him to his feet, wrapped his huge left hand around Cedric's throat, and lifted him up a foot above the floor. Cedric grabbed desperately at Mack's hand and tried to free himself from his iron grip. It was a wasted effort.

'Show him what you can do, Mack,' said Mellencamp, swilling his glass of cognac around in his hand.

'Look boss. One hand!' Mack replied, grinning inanely.

'Very good Mack. Very good.'

Mellencamp watched as Cedric choked and fought desperately to peel Mack's hand away from his throat. It took only a few seconds for his face to turn bright red, then slowly transform into a blue colour, his eyes bulging as the air was expelled from his lungs. Mellencamp smiled and chewed on the end of his cigar.

'Mack,' he said, blowing smoke towards the ceiling. 'Try not to piss on the carpet this time.'

Twenty Seven

'What the hell is going on in here?'

Milena Fonseca spun around. Standing at the entrance to Dominic Touretto's room was Linda Carter. The doctor looked wide eyed and baffled at the sight before her. Touretto was stark naked on his knees cradling his balls with one hand, and he had a deodorant stick wedged up his asshole. Fonseca was standing behind him with her cell phone in her hand.

'Were you taking photos of his ass?' Dr Carter asked. 'And what has he got wedged up there this time?'

Fonseca glared at the doctor. 'Why did you lock me in?'

Dr Carter frowned. 'What are you talking about? I didn't lock you in.'

Fonseca pointed at Dominic Touretto. 'He said you locked the door behind you when you went out.'

'And you *believed* him?'

'Did you lock the door?'

'No. Why would I?'

'Because you're a patient here. You're not a real doctor.'

Dr Carter raised her eyebrows. 'I've only been out of the room for two minutes and you've gone insane. And why is he naked?'

Fonseca took a deep breath and tried to collect her thoughts. She thought back to when Dr Carter had left the room earlier. She couldn't recall hearing the door lock. It was Touretto who claimed that Carter had locked it, but she hadn't actually heard a key turn in the lock. The sight of Touretto stripping off, with plans of sexually assaulting her had scrambled her brain. She hadn't had time to consciously process what was going on. She had been too preoccupied with defending herself and ramming the deodorant up his bum.

'She stuck a deodorant up my ass!' Touretto shouted.

Fonseca stood up straight and swung her right foot hard at his backside. The toe of her shoe connected with the end of the deodorant stick and kicked it further up inside him, out of sight.

'Oh ΓUCK!' Touretto slumped forward, his face thudding into the floor.

Dr Carter rushed over and grabbed Fonseca by the arm, pulling her away from him. 'HAVE YOU LOST YOUR MIND?' she yelled. 'What are you doing?'

'He tried to assault me. He told me that you had locked us in. He said that the asylum had been taken over by the patients and that you were one of them, posing as a doctor.'

Dr Carter let go of her arm. 'I did warn you he was a fantasist!'

'I know, but for a minute there, he had me convinced. It seemed to make sense.'

'This place will do that to you.'

'Fucking hell.' Fonseca felt embarrassed, although she was still trying to work out if there might have been any shred of truth in what Touretto had said.

'You looked me up on your phone just now, didn't you?' said Dr Carter. 'Surely there was a picture that will verify that I am in fact a doctor and not a patient here?'

Fonseca thought about it and nodded. 'Yes. The picture was very old. You look different now. And you've had a nose job.'

'Thanks for noticing.'

'It was mentioned in the file.'

Carter peered around Fonseca and took a look at Touretto who was still on his knees with his face pressed into the floor. 'I'd step aside if I was you agent Fonseca,' she said. 'He's about to ejaculate on your leg.'

Fonseca looked down. Touretto was masturbating furiously with his right hand. And he was aiming his erect penis in her direction. This guy was unbelievable. She put her right foot to good use once again. This time she took a longer back-lift and ploughed the meat of her foot into his jaw. His head flew back, and his neck made a cracking sound. The blow knocked him unconscious straightaway. He fell onto his back. His eyes rolled up in his head and his hand slipped off his penis. Not a moment too soon by the look of it.

Fonseca turned back to Dr Carter. 'I think I've seen enough of this place now thank you,' she said.

Dr Carter leant down over the body of Dominic Touretto and rolled him over into the recovery position. 'How did he get you to stick the deodorant up his bottom?'

'He didn't *get me* to do anything. It was self-defence. I rammed it up there to teach that rapist sonofabitch a lesson.'

'Okay. One problem with that though.'

'What?'

'He loves having stuff shoved up his ass. You've played right into his hands there. One of his favourite sexual fantasies is to be dominated by a woman. I hope you didn't squeeze his balls too.' She looked down at Touretto's balls. 'You did, didn't you?'

132

'He gave me no choice.'

'Of course. You should count yourself lucky. Squeezing his balls is usually enough to get him off. He's always asking the female staff to kick him or punch him in the balls. And there have been numerous times he's asked for anal examinations in the hope someone will stick a surgical tool up his anus.'

Fonseca wiped her hand on her shirt. 'So he really is insane?'

Dr Carter looked surprised. 'This is an asylum, *of course he's insane*. He might not have multiple personalities in the way he convinced the judge and jury in his trial, but he's definitely not normal. I, on the other hand am *most definitely* a doctor.'

'Yes. I can see that now. My apologies.'

'It doesn't matter. Now, was there anything else you wanted from him? Or can I get someone up here to revive him and remove that deodorant from his bum,' she paused before adding. 'Although not necessarily in that order.'

'Yes. I'm done here. Could you have someone call me a cab please? I need to get to B Movie Hell to meet up with my partner.'

'Certainly. Come on, I'll escort you back to reception if there's nothing else you want here.'

'There is one other thing I need,' said Fonseca.

'Yes.'

'I'd like to wash my hands a few times.'

'Obviously. I'll show you to the staff washroom where the good soap is.'

Dr Carter walked out, leaving Fonseca to look around the room one more time. For good measure Fonseca kicked Dominic Touretto hard in the balls and then grabbed his copy of *Gone with the Wind*. There were no two ways about it, she was taking that book with her. And the photo of the girl with the blue birthmark that was tucked inside it.

Twenty Eight

Munson cruised down the highway until he came to the dirt track on the left roughly a mile down, just like Luke the Fed Ex guy had said it would be. He steered the Mercedes off the road and onto the dirt track. The surface was uneven and full of potholes, but even so, it had to be better than driving across the field like the cops had done. He followed the dirt track for about a mile until he saw a cottage up ahead.

The police patrol car that he had seen driving across the field earlier was parked outside. A red door at the front of the cottage was hanging off its hinges, swinging slowly back and forth in the wind. If this was Litgo's house, then it looked like it had seen some recent violence.

Munson slowed his car to a crawl and pulled up next to the squad car. He killed the engine and waited to see if anyone poked their head out of the cottage door to see what the noise was. The place looked eerily empty, in spite of the open door and the police car parked outside. There was no sign of any movement anywhere. Something felt a little off. But that wasn't uncommon in B Movie Hell. Nothing seemed right about this town. He pulled his bottle of rum out of his jacket, unscrewed the lid and took another swig. A sip here and there was just about keeping his hangover at bay. He cursed the fact he'd been drinking the night before. If he'd known he'd be called into action he would have stayed sober, *probably*.

He slipped the bottle of rum back in his jacket and drew his pistol from its holster under his left arm. He opened the car door and climbed out onto the grass and stone beneath his feet. A gust of wind blew across him. The evening would be drawing in soon. It was already turning cold. He crouched down, concealing himself behind the police car, just in case there was any trouble ahead. A bunch of cops had already been gunned down by Joey Conrad. He had no intention of joining them in the morgue any time soon. He peered over the trunk of the police car and shouted out in the direction of the cottage door.

'This is Munson from the FBI. Anyone there?'

The door continued to swing slowly in the wind, ignoring him. No response came from within the cottage. He shouted out one more time.

'Anyone in there? Hello! Anyone?'

Still no answer.

He stepped out from behind the police car, pointing his pistol at the open red door of the cottage. And he edged forward. If someone was inside pointing a gun at him, he would be an easy target. But this was what he got paid so handsomely for, sticking his life on the line to hunt down killers.

He squatted down into a crouched position and made a run for it. He hurried up to the side of the cottage, making far more noise than he had intended to. He pressed his back up against the wall, right by the open door, ready to make a move to go inside. This was quite a predicament. On the one hand he wanted to take one more swig from his bottle of rum, but on the other hand, that was just a fucking dumb idea. And he shouldn't even be thinking about it. He needed to focus on the mission in hand.

He took a deep breath and peered slowly around the open doorway, his gun cocked and ready to fire if necessary. On the red tiled floor inside he saw a body on the floor. The body of a cop. He stepped inside the cottage straight into a kitchen. *A ransacked kitchen.*

With two dead cops on the floor.

One was lying on his back by the door in a pool of blood. The other was a few yards away lying face down in a similar state of splattered blood. Even though both of them had been executed with gunshots to the head, he recognised them as the two cops who had left the diner and driven across the field in a hurry to get to Litgo's.

Doing his best to avoid the blood, Munson trod carefully around them and made his way over to an opening on the far side of the kitchen. It led through to a hallway where he found the third dead body, lying face down on a fluffy red carpet. This one was different. This guy hadn't been shot. And he was wearing a Superman outfit, or upon closer inspection, a Super-*girl* outfit, complete with a set of crumpled fake tits underneath the costume.

'You must be Litgo,' Munson whispered to the corpse as he stood over it. The Supergirl costume was torn in several places and covered in blood. Much of the blood came from a gaping wound in his neck, which had the necktie from the Supergirl cape stuck in it. Someone had sliced him open from ear to ear. But that wasn't all. The slitting of the throat would have been the final, fatal cut. This guy had suffered for a while before that. He'd had some of his fingers cut off. Four on one hand, two on the other. That indicated a very real possibility of torture. If this was the work of Joey Conrad (and Munson was pretty sure that it was) then why would he torture Litgo? And where the hell was the girl who had fled across the field? Had she made it to Litgo's? And if so, where was she now? And where was Joey Conrad?

He checked all the other rooms in the cottage and found nothing of note. No more dead bodies, thankfully. No killer and definitely no pregnant girl. He did find a miniature bottle of rum though. It was called Cutthroat Rum, possibly a local brand, but certainly one he had never come across before. He slid it into his pocket with the intention of trying it later on.

He walked back into the kitchen and leant down over one of the two dead police officers. He unhooked the walkie-talkie from the guy's belt and sat himself down on one of the chairs around the kitchen table. He had a number of things to consider. There was one almighty mess building up in B Movie Hell. He checked his watch. Pincent would be home soon, and Munson definitely needed to talk to him to find out what the fuck was going on. There were so many questions. Like, why was it that Pincent couldn't talk to him on the office phone? Or his company cell phone? And what did Joey Conrad's arrival in B Movie Hell have to do with a mysterious pregnant girl, a bunch of unhelpful cops, a dodgy waitress and a dead transvestite in a shitty house in the middle of a field? The waitress at The Alaska definitely knew something, but she wouldn't tell him anything while the cops were there. He had to get the cops away from the diner. The best way to do that would be to radio in the murder of two of their officers at Litgo's.

Trying to piece everything together in his head was beginning to give him a headache, and the thought of the miniature bottle of rum in his pocket was hanging at the back of his mind. He decided to take a quick taste of it to see what it was like. Hell, maybe it would even provide some inspiration? He unscrewed the lid and took a long swig, downing almost half the miniature. It tasted foul, nothing at all like rum. He grimaced and put the lid back on the bottle. It was time to radio in the latest murders. He flicked a switch on the dead cop's walkie-talkie.

'Hello. This is Jack Munson of the FBI. I'm at Litgo's cottage in a field somewhere.' He suddenly felt a jarring sensation in his stomach as if he were about to throw up. He tried to ignore it and carry on. 'You've got two officers down here. I repeat two of your officers are down. Permanently. The Red Mohawk has struck again. Litgo the owner of the property is also dead. And he's lost some fingers, possibly been tortured.' The jarring sensation transformed into a stabbing sensation, causing his voice to stiffen. 'Your two cops have been executed by gunshots to the head. Over and out.'

He tossed the walkie-talkie back on the floor by the dead officer and rubbed his stomach. The pain subsided a little. He hoped that a whole bunch of the local cops would head out to Litgo's to investigate.

It would keep them busy for a while longer. That is, if they weren't busy enough already. After all, the bodies were starting to pile up all over town.

Munson liked the idea of heading back to the Alaska Roadside Diner and questioning the waitress again. He tried to remember her name. Carly? Carey? Candy? *Candy, that was it.* Questioning Candy when there were no cops present might just provide him with a few answers. She definitely knew more than she was letting on.

His stomach suddenly tightened again. And it rumbled. He felt the early warning signs of a bout of heartburn, or possibly vomiting. In fact, definitely vomiting. He hauled himself up out of the chair and made a dash for the kitchen sink. He made it in the nick of time. A huge splurge of vomit flew out of his mouth and over the dirty dishes in Litgo's sink. The pain in his stomach didn't ease though. He doubled over in pain, placing one of his hands down on the cold kitchen floor. What the fuck was in that rum?

Twenty Nine

Dr Carter was true to her word and called a cab for Milena Fonseca. Fonseca waited outside in the fresh air for it to arrive. It was a painfully long fifteen minute wait, but the thought of hanging around inside the asylum after what had happened in there just didn't appeal. Grimwald's Asylum was more insane than its title suggested and the staff weren't any more likeable than the patients. So Fonseca waited outside, with her stolen copy of *Gone with the Wind* tucked inside her jacket.

The air had turned cold by the time the blue cab pulled up. The driver wound down the window and called out to her. 'Hi. Are you Milena Fonseca?'

'That's me.'

The young man jumped out of his cab and came over to greet her at the asylum's front doors. 'Hi, I'm Darius from Johnny Cabs,' he said. 'Have you got any luggage?'

'No. I wasn't staying here. I just dropped in for a visit.'

Darius was olive skinned and in his early thirties. He was wearing a blue blazer with a matching hat, the kind a bus driver would wear. 'Where can I take you?' he asked.

'Johnny Cabs huh?' said Fonseca, reluctantly accepting a handshake from him and checking out the cab, which looked like it had seen better days.

'Yes Miss. Where can I take you?'

'B Movie Hell please. I'm meeting a friend there. I'm not sure exactly where yet, but I'll let you know on the way.'

Darius hurried over to the cab and opened the back door for her. It was a comforting moment of chivalry after the Touretto incident. She stepped in and he closed it behind her.

Fonseca took one last look back at the asylum as she pulled *Gone With The Wind* out from inside her jacket. She placed it on the seat beside her. She reminded herself not to touch the photo inside it again. That thing had been up Dominic Touretto's ass. She shuddered as the image of him naked popped into her mind. It was a relief when the cab pulled away and drove her out onto the main highway.

'How long will it take us to get there?' she asked.

'About fifteen minutes,' Darius replied, smiling at her in his rear view mirror. 'There's very little traffic and virtually no stoplights.'

Fonseca decided that twenty minutes was enough time in which to press him for some local knowledge. After all, if a cab driver in a small hick town didn't know all the local gossip then who did?

She leant forward from the back seat and spoke loudly and clearly *into* his ear. 'You live in B Movie Hell?' she asked.

'All my life,' he replied.

'You like it there?'

'What's not to like? Got a real good sense of community spirit there. Everyone looks out for everybody else.'

'That's nice. You got all your family there then?'

'Yeah. Is that why you're going? Visiting someone?'

'No. I'm with the FBI. Come about the killer that's just turned up in town.'

'Oh. That guy. Yeah it's terrible what's happened,' said Darius. 'Pete, the police officer he killed and beheaded was in the same class as my brother at school. I've known him my whole life. I'll tell you, I hope this Red Mohawk guy tries to get a ride in my cab. I'd like five minutes alone with him to show him what I think of him.'

'I wouldn't recommend that,' said Fonseca, conscious not to let on that she knew the true identity of the masked killer. 'He's clearly very dangerous.'

'Do you guys know who he is yet?'

'I can't say.'

'Why not?'

'Until we're one hundred percent sure it would be wrong to label anyone as the killer. So far he's been wearing a mask so it's not really possible to identify him.'

'Is it someone from the asylum? Is that why you were there?'

'No. I stopped off there to visit a friend of mine who works there.'

'Who's that?'

'Dr Carter.'

'Oh. Yeah she's nice.'

'Yes. She's delightful.'

'So what leads have you got on this murder case?'

'None that I can talk about.'

'But seriously, come on. I bet you do know who's behind the mask, don't you?'

'No,' Fonseca lied. 'But so far we don't think it's anyone local. Like you said, you've got a real good community spirit in B Movie Hell. If the killer was a local man I think you'd know before we did.'

'That's true. According to the news, he's driving round in an old yellow and red stock car that he stole this morning from Jackson's Motors. I know exactly the car they're talking about too. If I see it, we're going after him, okay?'

Fonseca smiled. 'Okay.' She suspected that Darius was all bravado and if he saw the car the chances of him following it and confronting the masked killer were probably very slim indeed. 'So your friend Pete who was killed, do you know if he had anything in common with any of the other victims?'

'Like what?'

'Anything. Did they have the same hair colour, personality, sporting heroes, anything really?'

Darius screwed his face up as he contemplated how to answer. It struck Fonseca that he wasn't too bright and by asking him such an open question she had given him far too much to think about. It seemed to be deeply troubling him.

'He's killed a few cops now,' he mumbled. 'Of the civilians he's killed, Arnold worked for Mellencamp, but Hank Jackson the car salesman worked for himself. I don't know if they have anything in common. There's another victim who was with the cops that got shot earlier today. He hasn't been identified yet.'

'You said Arnold worked for Silvio Mellencamp? What does Mellencamp do exactly?'

'Mr Mellencamp, oh he's got his fingers in everything. He pretty much owns B Movie Hell. He's the one who came up with the name for the town. He used to be a movie producer in Hollywood. Then he moved here and totally transformed the place.'

'Do people not mind that he changed the name of the town?'

'I think there was a little resistance at first but when it became clear that he was willing to invest his money in all the local businesses, people soon got over it. That was over fifteen years ago now.'

'Is he a good guy?'

'Yeah. He employs half the town. If people in B Movie Hell are out of work, the Mellencamp foundation finds work for them. Trust me, if he ever moved out of B Movie Hell the local economy would be knackered. I mean, he even part-owns the cab firm I drive for. It was him who came up with the name *Johnny Cabs*. And he designed the uniform too.'

'He sounds very original. I wonder where he gets his ideas.'

Darius shrugged. 'I don't know. Someone told me that Johnny Cabs featured in a movie once, but I don't recall the name of it.'

'Yes, I think it did. What do you know about girls?'

'Girls?'

'Yeah. Isn't there a place called The Beaver Palace in B Movie Hell?'

Darius frowned and took a hard look at her via his rear view mirror. 'Are you into girls then?' he asked.

'No. I'm just being nosy that's all. I heard that Mellencamp owned The Beaver Palace.'

'Oh, I wouldn't know about that sort of thing.'

'Of course. It's just that someone gave me a photo of a girl who looked like she might be an escort. Could you take a look at it for me? I'd be interested to see if you know who she is, seeing as you're a cab driver I figure you must know most of the local women right?'

'Sure. Let's see it.'

'It's in my book. Hang on a sec.' She opened the book onto the page with the photo in it. 'Do you have a tissue?' she asked.

'Sure. Hang on.' Darius reached over into his glove box and pulled out a white tissue. He handed it back to Fonseca.

She took the tissue and used it to pull out the photo from *Gone With The Wind*. She held the photo out in front of Daruis's face. He took his eyes off the road for a few seconds and slowed the car down. He stared hard at the picture and pulled his head back slightly to get a better view of it. And he sniffed.

'That photo smells a bit funny.'

'It's been stuck in *Gone With The Wind.*'

'Oh. That book must smell of shit then.' He stared hard at the picture, all the while screwing his nose up to avoid its foul odour. 'Who gave you that picture?' he asked.

'I got it from a dating agency.'

'A what?'

'A dating agency.'

'What's one of them?'

'Don't you have dating agencies in B Movie Hell?'

'That depends, what are they?'

'Never mind. It doesn't matter. Do you recognise her?'

Darius focussed his attention back on the road ahead. He slowed the car down a little more. They were approaching a bridge with a police car parked at the end of it.

'Hold on. We just have to make a stop,' he said.

'What for?'

'Just got to check in with the cops. They aren't letting anyone suspicious in. You'll be okay though. I'll vouch for you.'

He pulled up alongside the police car and wound his window back down. A grey haired old cop was leaning out of the driver side window of the police car. 'Afternoon Darius. Who you got with you?' he asked.

'She's from the FBI. Her partner is already in town.'

The cop peered through the window at Fonseca. He ran his eyes up and down as if he was checking her out. After a few seconds he smiled at her and nodded at Darius. 'Her partner already came through. Carry on.'

'Do you need to see any identification from me?' Fonseca called out.

The cop shook his head. 'Nope. You carry on little lady.'

Little lady? Fonseca took a deep breath through her nostrils and fought back the urge to call the guy a *patronising fat bag of shit.*

Darius thanked him and pulled away again, steering the car past the WELCOME TO B MOVIE HELL sign and onto the bridge that led into town.

'So do you recognise her?' Fonseca asked again.

'Who?' said Darius.

'The girl in the picture.'

'No.'

'I was told that she worked at The Beaver Palace. Would you like to take another look at the picture?'

'I don't recognise her. There ain't no girl in town like that.'

'The birthmark on her face is quite distinctive, don't you think?' Fonseca said taking another look at the girl for herself.

'Yeah. There ain't no girls in this town with birthmarks on their faces.'

'If there were…'

Darius let out a small laugh. 'Look lady, I need to concentrate on the road. There's a lot of speed traps around here. I can't afford to get caught again. I'm one ticket away from a ban.'

'Sure.' Fonseca sat back. She and Darius exchanged a quick look in the rear view mirror before he returned his focus to the road ahead.

Now that she was in B Movie Hell, it seemed like an appropriate time to catch up with Jack Munson to see how he was getting on. She pulled her phone out of her pocket and hit Munson's name on the speed dial. The phone rang for quite a while before he answered. He sounded half asleep.

'Hey Milena.'

'Hi Jack. How's it going?'

'Uh, where are you?'

'I'm in a cab. Just driving across the bridge into B Movie Hell. Are you okay? You sound a bit dazed?'

'Yeah. I'm fine. Been very busy here.'

'Are you still at the diner?'

'Nah. I left there already. The bodies are starting to pile up real quick here. I'm at a farmhouse now. A few miles away.'

'Okay, can you give me directions and I'll meet you there?'

'No. Don't do that. Go to straight to the Alaska Roadside Diner.'

'Why?'

'Because that's where I'll be going in a minute. See what you can find out from the waitress there. She knows more than she's letting on.'

'How so?'

There was a clattering on the other end of the line that sounded like Munson had dropped the phone.

'Jack? You still there?'

She heard him grunting and groaning for a while before he spoke again. 'Sorry about that,' he mumbled. 'Can the cab driver hear you?'

Fonseca glanced up at Darius. 'Probably yeah. Why?'

'Go careful. Everyone I've come across in this town so far seems to be a bit off. Everyone knows everyone else here and they aren't happy to see us.'

'Okay. I'll keep that in mind.'

'Did you get any useful leads or information from the asylum?'

'Actually yes I did. I'll tell you about it when I see you.'

'You didn't stay there long. Are you sure you got everything you could from that place?'

Fonseca glanced up at Darius to see if he was listening in on her conversation. He seemed to be concentrating on the road, but she lowered her voice anyway. 'I had to leave in a bit of a hurry. I had an awkward incident there. I think it was best for everyone that I left when I did.'

Munson seemed to perk up. 'Why? What happened?'

'Well, I had a minor misunderstanding which culminated with me anally raping one of the patients.'

Munson went quiet for a while before replying. 'Come again?'

'While interrogating one of the patients I had to stick a deodorant up his ass to teach him some respect. The doctor walked in on me and to be honest with you, things went kind of downhill from there. I got a little flustered and made a bit of an ass of myself.'

There was another long pause on the other end of the line before Munson spoke again. 'Milena,' he said. 'You're really starting to grow on me. I want to hear all about this when we meet up at the diner in a minute. It sounds brilliant.'

'Thanks,' she smiled for the first time in a long while. 'One morning hanging out with you and suddenly I'm raping suspects. Your influence must be rubbing off on me.'

'I'm glad to hear it. Did you wash your hands afterwards?'

'Do you really need to ask?'

Munson laughed. 'You know you can't go telling people that you raped a suspect. You'll get in trouble for that kind of thing.'

'I won't say anything if you don't, Jack.'

'Maybe it'll become a rumour around the office. Those things can really take on a life of their own,' said Munson, reminding her that she'd made a similar remark to him earlier.

'And I'll have to live with the fact that my rumour is actually true. I doubt it could get more ridiculous than it already is.'

There was a pause before Munson spoke again. His voice had softened. 'The rumour about me? What did you hear?' he asked.

'They say you shot a hostage but covered it up.'

There was another pause before Munson replied. 'There was a kidnapper with a gun to her head. I had to take the shot. He shot her. I shot him, half a second too late as it turned out.'

'And the evidence got burned,' Fonseca added.

'I'll see you at the diner in a few minutes,' said Munson, unsubtly switching the conversation. 'I just got some things to attend to here.'

Fonseca heard the sound of him flushing a toilet and decided it was a good time to end the call.

A few minutes later she arrived at The Alaska Roadside Diner. There were no vehicles parked in the bays out front. The place looked dead. Darius steered the cab off the road and parked up on the edge of the forecourt.

'That'll be twenty-five bucks,' he said, staring at her in the rear view mirror.

Fonseca reached into her jacket pocket and pulled out her money clip. She counted out twenty-five dollars and handed it to Darius. 'Thanks for the ride,' she said. 'Have a nice day. Sorry again about your friend Pete.'

'Yeah. Have a nice day Miss. Hope you catch that Red Mohawk guy before I get my hands on him.'

'Me too.'

Fonseca climbed out of the cab and walked up to the diner's entrance.

144

From his seat in the cab Darius watched her walk up to the diner. The glass door at the front was already open. She walked right in and up to the counter. Darius pulled his cell phone from the front pocket on his pants. He picked out a number on his speed dial and made a call.

A female voice answered. 'Hello, Beaver Palace.'

'Yo Clarisse, it's Darius. I need to speak to Mr Mellencamp.'

'He's kind of busy Darius, you know, what with all that's going on today.'

'I appreciate that,' said Darius. 'But I just gave a lady from the FBI a ride into town. And she's got a photo of a girl with a birthmark on her face. She's asking questions,' he paused before adding, 'if you know what I mean.'

There was a lingering silence on the other end of the line before Clarisse spoke again. Her voice sounded different this time. 'Putting you through now,' she said.

Thirty

Benny pulled up at the electric gates at the front of The Beaver Palace estate. Standing on the other side of the gates was an overweight, bearded security guard in blue jeans and a black T-shirt. He recognised Benny and gave him a thumbs up sign. A moment later the gates opened and Benny drove on through to the driveway that led up to the front of the Palace.

Baby had stayed silent ever since he'd warned her that Silvio Mellencamp wasn't best pleased with her and blamed her for the death of Arnold Bailey. She knew what that meant. It meant she was in for some kind of punishment, although hopefully not another gunshot wound like Benny had suggested. She'd been punished on numerous occasions in The Beaver Palace and the punishments were always severe.

She glanced over her shoulder out of the back window of Benny's squad car and saw the electric gates closing behind them. Her heart sank. Only a few hours earlier she thought she might have escaped this place forever, but she was back already. She feared that another chance to escape might not present itself for years. It made her feel tearful. She felt her throat tighten as the thought of what lay in wait for her within the walls of the mansion began to hit home.

Benny parked up by the front entrance. 'Time to get out, Baby,' he said, speaking to her in a pleasant manner, as if he had forgotten about the earlier tension.

Baby opened the car door and stepped out. There were a few more security guards milling around the grounds than usual. All of them were wearing jeans and plain black T-shirts. Mellencamp had obviously decided to beef up security in light of recent events. Baby didn't even recognise some of the new henchmen. And some of them were openly carrying firearms, which was extremely irregular. None of Mellencamp's guys were likely to be crack shots. Most of them were unfit or overweight, but even so, safety in numbers was clearly the order of the day. If the Red Mohawk showed up at Mellencamp's he'd get more than he bargained for.

Waiting for them at the front entrance holding the main doors open was Mack the Slasher. The sheer size of him filled out the door frame. He stood with his arms folded and a serious look on his face.

'Welcome back Baby,' he said.

'Hi,' said Baby, lowering her head as she walked past him and through the front doors. She didn't want to make eye contact with him because she was unsure about how much trouble she was in, if any. She made a point of holding her wounded arm though, to make sure he didn't grab a hold of it as he had a tendency of doing when he wanted someone to do as he said. Benny followed on behind her.

'Afternoon Slasher,' she heard him say. 'How's it going?'

She didn't hear Mack's response because within a second of walking through the door into the reception lounge she was deafened by a loud scream. It was a scream she recognised. It was followed by the gentle thudding of footsteps. Charging towards Baby with her arms open wide, desperate for a hug, was Chardonnay. She was dressed head to toe in skin-tight leopard print clothes. She jumped on Baby and hugged her tight. Baby wrapped her arms around Chardonnay and hugged her back, wincing at the pain in her arm from the bullet wound. Even so, it was nice to feel wanted for a change.

Eventually after being squeezed half to death, Chardonnay let go and stepped back. 'I was so worried. You've got to tell me all about what's happened to you! Where did you get shot?'

Baby raised her eyebrows. Chardonnay looked her up and down. Baby was wearing a blood stained sweatshirt. One sleeve was missing and there was a thick white bandage wrapped around the arm just above the elbow.

'Come on then?' said Chardonnay excitedly. 'Which arm did you get shot in?'

'This one,' said Baby pointing at the arm with the bandage on it.

Chardonnay's jaw dropped open. 'No way!' she gasped. 'Does it hurt?'

'A little bit. That'll teach me for going into town, won't it?'

'Well I've got something to cheer you up,' said Chardonnay, grabbing her by her injured arm. 'Come with me.'

She dragged Baby over to an orange sofa by the wall. 'Sit yourself here,' she said. 'We've all been given the night off, because, well, you know, there's a killer on the loose and all that.'

Baby sat down on the sofa. 'What are we doing?' she asked.

'We've got the big telly for tonight!' screamed Chardonnay, clapping her hands together like a sea lion on crack. She grabbed a remote control from a coffee table in the middle of the room and plonked herself down next to Baby. She flicked on the giant plasma television on the opposite side of the room and snuggled up to Baby.

'What are we going to watch?' Baby asked.

'Coyote Ugly of course!' said Chardonnay.

Baby had only been introduced to the brilliance of Coyote Ugly the night before. But even so, she was more than happy to watch it again. After all, it was about a girl who escaped from her job in a pizza place to become a star in New York. With Adam Garcia.

'Okay,' said Chardonnay. 'While John Goodman is on screen you can tell me all about your day.'

While the opening credits rolled, Baby began to regale Chardonnay with the details of her incredible day. Chardonnay listened open mouthed, occasionally interrupting with an "Oh no you di'ent!" or a "Get the fuck out!". Baby timed the story just right so that by the time the John Goodman scene was over she'd brought Chardonnay completely up to speed.

'Wow,' Chardonnay said while looking totally envious. 'I wish that had happened to me. You're so lucky!'

'I don't feel lucky,' said Baby rubbing her arm.

'Don't worry about that. The doctor is on his way,' said Chardonnay.

'What doctor?'

'The one who's going to patch up your arm and see about your pregnancy.'

Baby looked around. Mack and Benny had wandered off to Mellencamp's office so no one of any importance was within earshot. She whispered in Chardonnay's ear. 'I was never really pregnant.'

'Get the fuck out! No way!' Chardonnay screamed.

'Shhh. Don't tell the whole world.'

Chardonnay frowned as she processed the news. 'You'd better keep quiet about that,' she said. 'Don't let the boss find out. Apparently he's already blaming you for Arnold getting killed. If he finds out you weren't even pregnant, you'll be in big trouble.'

The feelings of anxiety Baby had endured for most of the day came rushing back. 'Hopefully the doctor will just make me take a pregnancy test. When it comes up negative I can just claim it was a phantom pregnancy.'

'I don't think the doctor has come to give you a test. I heard Clarisse say he was coming to do an abortion and to fix your insides so you can't get knocked up again.'

148

Thirty One

Candy had spent half an hour mopping up the blood from the diner's floor. It had been a painstaking job and her back was beginning to ache. The men's washroom was proving to be particularly tiring. There was blood everywhere. On the walls, the floor, the cubicle doors, in the urinals.

The local cops had taken all the evidence they needed from the crime scene, which basically meant that they'd had a bit of a look around and then taken some muffins and donuts from behind the counter. The B Movie Hell police department wasn't big on stuff like DNA evidence. They liked to work on old-fashioned methods like gut instinct and hunches. While eating donuts. It was a policy that had served them well over the years, but they had never encountered anything like The Red Mohawk before, and neither for that matter had Candy. She couldn't help thinking that the cops should be the ones cleaning up the crime scene.

Randall Buckwater and his new partner Gary had left her to clean up the mess created by the Red Mohawk, and she was pretty sure Gary had left an un-flushable turd for her to dispose of in the second cubicle.

She had propped the front door of the diner open in order to let some fresh air in to eradicate the smell of blood and shit. After cleaning the washroom, which smelt even worse, she headed back out to the diner area. When she got there she was greeted by the sight of a woman dressed smartly all in black in her early thirties looking around the place.

'Can I help you?' Candy asked.

'Hi. I'm Agent Fonseca from the FBI,' the woman replied with a smile.

'Sorry, we're closed.'

'I know,' said Fonseca stepping all over the newly mopped floor as she looked around under the tables and chairs.

'What are you looking for?' Candy asked.

'I'm assuming you met my partner Jack Munson earlier?'

'Oh yes,' said Candy. 'He was here. Do you have some identification, please?'

Fonseca reached into her jacket pocket and pulled out her FBI identity card. She held it up for Candy to get a look at it. A fairly pointless process really because Candy wouldn't know a real FBI badge from a fake one.

'What can I do for you?' Candy asked.

Fonseca slipped her ID back in her pocket. 'My partner told me you were very helpful when he asked you some questions earlier. Could you please tell me what you told him?'

'Yes, of course. Let me just put this mop and bucket away and I'll be right with you.'

'Thanks.'

Candy wheeled the mop and bucket through the dining area and round behind the counter. 'Can I get you a drink or anything?' she asked.

'A glass of soda water would be good, thanks,' said Fonseca sitting herself down on a stool at the bar. It was the same stool Arnold had been sitting on before The Red Mohawk sprung into action and chopped him up.

'Last person to sit there had his fingers cut off,' Candy informed her politely.

Fonseca looked down at the stool and the surrounding area. 'You've cleaned it up well,' she said, shifting herself across onto the next stool along.

'Thanks. You should have seen the mess in the men's room. That was ten times worse.'

'I'll bet. The men's room at the FBI is always a mess too, and we've not had a murder there in years.'

Candy wasn't familiar with FBI humour so she had no idea whether or not she should be laughing. 'One glass of water coming up. I'll be back in a sec.'

She left Fonseca behind and wheeled the mop and bucket through the PVC strip curtain and into the kitchen. She propped the mop and bucket up against a wall by the grill. The last thing she needed right now was to participate in another interrogation. The earlier one with Jack Munson hadn't gone well. Reg the chef was a far better liar than her and she felt anxious answering questions without him around. Unfortunately he was hiding out upstairs. Ever since he'd shot the girl with the birthmark on her face, he had wisely decided to stay out of the way of the cops and the FBI.

Candy washed her hands in the sink as she thought about the best way to deal with an interrogation from Fonseca. *"Keep your answers short!"* she told herself, repeating the thought over and over in her head. She made her way back out to the eating area where Fonseca was still seated at the bar. The FBI agent was playing around with a cell phone and not really paying attention to the waitress. Candy picked up a clean glass and filled it with soda water from the drink dispenser. She placed the glass down on the bar in front of Fonseca.

'One soda water,' she said. 'On the house.'

'Thanks,' said Fonseca, taking her gaze off her phone and looking down her nose at the soda water. 'Before we get started about what happened in here earlier. I wonder if you could just take a look at this for me. See if you recognise this girl.'

Fonseca grabbed a napkin from a dispenser on the counter. She used it to hold up a small Polaroid photograph for Candy to get a good look at. It was a picture of a young woman in lingerie. 'Ever seen her before?'

Candy stared closely at the photo. 'I don't know,' she said. 'She doesn't look familiar. I mean she's not a regular customer here. I'd know her if she was.'

'This girl has a blue birthmark on her face. Have you seen any girls in town with a birthmark like this? I'm told she might work at a place called The Beaver Palace. Do you know it?'

Before Candy could think up an answer the phone in the kitchen started ringing. 'I'd better go answer that,' she said. 'Could be the police.'

'They can wait,' said Fonseca firmly.

'No they can't,' Candy replied. 'I've got family and friends in this town and there's a serial killer going round cutting people's heads off, so I'm answering that phone whether you like it or not.'

She hurried back out to the kitchen, pleasantly surprised at herself for being so forceful with Fonseca. She grabbed the phone off the wall. 'Hi Alaska Roadside Diner, Candy speaking.'

A male voice on the other end spoke gruffly. 'Put Reg on the phone.'

'He's upstairs. I've got the FBI in here....'

'I know. Put Reg on the phone.'

Candy knew the voice on the other end of the line. It was Mack the Slasher. Not a man to be messed with. She put her hand over the phone and shouted up the stairs. 'Reg! Phone! It's Mack for you.'

Reg yelled back down. 'Coming.'

The creaking of floorboards above her head followed. She heard a door open, followed by a loud farting noise and then Reg's footsteps coming down the stairs. He soon appeared on the stairs, wearing slippers and blue sweatpants, and his undershirt. He looked like he'd been drinking. His eyes were a little bloodshot and his shirt was untucked. He ambled over to Candy and held out his hand to take the phone. 'What's he want?' he whispered as Candy handed it to him.

She didn't reply. Instead she gave him a serious glare. The kind she knew he would understand. He took a deep breath and spoke into the receiver.

'Hi Mack. How's it...'

Candy didn't wait around to hear the outcome of the conversation. She headed back out to the dining area to see Milena Fonseca who hadn't moved from her stool at the counter. This time the FBI agent held up her cell-phone. On it was another photo. This time it was picture of a man in his late twenties or early thirties.

'This is a guy named Dominic Touretto. You ever seen him?' she asked.

Candy studied the picture. She felt a sense of relief when she realised she had never seen the man before. 'He's not a local,' she said. 'If he's ever been in here then I don't remember him.'

'Okay,' said Fonseca. 'Would you say you normally know all the customers?'

'Pretty much yeah. This isn't a big tourist resort.'

'What about the killer in the mask this morning? Did you see his face?'

'Yes, but I didn't recognise him. Never seen him before.'

'But you got a good look at him?'

'Not really. When I took his order he was talking to himself so I avoided staring at him. He didn't put the mask on until just before he started chopping folks up.'

'But you saw what he looked like without the mask?'

'Yes.'

Reg walked into the diner through the PVC strip curtain. He tapped Candy on the shoulder. 'Candy, your friend wants to speak to you on the phone,' he said.

Candy turned around and looked at Reg. He nodded towards the phone in the kitchen. 'Don't worry,' he said. 'I'll speak with the FBI lady. Go take the call.'

Candy wandered back through the strip curtain and into the kitchen. She had taken barely two steps towards the phone before she heard a horrific sound behind her. It sounded like someone gurgling or throwing up. She raced back into the kitchen and saw a ghastly sight. Reg had thrust a large kitchen knife into Milena Fonseca's throat.

Candy covered her mouth with her hand, fearing that she might throw up. Reg tugged the knife back out of Fonseca's neck. The blade was covered in blood, much of which was dripping onto the newly cleaned floor. Even more blood was gushing out from a gaping wound beneath Milena Fonseca's chin. Before Candy could scream at him to stop, Reg plunged the knife back into Fonseca's neck. The FBI agent's jaw dropped. Her mouth was open and her tongue practically hanging out. Her eyes revealed a look of total shock at the sudden unprovoked attack. As Reg withdrew the blade for the second time he stepped back, treading on Candy's toes. Candy jumped out of the way. She watched in horror as Milena Fonseca's eyes dulled. The life drained right out of her and she slumped forward. Her head crashed down onto the bar with a sickening thud.

Reg turned to Candy. 'Get the mop,' he said. 'We gotta clean this up quick!'

Thirty Two

Mack led Benny up to Mellencamp's office on the upper floor of The Beaver Palace. He banged hard on the door with one of his enormous fists, then shouted through it.

'Benny Stansfield is here to see you boss!' There was no reply from within, so after a few seconds Mack twisted the doorknob and opened the door inwards. He gestured to Benny to go in. 'It's alright,' he said. 'He's had a busy day. He might be taking a nap. Just wake him up. He won't mind.'

'Thanks.'

Benny walked in and Mack pulled the door shut behind him. Silvio Mellencamp was behind his desk, taking a nap just as Mack had suggested. His head was leant back against the soft black leather on his chair. His eyes were closed and his mouth was slightly open. His gold dressing gown was wide open, but fortunately from where Benny was standing he was only visible from the chest upwards. He didn't seem to have heard Benny enter, or heard Mack close the door, so Benny cleared his throat quite loudly in order to grab his attention. Mellencamp didn't stir.

'Mr Mellencamp,' Benny called out. 'You awake?'

Mellencamp opened his eyes slowly, one at a time. 'Hold on a second,' he said before closing his eyes again.

Benny stood and waited. For about another twenty seconds Mellencamp remained seated behind the desk, not moving. His eyes stayed closed, only flickering occasionally. Waking up seemed to be quite an arduous task for the old fella. His mouth gradually closed and his lips curled up in a smile that bordered on being a grin. Eventually he shuddered and just as quickly he sat upright and opened his eyes.

'Okay, all done,' he said.

Benny approached the desk tentatively. He stopped in his tracks just short of Mellencamp's desk when he saw something moving. A young woman was crawling out from underneath the desk. She popped into view on Mellencamp's side. She had long dark hair and creamy brown skin. She was dressed in a black bra and matching thong with a pair of thigh high, high heeled boots. She stood next to Mellencamp and kissed him on the cheek.

'Will that be all?' she asked.

'Can you just wipe the sweat off my brow?' Mellencamp asked.

The young lady grabbed a tissue from a box on the desk and wiped his forehead with it. 'Is that better?' she asked.

'Lovely.'

She turned to Benny. And smiled. 'Hi Benny.'

'Hi Jasmine.'

Mellencamp patted Jasmine on the backside and then ushered her away. 'Tell Selena to drop by in half an hour,' he said. He took his eyes off her backside for a moment and smiled at Benny. 'Take a seat.'

Benny sat down in a chair opposite him. 'I got the girl back for you,' he said. 'She's downstairs watching a movie in your entrance lounge.'

'You mean Baby? You got Baby back?'

'Yeah. That's who you wanted, right?'

'Fuck yeah. How is she? Is she shaken up about what happened to Arnold?'

'Yeah, little bit. She's been shot too. Reg hit her in the arm with a shot from his rifle. It slowed her down.'

Mellencamp nodded. 'Yes I heard. Good old Reg. Never misses does he? I owe you each ten grand. You've really pulled me out of a hole here.' He reached into a drawer on his desk and pulled out a thick wad of fifty-dollar bills. He tossed it across the desk to Benny. 'There's ten for you. Don't spend it all at once.'

'I can take Reg's too if you like.'

'Not necessary. Besides, I need to keep some money in the desk drawer to pay the doctor when he arrives.'

'What doctor?'

'Clarisse managed to get the doctor from Lewisville to do a call out to take care of Baby. It'll cost me a small fortune mind.'

'Oh right. To sort out that bullet wound in her arm. It's not that bad you know. I think she's making a fuss over nothing.'

'Well that's nothing new. But actually the main reason for getting the doctor in is to carry out a termination. Baby's gone and got herself knocked up.'

'Really?'

'Yeah, that's why Arnold was taking her to Lewisville this morning. But now Arnold's dead and if I'm honest, I'm beginning to wish Reg had shot Baby in the head instead of the arm. It would have saved a lot of trouble.'

'You'd have had to pay him more than ten grand though, I'll bet!' Benny joked.

'I'll be paying him more than that anyway. He's just killed an FBI agent for me.'

Benny couldn't hide his surprise. 'What?'

'We've got two FBI agents in town.'

'Yes I know, but they're here to find the Red Mohawk aren't they?'

Mellencamp picked up a glass of cognac from his desk and took a swig. 'That's what they want us to believe,' he said, licking his lips. 'But the female agent dropped by Reg's diner earlier. She had a photo of Baby. And she was asking questions.'

'No fucking way!'

'Yeah. Sneaky bastards.'

'So how did Reg kill her?'

'Stabbed her in the throat.'

Benny grimaced. 'Eww, that must have been hard.'

'Not for Reg. He cuts pigs throats all the time out the back of the diner. He knows what he's doing.'

Benny tried not to visualise the image of Reg slaughtering pigs or female FBI agents. 'So what about the other agent?' he asked.

'We need to give him the Corey Feldman treatment.'

Benny frowned. 'What's the Corey Feldman treatment?'

'He can never be allowed to leave B Movie Hell.'

Benny understood what Mellencamp meant. Before he could comment, the walkie-talkie on his belt crackled into life. 'Benny, come in, this is O'Grady.'

'Excuse me a moment,' said Benny. He plucked the radio from his belt and spoke into it. 'Hey Chief, wassup?'

'The Red Mohawk has struck again Benny. Where are you?'

'I'm at Silvio's place. Just informing him of what's been going on.'

'Well you can tell him that we've just heard that your buddy Litgo's dead and apparently so are officers Leland Patchett and Hanran Lonnegan.'

Benny's jaw dropped. He felt his mouth go dry and his stomach tighten. He knew all three of those guys. Two work colleagues and a lifelong friend. He managed to force out a few words without throwing up. 'What the fuck?' he said.

Mellencamp had heard everything that Chief O'Grady had said. He looked concerned, far more so than he had a minute earlier. He rubbed his chin and looked deep in thought. 'The Red Mohawk went to Litgo's place?' he said, thinking aloud. 'That's weird. I was talking to Litgo less than an hour ago.'

O'Grady's voice crackled through the radio again. 'Hi Silvio.'

'Hey chief,' Mellencamp replied. 'What's going on here?'

'This Mohawk asshole went to Litgo's. It sounds like he tortured Litgo before killing him. Patchett and Lonnegan must have showed up and disturbed him because they're both dead too. Gunshots to the head. It was radioed in by an FBI agent named Jack Munson. Our guys are on their way to Litgo's place to confirm it. I think it's true because we can't get hold of Litgo or Patchett and Lonnegan. And there's no reason to suspect the FBI guy is lying.'

Mellencamp reached across the desk and snatched the walkie-talkie from Benny's hand. He spoke into it, spitting some cognac over it accidentally. 'Is the FBI guy at Litgo's right now?' he asked.

'Yeah, I think so. I've just sent two units there to find out what's going on. We'd have got there sooner if it hadn't been such a crazy morning. Guys are dropping like flies.'

Mellencamp silently cussed. 'Does this FBI agent know anything?'

'Like what?'

'Like anything about what goes on in my establishment?'

'No. I haven't even spoken to the guy yet. All's I know is, he turned up at Litgo's and found the latest bunch of dead bodies. Then he called it in on Patchett's radio.'

Mellencamp took a sharp intake of breath and pulled the walkie-talkie closer to his mouth. 'Chief, this FBI shithead, what's his name, Munson? He can't be allowed to leave town.'

'What? Why not?'

'I think he's come looking for Baby.'

Benny noticed that Mellencamp was spitting a lot over his walkie-talkie while he was talking into it. He reminded himself it would be worth wiping it clean before using it again.

Chief O'Grady's voice responded to Mellencamp through the walkie-talkie and all the excess saliva. 'No you're mistaken Silvio. The FBI are here for the Red Mohawk.'

'Then tell me why his partner turned up at The Alaska with a photo of Baby, asking questions.'

'Oh.'

'Yes, oh. This guy can't leave town. He's got to be eliminated. We've already taken care of his partner. When your guys get to Litgo's, if he's still there, tell them to take him down.'

'You mean kill him?'

'Yes.'

'That's a bit over the top isn't it?' said O'Grady.

'No it's not. We can't take any chances.'

'But surely it will mean a whole bunch of other FBI people coming to town? They're not going to let that go. There'll be hundreds of them coming here to find out what happened to their colleagues.'

Mellencamp laughed. 'I bet they don't. I can guarantee you these two FBI agents are here in an "off-the-record" capacity. Only one man will know they're here and that's the clown who sent them.'

'How can you be sure?'

'Trust me Chief. Just get rid of this Munson asshole. And burn the body. Over and out.'

Mellencamp switched off the radio and handed it back to Benny.

'We don't generally say over and out any more Silvio,' Benny said, taking the walkie-talkie and trying to keep his fingers clear of all the spit.

Mellencamp ignored him. 'Fucking FBI,' he said, thinking out loud and picking up his glass of cognac. 'I thought this shit was over and done with.'

Benny sensed that Mellencamp was overreacting and seemed a little paranoid. 'It's Pete's Neville's murder last night that brought them here. Maybe they're only asking about Baby because she was with Arnold when he got killed?'

'That is possible, but it's one helluva coincidence.'

'So, shall I take Baby somewhere else then? Somewhere safe?'

Mellencamp shook his head. 'Too risky. One good thing about that Red Mohawk coming to town is that I've beefed up security. This is the safest place to be right now. But we've got to get rid of that FBI agent before he contacts his boss and that fucking clown sends more of them here.'

Benny frowned. 'What clown? Who are you talking about?'

'Devon Pincent. I bet he's behind all this.'

'Devon Pincent?' Benny stiffened in his chair. 'Is that who I think it is?'

'Yeah. That sonofabitch.'

Thirty Three

The miniature bottle of Cutthroat Rum had done something evil to Jack Munson's insides. After throwing up in Litgo's sink and collapsing in a heap on the floor, he dragged himself across to the bathroom on the other side of the cottage. He spent another fifteen minutes throwing up in the toilet before he was able to compose himself. In the middle of all that he'd taken a phone call from Milena Fonseca and agreed to meet her at the Alaska Diner.

He washed some traces of vomit from his face and hair and splashed some water on his face. He couldn't work out if he'd just had too much rum or if the Cutthroat stuff had been spiked with something. Or maybe the stresses of just being back in the job had begun to get to him. It also occurred to him that Luke the Fed Ex delivery man at the diner had warned him about Litgo leaving traps around the place to catch out intruders. Maybe the rum had been poisoned? Either way, he'd lost some crucial time and he couldn't waste any more mulling over the possible causes of his sudden illness. He felt light-headed and in need of a lie down, but that wasn't an option. He'd radioed Litgo's murder in to the local cops with the intention of making himself scarce before they arrived. He should have been long gone.

He hurried back outside into the fresh air, still feeling distinctly under the weather. He climbed into his car and took a look at himself in the rear view mirror. He didn't look fit for work. It was time he took a break from sipping rum and faced up to the hangover that was trying to kick in.

He started the engine and reversed the car back out onto the dirt track. It was too late to go back the way he came. He could tell from the sound of the siren that the cops were coming up that way. The dirt track carried on past Litgo's so he followed it along in the hopes of finding his way back to the main highway. Unfortunately the dirt track led him on a merry dance, taking him further away from his arranged meeting with Fonseca at The Alaska Roadside Diner. By the time he'd got himself back on the highway and cruised up to the diner he'd wasted nearly half an hour. His car was leaning heavily to the right and making some strange noises too.

He pulled into the diner's parking lot and stopped as close to the entrance as he could. The place looked barren. There wasn't a customer in sight and all the cops that had been milling around earlier in the day were long gone.

He sat in the car for a few moments to get his shit together. He stared through the windscreen to see if he could spot Fonseca anywhere. She was supposed to meet him in the diner. He was sure that's what they had arranged. Or maybe the rum was playing tricks on him? So where the hell was she? He sensed that he stank of a mixture of puke and booze. There was no hiding it. Fonseca wouldn't approve. But then he didn't approve of her not being where she said she'd be.

He got out of the car and walked gingerly up to the diner's entrance. He tugged at the handle on the glass door. It didn't move. The damn thing was locked and bolted shut from the inside.

He peered through the glass for any signs of life. There was no movement, not even a stray cockroach. He banged hard on the door to see if he could catch anyone's attention. To his eternal relief, after just a few seconds, Candy the waitress appeared through the strip curtain from the kitchen out back. She stopped dead like she'd been freeze-framed when she caught sight of him at the door. She didn't look pleased to see him. She pointed at the sign above his head on the door. The sign that said closed. Then she mouthed the words *"We're closed"* just to overemphasise the point.

Munson shouted back through the door, *"I don't give a fuck. Open the fucking door! I need to take a piss!"*

Candy appeared to contemplate her options for a while before mouthing the word *"Fucksake!"* and then making her way round the counter to the entrance. She unbolted and unlocked the door.

'We're closed you know,' she said.

'I got that.'

'What do you want?'

'I'm meeting my partner Milena Fonseca here. You seen her?'

'No.'

'In that case I'll have a coffee while I wait for her.'

Candy looked like she was about to refuse, or at least attempt to, so Munson pushed the door further open and barged past her. He took up a seat at the counter. 'Black, two sugars,' he said.

'I thought you needed the toilet?'

'I'll go later.'

'Fine. I hope instant coffee is okay for you?'

'Nope. Put on a fresh pot.'

'I've just washed up.'

'I don't give a fuck. I'm feeling a bit queasy and I need the good stuff. Put on a fresh pot and then you and I can discuss what you know about the girl who was in here earlier.'

'What girl?'

'Don't give me that shit again. I'm talking about the girl who was with Arnold when he got chopped up. The girl who ran across the field to Litgo's and is now missing.'

'Oh, that girl.'

'Yeah. That girl.'

Candy picked up a jar of coffee from a shelf at the back. She unscrewed the lid and poured some of the coffee into a filter machine. 'I told you everything I know about her, which isn't much,' she said, avoiding Munson's stare.

'Candy,' said Munson, his stomach rumbling almost loud enough to drown out his voice. 'Look at me.'

The waitress put the lid back on the coffee jar and replaced it on the shelf. She turned and looked at Munson as he'd instructed.

He made sure he had her full attention and looked her firmly in the eye. 'If you don't co-operate with my investigation,' he said, barely moving his lips, 'if you test me in any way, I'll see to it that your shitty little diner gets shut down. Not just for a week, for good. And if you know anything about this girl and I find out that you've chosen not to share it with me, your days in B Movie Hell will be coming to an end. You'll be coming back to my headquarters with me.'

'I understand,' said Candy. She picked up a jug of water from under the counter and flipped open the top of the filter coffee machine. She began pouring the water in. She seemed fairly calm all of a sudden. Munson couldn't make out if it was false confidence or what. 'Coffee will be ready in five minutes,' she said.

'Good. Get me a fucking muffin too. I'm starving.'

'Certainly sir.'

Candy disappeared back out to the kitchen. Munson suspected that she could tell he was sick and a little drunk. Maybe that's why she wasn't so nervous? She thought she could outwit him. *Bitch.* His mood was seriously darkening. The drink and the nausea were taking him to places he knew he shouldn't go. He was becoming crankier by the minute. It was times like this when he was best off keeping a distance from other people. Because when he was this drunk, he had no tolerance for anyone.

He pulled his cell-phone from his pocket. It was irritating him that Fonseca hadn't showed up yet. He couldn't really leave the diner without her because she had no transport. He flicked through the menus on his phone and called her number. He stared hard at his phone. The display flashed up to show that he was being connected to Fonseca.

Half a second later he heard the song *As Long As You Love Me* by The Backstreet Boys coming through the PVC strip curtain from the kitchen area. It was Fonseca's ringtone and it was soon followed by Candy mumbling the word, *"Shit."*

Thirty Four

Baby was enjoying Coyote Ugly so much that she had succeeded in putting her worries to the back of her mind, for a while at least. But then halfway through the film at a really good bit where Piper Perabo and Adam Garcia are sitting on the hood of his car and staring up at the night sky, Mack came down the main staircase in a hurry.

He snapped his fingers. 'Baby. Up!'

Chardonnay yelled back at him. 'Can't you see we're watching a film?'

'Shut your fucking mouth you dirty little fuckbag!'

'Fuckbag?'

'Yeah. FUCKBAG!'

Mack was never in the mood for any backchat, but that was exactly what he always got from Chardonnay. Baby assessed his frame of mind very quickly and jumped up from the sofa. 'What's wrong?' she asked.

'You're coming with me,' Mack snarled.

He stormed over and grabbed Baby firmly by her injured arm. 'You're coming downstairs. I'm taking you to your room. Silvio's orders. You've had a big fucking day. The last thing you should be doing is laughing and joking while watching shit films on the big TV.' He looked over at Chardonnay who was pulling a face at him. 'You! Turn that fucking shit off!' he yelled.

Chardonnay was never one to follow orders so she used the remote control to flick the film forward to one of her favourite scenes. Mack didn't approve.

'I'll ram that remote up your ass again if you don't do as you're told!' he bellowed. Chardonnay paused the DVD and folded her arms in a sulk.

Mack dragged Baby away from the sofa and threw a parting shot in Chardonnay's direction. 'If I hear that fucking *Fight the Moonlight* song while I'm walking away, I'll come back and I promise you, you won't be able to walk for a week when I'm done with you.'

He yanked Baby's arm real hard and hauled her out of the lounge and over to the stairs that led down to the girls rooms. They passed quite a few of the other girls on their way to Baby's room. No one dared to look at them or speak a word. It seemed as if everyone knew what was in store for Baby.

There hadn't been any sign of a doctor arriving at The Beaver Palace yet, so she feared that this was something else. Mack had something unpleasant planned. The other girls all knew it. Baby recognised the look on their faces. It was the look that signified she was in trouble and that they were all praying for her that it wouldn't be life threatening.

When they got to Baby's room, Mack opened the door and pushed her inside. She was thankful that he had let go of her arm. His grip had been so tight he had left fingerprints on her. *On her bad arm of all places!* She had made a few whimpering noises to indicate how much he was hurting her but he had ignored them, and she knew not to overdo it because it would only encourage him to squeeze harder. *The insensitive prick.*

She walked over to her bed and sat down on it, staring at her feet and hoping Mack's intention was just to leave her there on her own to mull things over. Unfortunately Mack had other plans. He wasn't leaving. He closed the door behind him. And locked it.

'I'm sorry about this Baby,' he said. 'But I'm under instructions from Mr Mellencamp.'

Baby swallowed hard and made a point of rubbing her injured arm again to remind him that she was in a vulnerable state already. 'What's going on?' she asked.

'Take off your clothes.'

'Why?'

'Because I said so.'

'What about the doctor? Is he really coming tonight?'

Mack took a deep breath. 'I don't like having to ask twice. Now take off your clothes.'

'But…'

'Now!'

Baby leant down to untie her sneakers. Due to the pain of the bullet wound in her right arm and a general feeling of numbness due to the lack of blood flow she tried to do it with just her left hand, so her efforts were somewhat clumsy.

'Come on, hurry up!' Mack snapped.

'It's difficult. My arm hurts. I have been shot you know.'

'Fine. I'll help you.'

He reached forward and pushed her head back out of the way.

'Ow, careful!' she cried.

That was enough to piss him right off. He pushed her head all the way back down onto her pillow.

'Lie back. And lie still,' he said.

He walked around the bed and grabbed a hold of her sneakers, one in each hand. He didn't bother to untie them. Instead he yanked them both off with brute force and dropped them onto the floor. 'Can you lift your arms up?' he asked.

'Only the left one.'

Mack reached forward and grabbed her sweatshirt. In one swift and ungainly movement he yanked it over her head and then pulled the left sleeve off her arm. The other sleeve had already been ripped off earlier in the day so he didn't have to cause her too much discomfort. He threw the sweatshirt against the wall on the far side of the room. It left Baby in just her jeans and a bra. 'Can you undress yourself from here?' he asked firmly.

'Yes. But what for?'

'Because I told you to.'

Baby began unbuttoning her jeans. Once again it was a clumsy effort with just one good hand available to her. She managed to undo two buttons before Mack lost patience again. 'Take off your bra,' he snapped.

'That's going to be tricky,' she said. 'My arm should really be in a sling you know.'

Mack lunged forward and grabbed her by the throat. He lifted her off the bed with one hand, almost choking her, his grip was so tight. With his other hand he ripped off her bra, snapping the strap. He tossed it aside and then slammed her back down onto the bed. Next he forcefully yanked her jeans off, almost hauling her off the bed. Her panties came down slightly and before she could reach down to pull them back up he had ripped them off too. He climbed up onto the bed on his knees and loomed large over her. Yet again he placed a hand around her throat. When he was sure she couldn't move he reached over to her bedside table and pulled something out of the top drawer.

'This will only take a minute,' he said. 'And it will be easier if you don't struggle.'

Thirty Five

As soon as Munson heard The Backstreet Boys song *As Long As You Love Me,* he raced around the counter and through the PVC strip curtain into the diner's kitchen. The effects of the rum and the vomiting had been nullified for a moment at least. The Backstreet Boys had sobered him up the second he'd heard them singing. Something was very wrong here. And that cunt of a waitress held all the answers. Candy was standing in front of a table in the middle of the room. She had a guilty look etched into her face. The Backstreet Boys song was blaring out from a cell phone on the table behind her. Milena Fonseca's cell phone.

'Give me that *fucking phone,*' Munson snapped.

Candy stepped aside. Munson looked at his own phone in his hand. The display told him he was calling Milena Fonseca. He ended the call.

And The Backstreet Boys stopped singing.

He slid his own phone back in his pocket and glared at Candy. She instinctively raised her hands in self-defence. Munson barged past her, his shoulder knocking against hers. He grabbed Fonseca's phone from the table. His eyes were immediately drawn to a couple of spots of blood on the display.

'Where's my partner, Milena Fonseca?' he growled.

Candy swallowed hard. 'I don't know what you mean.'

'You know full fucking well what I mean. This is *her phone.* And it's got blood on it. If you don't tell me where she is and what's happened to her, in about five seconds it'll have your blood on it too.'

Candy didn't wait for him to start counting. 'She's with Reg.'

'Who the fuck is Reg?'

'The chef. He works here. She had a nosebleed. He took her to the hospital.'

Munson pulled his right arm back over his left shoulder then swung it back, slapping her across the face with the back of his hand. Even though he was feeling groggy, he could still throw a mean backhand slap and he was sharp enough to catch a waitress off guard. His hand connected with her face, crashing into her cheekbone and snapping her head back. The blow knocked Candy off balance and she staggered backwards into the grill. She managed to grab a hold of it to stop herself sliding to the ground.

'What are you doing?' she cried, her face revealing a sudden element of fear that had been lacking previously. 'You're an FBI agent you can't go hitting a woman!'

'I'm from the Seventies. And I can do worse, I promise you.'

Munson hoped to God he didn't have to do any worse. He hadn't wanted to lay a hand on her, but time was in short supply. He needed answers from her *fast*. He recognised the look on Candy's face in light of the threat of more violence. She was trying to work out how far he would go to get the information he wanted, questioning whether or not she could handle another blow from him, and where the next blow would land.

'I had nothing to do with it,' she blurted out. She straightened herself up and steadied herself against the grill.

'Nothing to do with what?'

'It got out of hand. She attacked Reg…'

Munson stepped into her personal space and grabbed her around the throat. He didn't squeeze, but he made sure she knew the threat was there. 'I swear, if the next word out of your mouth is a lie, or even if it's true but it sounds like a lie, I'm going to knock every single one of your teeth out. Now think carefully. What happened to my partner? Is she still alive?'

Candy was too scared to recognise that it was an empty threat. In years gone by Munson might have meant it and carried out a brutal assault on her to get the information he wanted, but those days were behind him. He was beginning to realise that he no longer loved the violence of his job the way he had as a young man. He just wanted her to answer his questions.

Tears began streaming down her face. Her cheekbone was glowing red where he had slapped her. She looked down at his hand around her throat and shook her head. 'No. She's dead,' she sobbed.

Munson's felt the air drain from his lungs. He released his grip on her throat and stepped back. His shoulders drooped and his heart sank. The words *"She's dead"* replayed over and over in his mind. 'Who killed her? You or Reg?'

'Reg.'

Candy looked fearful of what else he might do to her if he got the urge. But she was definitely more fearful of what he might do if she didn't answer truthfully.

'How did she die?' Munson asked. 'What did Reg do to her?'

Candy looked down at the floor. She sobbed some more, her whimpering became louder and more hysterical, much to Munson's irritation. Before he had to threaten to strike her again, she blubbed out an answer. 'He stabbed her in the throat,' she mumbled. 'It was horrible.'

Munson closed his eyes and visualised Fonseca's murder. Not because he wanted to but simply because it was all he could think about. Her death had been avoidable. If he hadn't been drunk and busy throwing up at Litgo's he wouldn't have arrived late. He would have been here to deal with Reg when Fonseca needed him. He'd started to warm to Fonseca. She had spirit and a sense of patriotic duty about her. He shuddered at the thought of her murder. She had died alone in a shithole diner, away from her family and friends in the middle of this godforsaken clichéd B Movie town.

He opened his eyes. The mental image of Fonseca's murder sobered him up some more and made him angry. Right now he had some serious shit to deal with. Decisions had to be made, like what to do with Candy.

'Why did Reg kill Fonseca? What did she do wrong? What made him do it?'

Candy looked away and he sensed she didn't want to answer. He reached out and grabbed her around the throat again, gently squeezing this time. Some snot dribbled out of her nose and more tears streamed down her face. He sensed that she was feeling sorry for herself. And it disgusted him.

'Could you pass me some tissues? she sobbed, wincing in the fear that he might hit her again or apply more pressure to her throat. Munson spotted a roll of kitchen towel on the sideboard. He relinquished his grip on her neck and grabbed a couple of sheets of the kitchen towel. He held them out in front of her and said nothing. She snatched them from him and used them to wipe her nose and face clean. And now that she was free from his grip she took the opportunity to slide down into a sitting position on the floor, with her back pressed up against the grill.

Munson picked up Fonseca's phone from the table. He looked at the spots of her blood on the display. The sight of the blood brought back the image of her murder in his mind again. He grabbed a sheet of the kitchen towel and used it to wipe the spots of blood from the display.

The blood came off easily enough and the touch of the tissue and his fingers pressing against the phone made its screen light up. Fonseca's phone came out of sleep mode and on it he saw a headshot photo of a man in his twenties. The guy was pretty ugly. Munson squinted at it to get a better look.

'Who the fuck is that?' he muttered out loud.

Candy sniffed and looked at the mess she'd made in the kitchen towel. 'That's the girl you're asking about,' she said.

He looked down at her and frowned. 'What?'

'That's why Reg killed her. She had a photo of the girl.'

Not for the first time that day, Munson wished he hadn't drunk so much rum. He was looking at a photo of a guy, not a girl. He swiped his fingers across the phone's display. A different photo appeared on the screen. A photo of a girl with a blue birthmark on her face. Munson felt a headache coming on. He rubbed his forehead and stared hard at the photo. He glanced down at Candy again. She looked terrified, like she thought he was about to kill her. But she was of little concern to him. It was the girl in the photo that was giving him a headache. What was it about her?

It took him longer to work out the answer than it should have done, but when he did work it out, he felt his legs go weak.

'Oh SHIT!' He blurted his thoughts out loud. 'Pincent, what the *fuck* have you gotten me into!'

Thirty Six

Silvio Mellencamp had given up on any chance of getting dressed. The gold dressing gown was staying on for the rest of the day. There just didn't seem to be any point in changing into anything else. The day had been full of so many interruptions, that he hadn't had a chance to say hello to all the girls that worked for him. And more importantly he hadn't had time to decide which of them would get to spend the night with him.

He poured himself another large cognac from a decanter on his desk and sat waiting for the next person to knock on his door. He'd been told by his receptionist to expect someone within a minute. And that was about two minutes ago. To amuse himself while he waited he counted down from ten in his head. He only got to seven before he heard two loud knocks on the door.

'Come in Reg,' he shouted.

The door opened and in walked Reg, the chef from The Alaska Roadside Diner. He was a close and loyal friend of Mellencamp's, going back years. Reg was wearing blue sweatpants and a dirty white singlet. His forehead was sweating profusely and he looked a little out of breath too.

'Evenin' Silvio,' he said with a tired grin.

'Hey Reg. Good to see you. How's things?'

Reg blew out his cheeks. 'It's been one helluva day.'

'Tell me about it. I'm still in my fucking dressing gown. Take a seat. Fill me in on what you've been up to.'

Reg pulled out the chair on the opposite side of the desk. He collapsed into it and let out a deep sigh. 'The walk up your stairs nearly killed me,' he gasped.

Mellencamp smiled and reached into his desk drawer. He pulled out two thick wads of twenty-dollar bills. He tossed them across the desk to Reg who caught them on his stomach. He grabbed them with his sweaty hands to stop them sliding onto the floor.

'What have you done with the FBI agent?' Mellencamp asked.

'I've got her body in the back of my truck,' said Reg. 'What do you want me to do with her?'

'Is that her blood?' Mellencamp asked, noticing a red stain on Reg's undershirt.

Reg tugged at his undershirt and pulled it away from his chest to get a better look at the stain Mellencamp was pointing at. 'I think that's ketchup,' he said.

'You sure?'

Reg rubbed two fingers on the red patch and then put them in his mouth and licked them. He rolled his tongue around for a few seconds. 'Actually, you're right, it's blood,' he said, shrugging. 'That bitch has bled on my best shirt.'

'That's too bad,' said Mellencamp. 'I'll get Clarisse to wash it for you later. While she's doing that you can indulge yourself with a few of the girls downstairs. On the house of course.'

'If I can muster the energy.'

'Let the girls do the work. Jasmine can sort you out without you having to make any effort at all. Trust me.'

'I'll keep that in mind.'

'Good. Now this FBI agent you killed. She has a partner. Some guy called Munson. Have you seen him?'

'Nah. Last I heard he was at Litgo's.'

'You know Litgo's dead now though?'

'I heard yeah. Tragic. Poor fucker never hurt anyone.'

The phone on Silvio Mellencamp's desk started ringing for the hundredth time that day. The sound of it had begun to seriously piss him off. He snatched at it and answered it before it could ring a second time. 'Yes,' he snapped.

One of the female staff was on the other end of the line. 'There's a Doctor Chandler from Lewisville Hospital here to see you,' she said.

'Oh good. It's about time. Send him up.'

'Yes sir.'

Mellencamp replaced the receiver on the phone and sat back. He stretched his arms out and yawned.

'You expecting someone?' Reg asked.

'It's the doctor. He's come to do Baby's abortion.'

'She's pregnant?'

'So she says, although the doctor doesn't know about it yet. He thinks he's come to fix that gunshot wound you inflicted on her earlier.'

Reg laughed politely. 'I should leave you to it then. What do you want me to do with the FBI agent's body?'

Mellencamp swilled his glass of cognac around while he pondered what to do. 'Don't worry about that,' he said. 'I'll get some of my henchmen to throw her in the incinerator later on. You can stay here for a while because I've got another job for you. You'll like it. It'll appeal to your twisted sense of humour.'

There was a gentle knock on his door. 'Come in,' Mellencamp called out.

The door opened and a young gentleman in a brown tweed jacket, light blue shirt and a pair of creased beige chinos stepped inside. He had thick brown hair that looked like it hadn't been washed in a week. He was also wearing a pair of spectacles that were held together on one corner by a piece of sticky tape. He looked more like a schoolteacher than a doctor. 'Are you Mr Mellencamp?' he asked, timidly.

'Dr Chandler, I presume?'

'That's right.'

'Well come on in then. Would you like a drink?'

Dr Chandler stepped into the room and closed the door behind him. In his right hand he was carrying a brown leather briefcase.

Reg stood up from his seat opposite Mellencamp. 'Hey, you can sit here doc,' he said.

'Thank you. That's very kind of you.'

Dr Chandler perched himself on the edge of the chair and placed his briefcase on his lap, holding onto it tightly with both hands.

'This is a very nice place you have,' he said, throwing a glance around the room.

'I know,' Mellencamp replied. 'Do you know why you're here?'

Dr Chandler nodded. 'I understand you have a patient with a gunshot wound in her upper arm that needs tending to.'

'That's correct. She's been shot in the arm. It's not terribly serious, at least I don't think it is, but then I'm not a doctor which is why I thought it best to get you in to take a look at it.'

'I'm not a specialist on bullet wounds,' said Dr Chandler. 'But I do have some experience.'

'That's okay. You were recommended because this is one of those incidents where it's difficult to get quality healthcare without any awkward questions being asked.'

Dr Chandler frowned. 'You mean you didn't want to take her to the hospital?'

'That's correct. Lewisville is a long way to go. And in case you hadn't noticed there's a nutcase in town chopping people up, so the hospital is probably snowed under with emergencies right now.'

'Actually it's not too bad,' said Dr Chandler. 'I've been there all day. It's the morgue that's busy.'

'Yes, thank you for that,' said Mellencamp, not appreciating the interruption. 'But there's also another issue. The patient you'll be looking at has a history of behavioural problems, the kind that can't be explained away easily in a hospital with nosy doctors and administrative types around.'

172

Dr Chandler smiled. 'That's fine. Confidentiality is one of my strong points. It would never cross my mind to discuss a patient with anyone in say, the police department.'

'That's good,' said Mellencamp. 'And when you say police department I'm assuming you include the FBI in that?'

'Of course.'

'Excellent. So you've done this kind of thing before then?'

'As I said, I don't have a great deal of experience with gunshot wounds, but I have been in the operating room before when other doctors have tended to them. I'm fairly clued up on the etiquette.'

'Well that's a relief,' said Mellencamp. 'There is one other thing though.'

'Yes?'

'The patient is in the very early stages of pregnancy and we need you to carry out a termination as well as tending to the bullet wound.'

Chandler grimaced. 'Oh.'

'Is there a problem?' asked Mellencamp.

'Well, I have *even less* experience of terminations. I know how they're done, but I've never actually carried one out. And I'm not sure I have the right surgical equipment with me.'

Mellencamp waved a dismissive hand. 'You know more about these things than anyone else here. You'll be fine. The pregnancy isn't that far gone. I doubt you'll need too many tools.'

Dr Chandler looked unconvinced. 'Well, yes but I don't have anything to sedate the patient. I mean, I could do a kind of hack job, if you'll pardon the term, but it would be extremely painful and distressing for the woman in question, particularly one who has already suffered the trauma of a bullet wound.'

Mellencamp reached into his desk drawer and pulled out a thick bundle of cash. He placed it on the desk in front of the doctor. Dr Chandler stared at the money.

'How much is there?' he asked.

'Five thousand dollars. That's the upfront payment. When the job is done there's another five for you, you know, as a thank you for coming at such short notice. And for the confidentiality, of course.'

The doctor stared hard at the money as he took a moment to weigh up his options. Eventually he took a deep breath and replied. 'Of course. Well, I guess I'll be happy to give it a go Mr Mellencamp. I've not carried out an abortion before, but I think I know enough about how they work to be able to do a decent job.'

'Excellent. That's all I'm asking for. Just give it your best shot.'

Dr Chandler reached across the desk and picked up the bundle of cash.

'There is one other thing I forgot to mention,' said Mellencamp, causing the doctor to hesitate and take his eyes off the cash momentarily.

'What's that?' he asked.

'Well, the girl doesn't actually want an abortion. She's mentally unstable and confused. As her legal guardian I'm making the decision to have the termination for her.'

Dr Chandler looked horrified. 'She doesn't *want* a termination?'

'She's confused, that's all.'

'But I told you I don't have anything to sedate her with. Do *you* have anything? Because if she's going to struggle then this could be extremely dangerous.'

'I've taken care of that,' said Mellencamp. 'We've tied her to a bed. She's bound and gagged. She won't be able to put up a struggle, or even scream if you do her any damage.'

The doctor looked at the bundle of cash in his hand again. 'Five upfront and another five afterwards,' he said, thinking out loud.

'That's right.'

'That's for the abortion, right?'

'Uh huh.'

'So, I should expect say, another five for tending to the gunshot wound as well?'

Mellencamp raised his eyebrows in surprise, but he swiftly followed it up with a big grin. He nodded at Reg. "I like this guy!' he said.

'Me too,' Reg agreed like a total kiss-ass.

Mellencamp reached back into his drawer and threw another bundle of cash onto the table. 'There you go,' he said. 'Another five up front.'

Dr Chandler opened his briefcase and piled the cash into it, then quickly sealed it shut. 'So where do I find the patient then,' he said, standing up.

'Reg here will take you down to see her. And he'll sit in and oversee the whole thing to make sure you don't have any unforeseen problems. That okay with you?'

'That's fine with me Mr Mellencamp.'

'Good.'

Reg opened the door for Dr Chandler. 'I'll lead the way,' he said. 'We're going down to The Booty Parlour. You'll like it.'

Mellencamp called over to him. 'Reg, Mack is down there with Baby at the moment. When you get there, tell him he can have a break. He can take ten minutes to do what he likes with one of the girls then I want him back up here. I've got an important job for him.'

Thirty Seven

Munson crouched down in front of Candy and held Fonseca's cell phone in front of her face. He made sure she got a good look at the picture of the girl with the blue birthmark on her cheek. 'You know who this girl is don't you?' he barked.

'She was the girl with Arnold this morning,' said Candy sobbing.

'I know that. You know who she is though, don't you?'

'No.'

He grabbed her by the face, squeezing her cheeks hard and keeping her face pointed directly at his. 'You know her, don't you?'

Tears streamed down Candy's face. 'Yes.'

'What's her name?'

'Baby.'

He squeezed her face even harder. He could feel his strength returning, as if the effects of all the alcohol he had consumed were beginning to wear off.

'Baby. Everyone calls her Baby. She's one of the girls at The Beaver Palace.'

'Did my partner Milena Fonseca know who she was?'

'I don't think so.'

Candy's sobbing grew louder, and more annoying. Munson slid his hand down from her face to her throat and squeezed gently, but firmly enough to let her know he was willing to haul her up by it if he had to.

'Is Silvio Mellencamp behind all this?'

'He runs this town. He's behind everything. He'll never let you leave. Half the town is looking for you already.'

'What?'

'I'm just telling you because I want to do the right thing.'

'Do the right thing? It's a bit fucking late for that.'

'Mister, I'm trying to help you out. They're going to kill you.'

'*They? Who's they?*'

'The cops, Reg, Mellencamp's henchmen, basically anyone in this town. There's a bounty on your head.'

'That's ridiculous. You're talking shit.'

'I'm not. That's how things are done in B Movie Hell. You should leave town now. Forget you were ever here.'

Munson reached down and hauled Candy up off the floor by her throat. 'You've already killed an FBI agent. There's no way you're getting away with this.'

Candy wiped some more snot away from her nose with the clump of kitchen towel she was clasping in her hand. 'So where's the body then?' she sneered, indicating that she was tiring of his intimidation.

Munson looked around. 'Well, I don't know. But it's in B Movie Hell somewhere.'

'Face it mister. You're in over your head. When someone dies in B Movie Hell, that's it. They're gone. Vanished forever. Ask all the questions you like. She's gone.'

Munson still had a firm grip on her neck. He slipped Fonseca's phone into his pocket to free his other hand. Then he yanked Candy forwards and swung her round disorientating her. Before she had a chance to steady herself he wrapped an arm around her neck and put her in a chokehold. She didn't have the strength to put up a struggle, so within a matter of seconds he had rendered her unconscious. He'd not had to choke anyone into a state of unconsciousness for a long time, but the old skills hadn't deserted him just yet. He let go of her and eased her body down to the floor.

He figured she'd be out cold for a few minutes, buying him just enough time to find something to tie her up with. He couldn't allow her to contact anyone and inform them of his whereabouts, or what he knew. As he looked around the kitchen for some rope or binding he caught a whiff of the smell of fresh coffee coming from the diner. He had time for one cup of the stuff. Hell, he needed at least one cup. Caffeine was a priority. He had to figure some serious stuff out. And quick.

He tied Candy to a table leg in the kitchen using her apron strings. The knot he'd tied wasn't perfect but it would be strong enough to keep a waitress incapacitated for a fair time. He headed back out into the kitchen and waited for the filter coffee to finish brewing. He cast his mind back to the asylum and the questions he and Fonseca had been asking the staff. The pieces of the jigsaw were beginning to fall into place. No one at the asylum knew how Joey Conrad had escaped. Munson now knew why that was.

He pulled Fonseca's phone back out of his pocket. He took one more look at the picture of the girl before he flicked through the phone's directory until he found Devon Pincent's home number. He hit the speed dial. Pincent answered almost immediately.

'Hi Milena, how's it going?'

'Milena's dead.'

'Jack?'

'Yeah. We need to talk.'

'Seriously? Where's Fonseca?'

'She's dead. Devon, you got that woman killed.'

'Who killed her?'

'The same people who are probably going to kill *me* any minute now.'

On the other end of the line, Pincent took a deep breath. 'Was I right to send you there Jack?'

'You should have told me what was going on.'

'I wanted to. I've been waiting for you to call for ages. What have you been doing?'

'I've been busy trying to work out what's going on here. And following a trail of dead bodies around B Movie Hell. Why didn't you tell me what was going on? Or at least drop me some hints?'

'I tried to, but I couldn't take any chances with Fonseca around. I got in trouble for this once before, and I was wrong about it that time.'

Munson thought back to something Fonseca had said earlier. 'You were using company resources for personal use, weren't you? That's why you got in trouble.'

'Yes.'

'I get it now. I should have worked this out back at the asylum. I just haven't been using my brain much these last few months so I'm a bit off my game. I've got it now though. Joey Conrad didn't escape from the asylum, did he?'

Thirty Eight

Reg led Dr Chandler down one of the Beaver Palace's many long corridors until they reached an elevator at the end of it. He pressed a button in the wall and the doors parted immediately. Both men stepped inside and turned around to face the doors as they closed. Reg pressed the button on the control panel to take them to the basement.

'Been a doctor for long?' Reg asked, not particularly caring about the answer.

'I qualified two years ago.'

'That's nice. You know that if you ever speak about anything you see here, you're a dead man, right?'

Dr Chandler swallowed hard and nodded to show he understood. 'To be honest with you, I've always wanted to come here. This place is legendary. Do you come here much?'

'All the time.'

The lift doors opened and they were greeted by the sight of a whole bunch of women walking around outside the elevator. They were all wearing sexy lingerie. Reg had seen them all before, with and without the undergarments. Dr Chandler on the other hand, looked wide eyed at all the flesh on show.

'This is the basement, also known as The Booty Parlour,' said Reg. 'Don't get a boner just yet. You've got some surgery to do first remember?'

'Yeah.'

Reg led the way through the parlour. The girls in the lingerie all stopped what they were doing and watched the two men walk past. A few of them smiled politely at Reg, but the sight of Dr Chandler and his brown briefcase brought only looks of scorn, fear and in some cases contempt. It seemed that they all knew what was about to unfold in Baby's room.

'It's just down here,' said Reg pointing down a corridor. Up ahead he saw Mack the Slasher standing guard outside Baby's room.

'Hi Mack,' he called out.

Mack raised a hand and saluted him with a wry smile.

'Is she ready?' Reg called out. 'The doctor's here.'

Mack nodded. 'Oh yeah, she's ready. She struggled a little bit at first, but she's calmed down now.' He opened the door and held it for Reg and the doctor as they approached.

Through the opening Reg could see the lower half of Baby. She was completely naked and tied to a large bed in the middle of the room.

Reg stopped and stepped aside. He gestured for Dr Chandler to go ahead of him. The doctor looked up at Mack and smiled politely as he sidled past him and into Baby's room. Reg hung back and spoke to Mack. 'Did she give you any shit?' he asked.

'Nothing I couldn't handle. She's hurt her arm so I had to help her get undressed, but tying her to the bed was easy enough. She won't be able to put up a struggle. I've done all the hard work for you.'

'Good,' said Reg. 'Silvio said I should sit in on this. He said you can take a ten minute break, but then he wants you to head up to his office. He's got some kind of job for you.'

'Good. I can't say I was particularly looking forward to sitting in on an abortion. Not my kind of entertainment.'

'Me neither, but I'll try anything once. Look, just keep the other girls away from here. Some of them are giving the doctor filthy looks.'

'Don't worry about that. I'll keep them in line.'

'Cool. I'll let you know when we're done.'

Mack wandered off to the reception area of The Booty Parlour. Reg took one last look around and then followed the doctor into Baby's room. Baby was writhing around on the large king size bed. Her wrists and ankles were bound with rope and tied to the four corners of the bed. There was a thick strip of brown masking tape wrapped across her mouth. The pink duvet underneath her was ruffled where she had been trying to wriggle free. And standing at the end of her bed was Dr Chandler. He had set his brown leather briefcase down on the duvet between her legs. Baby was staring wide-eyed at the doctor and his bag of tricks.

Reg closed the door behind him and turned the key in the lock to prevent any unwanted visitors interrupting proceedings. When he turned back around he saw Baby struggling to free herself from the binding on her wrists and ankles. She was tied up so tight she had no chance of breaking free, just like Mack had promised. She twisted her head to the side and looked at Reg with pleading eyes. He watched her try to scream out to him for help. The brown masking tape over her mouth stifled any chance of that. She continued to struggle, the muscles in her arms and legs straining hard as she attempted to loosen the binding, but it was all to no avail. Reg smiled at her and spent a few seconds admiring her naked body, making sure she could see him eyeing her up, in the hope it might make her feel even more uncomfortable. He leant down to brush some hair out of her eyes and whispered in her ear. 'Don't worry Baby. I'll be here if anything goes wrong.'

He turned and nodded at Dr Chandler. 'Okay doc. She's all yours.'

The doctor took a deep breath and flicked open the handle on his briefcase. He looked nervous. He smiled apologetically at Baby. 'I don't want to hurt you,' he said. 'So please don't struggle.'

Thirty Nine

By the time Officer Benny Stansfield left The Beaver Palace, the night sky had drawn in. It had been a long and very stressful day and all he wanted to do was get home and see his wife. He called her to let her know he would be home within half an hour and then switched off the police frequency on the car radio. He'd had enough of listening to the repetitive reports of the day's murders.

 He flicked through the CD's in his glove box, while keeping one eye on the road. He picked out the soundtrack to the movie *Drive* and slipped it into the CD player. He flicked forward to the song *A Real Hero*, and began singing along to the parts he knew. He weighed up the day's events as he sped down the road. *He really had been a real hero.* He'd rescued Baby from Litgo's place just before the Red Mohawk showed up, and then he'd returned her safely to The Beaver Palace. And now he wanted nothing more than to put his feet up at home and crack open a bottle of red wine to share with the wife.

He'd travelled less than a mile from The Beaver Palace when he spotted something that sent a shiver down his spine. A yellow stock car with a red stripe through the middle of it was parked on the other side of the road by some bushes. There was no one sitting in either of the front seats. But this was definitely the Red Mohawk's car.

He eased off on the gas and pulled over a safe distance away. He stared across the road at the yellow car and weighed up his options. Potentially this could be worth another hundred grand, not to mention the fame and notoriety that would go with being the hero cop that caught the worst serial killer in B Movie Hell's history. However, this stretch of road was also isolated, unlit and covered on either side by thick woodland. That complicated things. A lot.

He kept the engine running on his black and white Plymouth Fury and turned the volume down on the car radio. His hand settled on the handle of his handgun. He pulled it out of its holster on his belt and flicked open the barrel to check if it was loaded. Every chamber had a bullet in it. That meant he had six shots. Six shots at becoming a real hero. He swallowed hard and nodded to himself. His mind made up, he quietly opened the car door and stepped out. The road outside was deadly silent. There were no chirping birds, no scurrying feet of rodents. Nothing. Not a sound. He edged across the road, with his gun pointed and ready to fire. There was definitely no one in the front seats of the stock car. He moved towards the rear of the car and peered in through the back window. He pressed his face up against it to get a good look inside. There was no one on the back seat either. He stepped back and crouched down to check underneath the car, his foot crunching on a small stone and finally punctuating the silence around him. There was no one under the car either. His heart was beating fast. And loud. His palms were sweating and his trigger finger twitched as he edged around to the back of the car and peered into the woodland. There was no sign of any movement. Remembering all the cheesy horror movies he'd seen in his time, he spun around, fearful that someone might be behind him, creeping up on him. There was no one, no sign of any movement at all.

He turned back to the car but kept his gun pointed into the woodland. He reached out with his spare hand and checked to see if the trunk would open. The metal lock was ice cold against his thumb, but to his surprise it flicked open easily when he pressed it. It bounced up half an inch and then settled back down, slightly ajar. Benny stepped away from it and reached forward to flick it open with the barrel of his gun. He was well aware of how ridiculous it was to think that the killer might be hiding in the trunk of his own car. But in dangerous times like these Benny wasn't willing to take any chances. A hundred thousand dollar reward was at stake for the execution of the Red Mohawk, but more importantly Benny's life was at stake too.

He flicked the trunk open and hopped back a step just in case. Nothing jumped out at him so he took a deep breath and squinted his eyes to get a good look inside. The lack of any light made it difficult to see anything at first. But after a few seconds he caught sight of something. *Something big.* He edged closer and peered inside, ready to jump back again if anything pounced. Before he even had a chance to focus on what was inside he heard a noise from the woodland. It was something scurrying around. Probably a rodent of some sort, but even so, it was enough to make him spin a full three-hundred-and-sixty degree turn with his pistol aimed. When he was confident there was no one in sight he calmed himself by concentrating on breathing slower, then he took a closer look inside the trunk of the car.

The large object he had seen was exactly what he feared it would be. A corpse. Another dead body to add to the ever-growing list. This latest victim was a man. It was hard to tell how old he was. He had thick hair that was covering much of his face. Benny leaned in and flicked some of the hair away to get a closer look. His hand touched on some dried blood that was matting several strands of hair together. The dead man wasn't anyone he recognised. Benny knew all the local residents, so who the fuck was this guy?

The corpse was wearing a stained blue T-shirt but no pants, just a pair of white boxer shorts. What Benny needed was a wallet with some form of identification for this latest victim.

He took another look around the road and surrounding woodland area to make sure no one was sneaking up on him then began feeling around in the trunk behind the dead body. There wasn't anything back there. He reluctantly rolled the body onto its side to see if there was anything underneath it. The body was cold and hard. Prodding and poking a dead guy was never a fun experience, particularly when it was dark and there was a possibility of sticking his hand into an open wound. He found nothing, not even some loose change. No identification, no handkerchief, not a damn thing. He took one last look around and decided to radio the discovery in to the station. He was just about to walk away when a gust of wind blew a piece of evidence his way. He wasn't sure how he'd missed it, but a small slip of white notepaper blew up out of the trunk. He reached up and caught it before it disappeared down the road. He held it up in front of his face. There was a handwritten message on it. In the fading light it was hard to make out the words. But now that he was confident he was alone he replaced his pistol in its holster and pulled out a small torch pen he kept in his top pocket. He shone it over the piece of paper and squinted to get a closer look. The message was written in red ink. It read

Silvio Mellencamp. The Beaver Palace, 100 Arlington Road, B Movie Hell.

For a moment he wondered why a stranger would have Silvio Mellencamp's address written down on a piece of paper. It offered no clue to his identity. At least, it didn't until Benny read the words that were written beneath the address in bold lettering.

GUNSHOT WOUND. FEMALE. UPPER ARM.

Forty

Reg walked around to the end of the bed and stood alongside Dr Chandler.

'Mack's done a great job tying her up, hasn't he?' he remarked, looking down at Baby's naked body. The girl looked so vulnerable, so helpless and so utterly terrified.

'He certainly has,' the doctor replied.

Reg couldn't help but stare at Baby's milky white skin. He had seen her naked body on a few previous visits to The Beaver Palace but he never tired of the sight of it. Everything was so firm, yet so supple. And now that she had her voice silenced by the tape over her mouth she was much less annoying than usual. He wished that he could have had five minutes alone with her before the doctor got to work. Unfortunately it was too late to even consider suggesting it. Now that the doctor was in the room with them and preparing to carry out a hatchet job of an abortion the opportunity had been missed. He was itching for an excuse to touch her though.

'Would it help if I held her down as well, just to be on the safe side?' he suggested.

Dr Chandler took off his brown tweed jacket and set it down on the floor at the end of the bed. 'It's okay,' he said. 'She's not going anywhere.'

Baby was still writhing around, frantically screaming through her nose, her face etched with the fear brought on by the sight of Dr Chandler standing at the end of her bed, rummaging through the contents of his leather briefcase.

Reg wasn't paying much attention to the doctor. He was too busy staring at Baby. Eventually Dr Chandler appeared to find what he was looking for. He tapped Reg on the arm.

'There is one thing you could do for me,' he said. 'Would you mind putting on some music, please?'

'Music?' Reg was puzzled and took his eyes off Baby's tits for a moment to see if the doctor was serious. 'What do you want music for? Does it help calm the patient?'

Chandler smiled. 'No, but it will help to drown out the screaming. So if you could put something on, the louder the better, that would be great, thanks.'

Reg shrugged. The idea made sense, kind of. He walked over to the stereo system in the corner of the room by the door. Each of the bedrooms had a stereo system and a selection of compact discs (mostly

185

by Barry White) that were played to death, particularly when any of the local overweight sweaty old men paid the girls a visit.

He picked up a CD called *Classic Soul Favourites* and slipped it into the CD player. Out of the corner of his eye he could see Baby still frantically trying to break free from the binding on her arms and legs. She knew what was coming.

"It serves her right," Reg thought to himself as the first track on the CD started playing. He listened to it for a few seconds before recognising it as the Sam and Dave track *Hold On I'm Coming*. A highly appropriate track for The Beaver Palace. He reached for the volume switch and turned it up a little. It was as loud as he would normally have it in his own house, but he noted that he could still hear Baby's stifled screams, so in accordance with the doctor's request he twisted the volume knob a little more until the song was blaring out at the kind of levels only a teenager could listen to.

'That ought to do it,' he said, swiftly realising that his own voice was being drowned out by the music. He turned to the doctor.

'I said that ought to…'

Dr Chandler was still standing at the end of Baby's bed. His briefcase was still open but he hadn't pulled any surgical tools from it. He wasn't holding any kind of instruments in his hands. The only thing he had pulled out of the briefcase was a rubber mask. While Reg had been busy fiddling with the stereo, the doctor had taken off his glasses and slipped the mask on over his head, and was now straightening it up so that he could see clearly through the eyeholes. It was a yellow skull mask with a red stripe of hair on top. The skull-face on the mask was grinning at him.

It took about a second for Reg to process the information, analyse it and interpret exactly what it meant. But it felt like one hell of a long second. He looked over at Baby. She still had the same terrified look on her face as before, but only now did Reg fully understand why. She had known who the doctor was the moment he walked in. And while Reg had been busy dicking around with the stereo system she had been watching the doctor transform into The Red Mohawk.

Reg found himself rooted to the spot, taken completely by surprise. Did he have time to run? Did he need to run? *Fuck Yeah*. He needed to run. His major problem was he'd locked the bloody door when he came in. His chances of unlocking it and getting the fuck out before the Mohawk got his hands on him were slim.

While all these crazy questions and plans were running through his head The Red Mohawk reached into his briefcase and pulled out a large shiny silver meat cleaver. He was staring at Baby, almost as if

186

he'd forgotten about Reg. And then he spoke, just loud enough to be heard over the music.

'I want you to watch this,' he said. 'It's going to be bloody.'

Reg was suddenly sweating profusely. His mouth had gone dry and he wasn't sure he'd be able to answer, or even know what his answer might be. Instinct took over and he spluttered out a response.

'I... I don't think I need to watch it,' he stammered. 'I'll leave you to it.'

The masked man took a step back from the bed and turned to his head slightly so he could stare at Reg. He tilted his head to one side then spoke in a chilling voice. 'I was talking to the girl,' he said.

No further hesitation was required. Reg rushed to the door and grabbed the handle. He frantically turned the key in the lock. His mind had gone blank and he couldn't remember which way to turn it. By the time he eventually got it right and yanked the door open, the masked killer was right behind him. Reg only managed to get the door open a few inches before one of The Red Mohawk's hands slammed it shut again. The same hand then grabbed Reg by the throat and lifted him up off the floor. Reg was dragged away from the door and slammed against the wall.

'Wait,' Reg pleaded. 'We can talk about this. I'm just a chef! *I'm just a chef!*'

The masked killer did not respond verbally. Instead he held up the meat cleaver to make sure his prey got a good look at it. Reg could see the dried stains of blood from earlier victims still on the silver blade. The masked man's fingers were whitening as he tightened his grip on the cleaver's wooden handle. He moved the cleaver downwards slowly, ensuring Reg could keep track of its whereabouts. He stopped when he reached the gap between Reg's legs, just below his balls. Then he twisted the meat cleaver over in his hand so that the blade was facing upwards.

'Oh Jesus, there's no need for this,' Reg spluttered.

'That's right,' said the Red Mohawk. 'But it's happening anyway.'

Forty One

'Joey Conrad didn't escape from the asylum, did he?'

'No he didn't,' Pincent admitted.

Munson thought about how sloppy he had become during his time away from the agency. In years gone by he would have worked this out much sooner. He and Pincent had always had an almost telepathic understanding, brought on by working together so often in pressure situations. The clues had been there all along. If he hadn't had so much to drink he might have figured out what was going on much earlier. He could have saved the life of Milena Fonseca, and more importantly he could have contacted Pincent and put a stop to everything. But now it was too late. Things had gone too far.

'It's time to come clean Devon. What the fuck is happening? Tell me the truth. Is this girl in the picture who I think it is?'

While he waited for Pincent to answer he grabbed a white mug from one of the shelves and set it down on the counter. He picked up the freshly brewed jug of filter coffee and lifted it from the hotplate. Before he had a chance to pour any coffee into the mug, Pincent answered. His voice wobbling a little as he spoke.

'It's Marianne.'

'I fucking knew it.' Munson rubbed his forehead. His headache was getting worse. 'How is that possible?'

'I never gave up looking for her. That's how it's possible.'

'But she's dead.'

'They never found her body Jack. I've been telling you that for years.'

Munson filled the mug on the counter to the top with coffee. 'This is fucking insane. What happened? Did she get away? Why didn't they kill her when they killed Sarah and Annalise?'

Pincent didn't answer.

Munson stuck the coffee jug back on the hotplate. 'They *did* kill Sarah and Annalise, *didn't they?*' he asked.

'Yes. Of course they did. We all saw the remains didn't we? But there was never any proof that Marianne was dead. I never gave up hope.'

'But it's been fourteen years. How did you know?'

'Jack, if you'd ever had kids you'd understand. You find out your wife and two daughters have been murdered and it rips your insides out. But then someone tells you that they can't find any trace of your youngest daughter. There's no body parts, no remains, no DNA. You don't just give up like that. You keep looking for her.'

Munson picked up his mug of coffee and took a sip. It was good stuff. As he savoured the taste and wondered where he might find some sugar, he thought about the emotion he could hear in his friend's voice. He remembered exactly how terrible it had been fourteen years earlier when Pincent lost his family. His wife and two daughters were snatched from a safe house. The virtually unrecognisable remains of his wife and eldest daughter were found in a burned down house a week later. His youngest daughter Marianne, aged only five had never been found. Munson had naively assumed that Pincent had accepted the fact he would never see her again. He'd assumed wrong.

'So you found out she was in B Movie Hell. *How?*' Munson asked.

'Believe it or not, it wasn't me that found out. For the last few years I've been convinced that she was in Detroit. I damn near lost my job sending agents to investigate and harass the Palluca family. I was sure they were responsible for what happened to Sarah and Annalise. We were investigating the Pallucas at the time all those years ago. We were getting close. I always thought they kidnapped my family to scare us off. Instead it turns out it was this small time fucking porno producer we were trying to shut down.'

'But how did you find this out?'

'I didn't. Joey Conrad did.'

'Eh?'

'Another patient at Grimwald's escaped a while back. He came back with a photo of this girl he'd met at a place called The Beaver Palace in B Movie Hell. Conrad recognised her from the birthmark and wrote me a fucking letter. Can you believe that? I always knew he was a good kid.'

Munson took another sip of the coffee and looked out the front window of the diner. His car was still the only one parked outside.

'So, you went to Grimwald's and you let Joey Conrad out? And you sent him to B Movie Hell to get Marianne back?'

'That's right Jack. I gave him the mask, the clothes, the meat cleaver and all the fucking guns and ammunition he wanted.'

Munson nearly spat out his latest mouthful of coffee. 'Oh Jesus. What the fuck were you thinking?'

'What the fuck was I thinking? I was thinking I want my baby girl back. Fourteen years they've been hiding her in that shithole town. Everybody in that town knows everybody else, Jack. They all knew she was there. And not one of them said anything. Mellencamp funds everyone's business in that place. Those residents that aren't scared of him, are paid by him. I sent Joey Conrad in there and let him loose on those bastards.'

Munson couldn't believe what he was hearing. 'He's killed half the goddamn town, Devon! There's a lot of innocent people that have died here. This could have been done through official channels. You'll fucking fry for this.'

'Only me, you and Milena Fonseca know about it. If you clean this up for me, no one needs to ever know what happened.'

'What about the asylum staff? They must know.'

'They turned a blind eye. Ask them how he escaped.'

'I did. They said the security was crap.'

'There you go.'

'I should have known right there and then. *Fuck*, Devon you'll never get away with this!'

'I don't care. I want my Marianne back. And I want everyone in B Movie Hell to suffer for what they've done.'

'There's better ways to do this. Official ways.'

'Search warrants and stuff like that? Don't make me laugh, Jack. You know how that would pan out. In a town like B Movie Hell, my baby would vanish the minute a search warrant showed up. I couldn't risk losing her again, not when I'm this close. You and me, when we worked together on that goddamn operation that we're not supposed to speak about, we worked fucking hard at training Joey Conrad to be the perfect killing machine. I finally got to put him into action. Operation Blackwash is a success after all.'

Munson felt the caffeine kicking into his system, re-energising him. He puffed out his cheeks. 'Are you trying to say that by training Conrad, I'm somehow equally responsible for this mess?'

'No. You don't need to be linked to any of this. Your name isn't anywhere in the Blackwash files. I erased it. No one knows you were involved and no one knows you're in B Movie Hell right now.'

'So why the hell am I here then?'

'Because Milena Fonseca found out about Conrad's escape. She wanted to go public with it. I convinced her to let you clean it up, but then she insisted on going with you. I couldn't tell you what was going on. Not while I was in the office, or using the office phones. This is totally off the record.'

'You should have just sent me instead of Joey Conrad. I could have dealt with this.'

'No offence Jack, but you're not exactly Liam Neeson these days. You're a washed up drunk, so you weren't my first choice to rescue my daughter. I wanted the killer from the Halloween movies.'

Munson finished off the last dregs of his coffee. He was feeling much better after his earlier vomiting incident. 'So what do you want me to do now?'

'Now that Fonseca is dead, you don't need to be there. Let Joey Conrad do his thing. You can come on home. I'll make sure you get paid somehow. All you have to do is keep quiet about this, just like I kept quiet when you shot that girl.'

'Thanks for nothing Devon.' Munson hung up the phone. The image of a kidnapper holding a gun to a girl's head flickered in his mind for the millionth time. He shuddered and blanked the image out. He had to concentrate on the matter at hand. He remembered Marianne Pincent well. As a five-year-old, she had been a beautiful, fun little girl with the world at her feet. But what could *he* possibly do to help get her back? Joey Conrad was supposedly going to rescue her, in what was basically the most immoral and ridiculously vengeful rescue mission of all time.

As he pondered what to do, the phone in his hand started vibrating. The Backstreet Boys song began playing. He answered the call expecting it to be Pincent calling back.

'What?' he snapped.

A boy's voice spoke on the other end. 'Hi, is my mom there?'

Munson ended the call. He threw the phone across the room. It smashed against a wall underneath one of the windows. Milena Fonseca had a kid. Maybe two kids, who knew? One thing Munson knew for sure was that those kids would soon find out their mother was dead.

He thought about Marianne Pincent. She had lost her mother and sister when she was just five years old. She'd lost her father too, but she could still be reunited with him.

He took a deep breath and reached into his pocket for his bottle of rum. He pulled it out and unscrewed the lid. He stared at it and deliberated whether or not to take a swig. Immediately the image of a man holding a gun to a girl's head flashed into his mind again. The girl was only eighteen years old. She was terrified. Her kidnapper, a vile greasy thug in his forties was threatening to shoot her. And it looked like he was going to do it too. So Munson did what he had been trained to do. He fired a shot.

It hit the girl in the side of the head.

A second shot hit the kidnapper between the eyes, killing him instantly. Munson would never forget rushing to the girl's side and cradling her in his arms as she took her last breath. Ninety-nine times out of a hundred he would have hit the kidnapper with his first shot.

Ninety-nine times out of a hundred.

But that day was the one time in a hundred when for no explicable reason his aim was off. He'd had to live with that mistake ever since. Drinking hadn't helped.

His mind flashed forward to the present and he the imagined throwing up again like he had done at Litgo's earlier after drinking the evil rum. It wasn't a pleasant thought. He placed the bottle of rum down on the diner's counter and whispered a promise to himself.

"Get Marianne Pincent back to her father. Make amends."

Forty Two

Benny slammed the trunk of the yellow stock car shut. He grabbed his cell phone from his pocket and called the number for The Beaver Palace. His fingers were trembling as he put the phone to his ear. The dialling tone kicked in straight away. It rang once. Benny expected it to be answered immediately.

It rang a second time.

And a third.

Then a fourth time.

And a fifth.

It just kept on ringing.

Normally the phone at The Beaver Palace was answered within two or three rings, unless it was engaged. This was a bad sign. What the hell was going on?

He hung up the phone and rushed back to his squad car. He dived inside and yanked the CB radio off its handle. It wasn't just his hands that were trembling now. His whole body was shaking. He flicked on the power switch on the radio and yelled into the mouthpiece. 'This is Benny. Come in please!'

He waited for a response. Surely the police station would respond quicker than The Beaver Palace? He thought about how he had planned to head home for a quiet bottle of wine with his wife. That idea was going to have to be put on hold. After an indeterminable length of time a female voice answered his call via the radio. 'Hi Benny. How you doing?'

'Put me through to Chief O'Grady right now. It's urgent.'

'Charming. You not even got time for a....'

'Jenny, will you just put me through for Godssake? It's urgent. I know where the Red Mohawk is.'

'The chief's not here right now Benny. He's doing another press conference. Anyone else I can get for you?'

Benny spent a few seconds cursing to himself. He had to make a decision. In fact, he decided it might be best to take charge of the situation anyway. 'Jenny, get a hold of everyone and tell them all to head to Mellencamp's right now.'

'What do you mean *everyone?*'

'Exactly that. *EVERYONE!*'

'What should I tell them?'

'Tell them the Red Mohawk is at The Beaver Palace. He's gone there disguised as a doctor.'

'How do you know? Have you seen him?'

'I found the dead body of the doctor in the trunk of the Red Mohawk's car. I think he's taken the doctor's car and gone to The Beaver Palace.'

'Okay. Where are you? And what are the instructions for everyone?'

'I'm a mile down the road from Mellencamp's. You can't miss me. My car is parked by the yellow piece of shit car the killer stole from Hank Jackson this morning.'

'Should I tell everyone to meet you there?'

'Yes. It won't be hard to spot me. I'm in my car. I'm on one side of the road and that fucking yellow and red stock car is on the other. Get everyone here in ten minutes. That's as long as I can wait. Then I'm heading into The Beaver Palace. Anyone arriving after I've left should just head straight there. But tell them all to come in riot gear if they can. And bring guns. Lots of guns. And lots of ammunition. And make sure you send *everyone!*'

'You want the whole police force?'

'I want everyone in town who owns a gun. And everyone who doesn't. Send everyone. It's time to take this fucking sonofabitch down.'

'Sure thing Benny. I'll call you back in a minute with an update.'

Benny hung the CB radio back on the dashboard and used his phone to call The Beaver Palace again.

And just like before, the phone rang and rang. And no one answered.

Forty Three

Baby turned away in horror a split second before she heard Reg the chef scream out loud. He screamed like a bitch too. The Red Mohawk's meat cleaver was put to work in a big way. As Baby looked away, she tried to blot out the sounds of Reg's body being sliced apart. She'd never been so grateful to hear Sam and Dave singing *Hold On I'm Coming*. Without them she might have heard a lot more of the gruesome violence.

She knew she could well be the next person on the sharp end of that meat cleaver. She'd already wasted the best part of half an hour trying to wrestle free from the binding that Mack had used to tie her to the bed. She had practically given up trying five minutes earlier, but circumstances had changed since then. Right now she was revitalised and mustering every last ounce of strength she had to try and break free. She was also twisting her mouth one way then another in the hopes of loosening the tape across it. Every strain, every pull, all of it was in vain.

There was no way of getting away from what was happening to Reg though. She could turn her eyes away from it, and Sam and Dave could drown out some of the horrific noises, but nothing could prevent specks of Reg's blood from spraying onto her legs and stomach.

Unlike earlier in the day when she had poured some syrup of ipecac down her throat, Baby now had no need to take any drugs to make herself sick. The urge to vomit was undeniable. She prayed that someone would come to her rescue. Mack the Slasher was outside somewhere, as were half a dozen of the girls, but with the loud music blaring out of her stereo none of them would have heard Reg's fading cries for mercy.

She'd often heard people talk about how their life flashed before their eyes during the moments when they thought they were going to die. She felt herself become lightheaded. Everything was suddenly blurred around the edges. Nothing seemed quite as real as it had done moments earlier. She was slipping into a state of shock. Up above her on the ceiling she saw an imaginary cinema screen unfolding before her eyes. On it she saw images of her own life flashing away, strobe-like in a high-speed montage. *Flickering visuals of her mother and father. An early Christmas with presents underneath a large green fir tree. Memories of her early days at The Beaver Palace.* She saw the older women telling her bedtime stories from a book of fairy tales. Her favourites had been Rapunzel and Sleeping Beauty. She had longed for a knight in shining armour or handsome prince of her own who would one day come to take her away from B Movie Hell. If a knight or prince was going to do any such thing, he would need to get a serious hurry on because time was running out fast.

The cinema screen above her rolled up into a cylinder and faded away. Baby stopped struggling and resigned herself to her fate. An odd moment of calm came over her. She stared straight up at the ceiling just like she'd done on her infrequent visits from the local dentist. Endure what was to come and focus on the ceiling, it was something Clarisse had always told her to do. It worked with dentists and sometimes with repulsive clients. Right now anything was better than looking across at the remains of Reg or the man who was mutilating him. Where the imaginary cinema screen had once been she now saw the silhouette of a masked man with a meat cleaver, chopping up a dead carcass.

The Sam and Dave song came to a climax and faded out. It signalled the end of Reg's annihilation.

His killer, The Red Mohawk loomed large into Baby's peripheral vision. She froze when his mask came into view above her head. She saw his meat cleaver at his side, his hand gripping it tight. Both the mask and the cleaver were splattered with blood. The cleaver dripped with the stuff, thick and clotted, like jam. Baby wondered if her blood would look the same.

He stepped closer and stared down at her. Baby stayed totally still. For reasons she couldn't explain she was desperate not to make any sudden movements. She just lay there, breathing through her nose and trying with all her strength to remain calm. The masked man just stared at her. She waited for him to say something. To attack her. To chop her into bits. But he said nothing. He did nothing.

After an incredibly long and awkward pause she turned her head, careful to avoid any sudden movements. She looked into the eyes behind the mask.

The silence was broken by the deep voice of Barry White warbling out of the stereo system. He drooled out the words *"It feels so good",* the opening line of his song *I'm Gonna Love You Just A Little Bit More.*

And in one swift movement the Red Mohawk swung his meat cleaver down towards the bed. Baby screamed behind the tape and screwed her eyes shut. This was it.

But it wasn't it. Instead of unbearable pain, she felt instead, the sudden release of tension on her left side. Her arm flapped across her body. It took her a moment to realise that the cleaver had sliced through the binding, rather than her flesh. She continued to lay there motionless, wondering if cutting her free was intentional or not.

Another swift swipe from the meat cleaver freed her left leg. She instinctively pulled her knee up to her stomach, as far away as possible from the meat cleaver. She looked up at the horrible masked figure walking around the bed. Even though he had cut two of her limbs free, the sight of him raising the meat cleaver above his head ready to swing it down at the rope tying her right leg to the bed still made her flinch. He wasn't paying much attention to her now. She picked at the corner of the tape on her mouth and peeled it away sharply. It stung, as she expected, but this wasn't the time to be fretting about such things.

'Who are you?' she asked.

The hideous masked figure cut the rope on her other leg and looked up. 'Do you know who you are?' he asked.

Baby looked up at the ceiling again. The imaginary cinema screen flashed up more images of her parents and the Christmas tree. It made her frown. 'I don't remember,' she said, staring at the images of her parents and feeling an emptiness in the pit of her stomach that she hadn't felt since childhood.

'You're Marianne Pincent.'

He swung the meat cleaver down one more time to free her right hand. She took her eyes off the ceiling and sat upright, dragging her knees up to her chest to cover as much of her naked body as she could. She skittered back across the bed, keeping as much distance as possible between them. The room felt cold all of a sudden, enough to make her shiver. She looked across at him in the hope he would elaborate on the revelation that she was Marianne Pincent, a name she recalled. A name she remembered from childhood, albeit only faintly.

He pulled the mask off and shook his head to loosen his thick brown hair, which had been flattened underneath it. He wasn't nearly as grotesque or terrifying without the mask. He put his meat cleaver down on the bed, staining the pink duvet with blood. He ran his hand through his hair and took a deep breath.

'I'm Joey Conrad,' he said. 'Your father sent me. I've come to take you home.'

Forty Four

Munson placed his cell-phone onto the dashboard of his Mercedes. He had tuned it into receive the local police radio frequency. There was plenty of talk going on, mostly back and forth between cops and the woman on the reception at the local station. The crux of it all was that Benny Stansfield had requested for every cop to head towards The Beaver Palace. He'd set up a roadblock and was planning on taking an army of cops to the Palace to confront The Red Mohawk. Munson took one positive from the whole thing. The cops were more interested in killing Joey Conrad than they were in finding him and stopping him from leaving town.

He started up the car and turned on the headlights. There were no other cars around. He took one last look at the diner. The lights were all turned off. He had left Candy on the floor in the kitchen, tied to a table leg with a cloth gag across her mouth. He still felt bad about leaving her like that, but he reminded himself that she was wrapped up in all of this. She had willingly taken part in the cover up, the hiding of Marianne Pincent. And she'd sell Munson out to Reg or anyone else the minute they turned up at the diner. Besides, with Joey Conrad on the rampage she was probably safer stuck in the diner anyway. The only residents of B Movie Hell that stood a chance of surviving through the night were the ones with the good sense to stay locked in their homes.

The highway was still fairly quiet but with all the cops likely to show up soon, he had to consider how safe it was to be seen on the road. His thoughts were interrupted by the voice of the receptionist at the police station. She crackled into life again through the radio on his phone.

'Calling all units. A black Mercedes fitting the description of Jack Munson's car has been spotted parked at the Alaska Roadside Diner. Is anyone in the vicinity?'

Fucking Hell.

A male voice answered almost immediately. 'This is McGready. Me and Simcock are half a mile away. We were heading to The Beaver Palace but we can make a stop and check it out. We'll be there in a couple of minutes.'

'Thanks Ken.'

'No problem.'

'Ken.'

'Yeah.'

'If you see Munson…. if he's there, the chief says to shoot on sight. He cannot be allowed to leave B Movie Hell.'

'Got it Stephanie. Over.'

Just as Munson had suspected and Pincent had more or less confirmed, the cops were after him. He was on his own in B Movie Hell with only one possible ally and that was a serial killer in a Halloween mask whose mental state meant he was completely unreliable. It made Munson smile. *He hadn't felt so alive in years.*

He switched off the headlights on his car. If the cops were looking for his Mercedes then he had to do everything possible to keep a low profile. He pulled out of the diner's parking lot and on to the highway. He considered the possibility of stealing a car. The cops were looking for his black Mercedes. Driving around with the lights off would make him hard to spot from a distance but it might not be the best way to evade them. The car lot from which the Red Mohawk had stolen a car earlier was probably unmanned right now, but it was a couple of miles back down the road. It was too risky. And besides, he needed to get to The Beaver Palace as soon as possible. That was where the action was.

It was hard to believe after all these years that Marianne Pincent was being held there. Munson remembered what had happened like it was only yesterday. He remembered vowing to do everything he could to help find her. He had meant it at the time too, but after six months with absolutely no leads he had given up the ghost. Pincent hadn't. Hell, from the sounds of it he'd thought of nothing else ever since. Everyone else had presumed that a girl with such an identifiable birthmark would have been easy to find. When she hadn't shown up after a few months it hadn't been unreasonable to work under the assumption that she would never be found. Most folks quietly believed that she was buried in a shallow grave somewhere. Everyone that is, except her father.

After driving in darkness with no headlights for about two miles and not encountering another vehicle or pedestrian he finally saw some signs of life. Up ahead around a bend he saw flashing blue and red lights. In his rear view mirror he saw another one appear in the distance behind him almost immediately. The blue light up ahead wasn't moving in any direction. It had to be the Benny Stansfield roadblock. This was Munson's cue to get off the highway. He steered his car off the road and into the woodland, disappearing behind a clump of bushes just before the police car behind him raced past with its siren blaring.

He parked up out of sight of the road and switched off the radio on his phone. He grabbed the phone, checked he still had bullets in his handgun and then climbed out of the car.

He had managed to avoid being spotted by either of the squad cars, but there was no way he would get past that roadblock. He was going to have to go around it. And if he was going to make it to The Beaver Palace, he was going to have to do it on foot. And quickly.

He crept through the woodland towards the flashing blue lights, making sure he never ventured too close to the highway. If he was spotted he was liable to get killed pretty quick. *"Shoot on sight"* the bitch at police HQ had said.

The blue lights continued lighting up the night sky but the siren on the squad car that had just arrived was switched off. There followed a moment of beautiful silence that ended all too quickly. Munson heard the sound of car doors opening and closing up ahead.

He trod carefully to avoid any loud snapping twigs and crept up to a spot where he hid behind a large tree so he could hear what was being said. At first all he heard was little more than small talk, until finally someone said something that pricked his ears up.

'Here comes Randall.'

'He'll be pissed,' another voice replied. 'He still hasn't had a night off.'

Sure enough Munson heard another vehicle approaching. Coming round a bend in the road was a metallic blue pickup truck. It bounded down the highway rattling and banging as it went. The driver pulled over and parked up by the side of the road behind the two squad cars not far from where Munson was hiding. Munson ducked out of sight, careful not to make a noise. He heard the truck door open and through the trees he saw a tubby old guy in a pair of denim dungarees and a red shirt jump out onto the ground. It was Randall, in his civvies.

'What's going on Benny?' Randall asked.

'The Red Mohawk is at The Beaver Palace,' Benny replied.

'So then why the fuck are you waiting around here?'

'We're waiting for backup. The riot team are coming. We're gonna take that sonofabitch down.'

'You've gotta be kidding,' Randall groaned. 'That psycho will have killed everyone by the time you guys get there. Let me go on ahead. I'll shoot the fucker down with my new shotgun.'

'Can't let you do that just yet Randall.'

'Why the fuck not?'

'I've been trying to call The Beaver Palace for the last five minutes. No one is answering. It could be chaos there already.'

'Goddamn it Benny. All the more reason to let me through then! This guy killed my partner last night, and he's killed a couple more of our guys today. I can't just stand by here while you guys dither and fuck about. Let me through. I'm in the mood to bag me a serial killer.'

'Calm down Randall for fuckssake.'

'You calm down Benny. I'm not a cop tonight. This time it's personal.'

'Jeezus! Could you be any more of a cliché?'

'Yes I could. I've always followed the rules, done everything by the book. Well not any more. From now on, I'm a cop living life on the edge. If the chief has to call me into his office to chew me out in the morning, well that's fine. I play by my own rules from now on.'

'You've been drinking haven't you?'

'All afternoon.'

'And watching Lethal Weapon again by the sounds of it.'

'Bits of it. And Die Hard.'

Another nearby cop threw an opinion into the mix. 'Benny, I say let him through. Randall is badass. If he wants to go on in ahead of us I ain't got no beef with that.'

While Benny, Randall and the other officers argued the merits of whether or not Randall should be allowed to go on ahead to The Beaver Palace, Munson took his chance and crept out of the woodland up to the side of Randall's pickup truck. He hauled himself up quietly onto it and rolled into the back. He landed on something soft and ducked down out of sight, laying flat out on his back staring up at the stars and listening in on the rest of the conversation.

'Okay, Randall. You go on ahead. I'll try calling Mellencamp again to let him know you're coming. If he's still alive, that is.'

'Good. You do that. I'll see you there,' said Randall.

Munson heard Randall's boots crunching on the small stones on the highway as he walked back towards the pickup truck. He climbed in and slammed the door shut behind him. He muttered some clichéd lines from a few eighties action movies to himself before he started up the engine. Pretty soon he was driving recklessly along the highway to The Beaver Palace with Munson hitching a ride in the back.

Forty Five

Clarisse was naked from the waist down and bent over the reception desk in The Booty Parlour. Mack the Slasher was standing behind her with his pants around his ankles. Silvio Mellencamp had given him a ten minute break and told him that he could have any one of the girls he wanted. Unfortunately for Clarisse, Mack always wanted her. And always from behind, over her desk.

She was holding on tight to the end of the desk and using her elbows to hold down some of her notepads and stationery (all of which often ended up on the floor during one of Mack's vigorous poundings). He wasn't blessed with any kind of rhythm, sexual technique, or imagination for that matter, all he knew was brute force, and only in a back and forth motion. And when he slammed his hips forward while fucking her he did tend to make the desk shake quite violently.

From the second he had pulled her underwear off and thrown it away wantonly in the throes of passion, the phone on her desk had been ringing almost non-stop. At the last count she had missed six calls. Mr Mellencamp didn't like her missing calls but seeing as it was his fault she was being rammed from behind by his right hand man, she felt justified in not picking up the phone.

Several of the other girls had walked past and ignored the ringing phone. It was a well known fact that when Mack was fucking Clarisse over the desk (which was often) he couldn't climax if anyone was talking, so someone answering the phone and having a conversation in front of him would have thrown him right off his stroke.

'I think someone's desperate to get through Mack,' Clarisse said through gritted teeth, while stopping a stapler from sliding off the desk.

'Shut up,' Mack snapped. 'I'm nearly done. Stop putting me off.'

'Well hurry up then.'

As usual, Mack's technique wasn't doing much for Clarisse, so while she pretended to have an orgasm she thought about Baby. The word was out that a doctor had arrived and was in Baby's room right now performing an abortion. Mack had refused to discuss it with her, but there was a hell of a lot of noise coming from Baby's room down the hall. A couple of the other girls were loitering near it to see if they could hear what was going on. The only thing that seemed to be coming out of the room was a lot of loud music. From where Clarisse was, with her face partly buried in the desk it was hard to make out what song it was. She definitely hadn't heard any screams from Baby but that didn't mean there hadn't been any. It was just because the music was so damned loud.

Eventually the song that had been playing so loudly (and distracting Mack) came to an end. A brief silence filled the reception area and Mack was finally able to shoot his load without any noise distracting him. He let out a relieved sigh.

'That's it. I'm done,' he said triumphantly, pulling up his pants. He slapped Clarisse across the ass, like he always did, then leant forward and kissed her on the ear. His lips were drenched in his own saliva, It felt cold and sticky on Clarisse's earlobe.

'I'll be upstairs if you need me,' he said, buttoning up his pants. 'See ya later.'

He trotted off to the elevator by the side of the reception area. Clarisse took a few seconds to catch her breath. She remained in position, bent over the desk holding onto a stapler in one hand and a hole punch in the other. When she heard the elevator make a pinging sound as the doors opened, she stood up and straightened the items on her desk. Mack stepped into the elevator and disappeared up to one of the higher floors.

Once everything on her desk was straightened and back in its rightful place she took a look around to see what had happened to her underwear. The standard attire for working on reception varied from semi naked to virtually naked, so most of the time Clarisse simply wore a bra and thong. She still had the bra on but as usual Mack had tossed the thong away somewhere that might take her five minutes to find it. In the past she'd discovered some of her thongs on top of lampshades, in plant pots and on one occasion on a blind customer's head.

She didn't get far before the phone rang again. It had stopped ringing at about the same moment as Mack had emptied his balls. Clarisse sighed. Someone was obviously desperate to get through. The hunt for her thong would have to wait a little while. She picked up the receiver.

'Hello Beaver Palace.'

'Clarisse? Is that you?'

'Yes.'

'It's Benny Stansfield. Put me through to Silvio, right now.'

'What's it about?'

'You've got a doctor in the house.'

'Yes, I know. He's in with Baby right now.'

'Clarisse, it's not a doctor. The doctor's dead. You've got the Red Mohawk in there.'

'What?'

'Put me through to Silvio and get the fuck out of there!'

Forty Six

Silvio Mellencamp finally felt relaxed. He was slouched back in the chair behind his desk with a cigar in one hand and a balloon snifter glass half full of cognac in the other. He closed his eyes and his face broke out into a broad smile. And then typically the phone rang again.

He sighed and placed his glass of cognac down on the desk. 'Never a minute's peace,' he grumbled to himself.

He kept his eyes closed but felt around on his desk until his hand settled on the phone. He picked up the receiver and put it to his ear.

'Silvio speaking.'

'Hi Silvio. It's Benny. Are you okay?'

Mellencamp opened his eyes. 'Who said you could stop sucking?' he snapped.

'Pardon me?' said Benny.

'Not you Benny. I was talking to Selena.' Beneath his desk, on her hands and knees was Selena, one of the girls from The Booty Parlour in the basement. She was fairly new and not familiar with Mellencamp's rules about blowjobs.

'Sorry,' she replied, massaging his balls a little before sliding his dick back into her mouth.

'Honestly,' said Mellencamp. 'You just can't get the staff these days Benny.'

'Silvio. Listen to me, the Red Mohawk is in there with you!'

'What?' Mellencamp glanced down to make sure it was Selena's mouth wrapped around his dick. Fortunately it was. 'What are you talking about?'

'That doctor who came to do Baby's abortion. He's dead. I found him in the trunk of a car. The guy who killed him and took his place is The Red Mohawk. He's in your building right now.'

'Holy shit.' Mellencamp could tell from Benny's voice that he wasn't joking around. The cop was speaking at a hundred miles an hour. 'Are you guys on your way here?'

'We will be soon,' Benny replied. 'I'm just waiting for the riot squad guys to show up. Randall is already on his way, but in the meantime make sure you stay away from that doctor!'

Before Mellencamp could answer, the door to his office burst open. Mack strolled in with a big grin on his face.

'Hey boss,' he said.

'Mack. Benny says the doctor is dead.'

Mack frowned. 'No he's not. I just let him and Reg into Baby's room. He looked fine.'

'That wasn't the doctor. Seriously who told you to stop sucking?'

'Huh?'

'I was talking to Selena.'

'Oh.'

Selena called out cheerfully from under the desk. 'Hi Mack.'

'Hi Selena. How's it going?'

Mellencamp took a puff on his cigar, then placed it in the ash tray on his desk and used his free hand to push Selena's head back to where it should be. 'Mack, get everyone down to Baby's room. That doctor who went in there is an imposter. Dr Chandler is The Red Mohawk. Send everyone down there and kill that sonofabitch.'

'The doctor is what? The Red Mohawk?'

'Yeah. He's the guy that killed half the town today. Get down there and shoot the bastard or break his fucking neck, I don't care which. Use the intercom system to tell everyone.'

Mack finally cottoned on to what was going on. He hurried over to a varnished wooden cabinet beneath the television on Mellencamp's wall. On it was an intercom system with a microphone that Mellencamp frequently used to call girls to his room when he couldn't find them. The intercom was linked up to all of the speakers in the building. Mack picked up the microphone, switched it on and made an announcement to the whole building. 'Everyone, this is Mack. I have an important announcement from Silvio. All henchmen are to head down to The Booty Parlour immediately. The Red Mohawk is there in Baby's room. He's disguised as a doctor. If you see him, shoot on sight. Shoot to kill.'

Mellencamp interrupted him. 'Tell them about the hundred grand!'

'Oh and yeah, remember there's a hundred grand for the man who kills The Red Mohawk.'

'Good,' said Mellencamp. 'Now get down there and kill that sonofabitch. Call me when it's done.'

Mack nodded and strode confidently back out of the room, slamming the door behind him. Mellencamp picked up his cigar from the ashtray and spoke into the phone again. 'Did you hear that Benny. Everything's under control. We'll have that muthafucker any minute now.'

'I'll send the riot squad anyway.'

'Thanks Benny.'

206

Mellencamp hung up the phone. He picked up his glass of cognac and took a sip.

'Is everything all right?' he heard Selena ask.

'Oh for fuckssake!' he yelled, standing up. 'Go and get Jasmine will you? And tell her to bring some yoghurt. And an oven glove.'

Forty Seven

Without the mask, Joey Conrad looked like a normal guy. It was odd, because Baby didn't feel threatened by him when he looked like this, but if she was going to get out of The Beaver Palace in one piece she wanted the killer who had showed up in the diner wearing the mask and the red leather jacket and black jeans. Not the guy in the creased chinos and the crap blue shirt with the brown leather briefcase.

He barked an order at her. His voice was just the same, confident and aggressive. 'I'll give you two minutes to wash that blood off and another minute to get dressed. Then we're getting the hell out of here,' he said.

Baby looked down at all the traces of Reg's blood that were splattered over her body. There wasn't an excessive amount, because most of the blood fell short of the bed. But there was enough to make her want to get rid of the stuff. *And soon.*

She rushed into the bathroom and jumped into the shower. The water was freezing, but she wasn't going to wait for it to warm up. She wanted to get out of The Beaver Palace as fast as possible. She refused to think about the fact that her way out was with a homicidal maniac. Out was out.

She scrubbed furiously. It wasn't just Reg's blood she wanted off of her, it was the stink of him. The stink of the whole place. As she watched his blood wash away down the drain hole at her feet she hoped it would be the last shower she ever took in The Beaver Palace.

When she was sure every trace of Reg was gone she jumped back out of the shower and grabbed a pink towel from the towel rail. Another thirty seconds were eaten up drying herself off before she darted back into the bedroom.

She was greeted by the sight of Joey Conrad slipping his red leather jacket on over a black T-shirt. The briefcase he had brought in with him when he'd disguised himself as a doctor was on its side on the bed. It had been emptied, yet there wasn't a stethoscope in sight. The case had contained nothing other than The Red Mohawk's clothes and weapons.

As Baby rifled through her clothes drawers she watched him in the mirror above her dresser. He had a brown leather contraption wrapped around his shoulders, containing a number of holsters for concealing weapons. He'd finished putting on his red leather jacket before she managed to identify what any of the weapons were.

As she slung on a sleeveless red T-shirt and a pair of jeans, she saw him pick his rubber face-mask up from the bed. He slid it on over his head and fixed it straight so he could see through the eyeholes. The mask was as hideous as ever, even though she now saw the man underneath it as an ally and her best chance of escaping from B Movie Hell.

'You've got one more minute,' she heard him say.

She grabbed her sneakers from where Mack had thrown them onto the floor earlier. Her arm still hurt from the bullet wound, but thanks to the adrenaline rush she was getting from all the excitement she was pretty sure it wouldn't hinder her in getting the sneakers on and tied up.

As she slipped them on, she heard a loud crackling noise. A set of speakers in the corners of the room that had previously been playing music suddenly burst into life. She knew what that meant. This was an announcement from Silvio Mellencamp. His office was synched into all the speakers in the building. Mack's voice followed the crackling noise.

"Everyone, this is Mack. I have an important announcement from Silvio. All henchmen are to head down to The Booty Parlour immediately. The Red Mohawk is there in Baby's room. He's disguised as a doctor. If you see him, shoot on sight. Shoot to kill."

Baby was sitting on the end of the bed tying up her sneakers. Once more she looked into the mirror on her dresser. The evil grinning yellow mask on her rescuer stared back at her.

'We've just lost our element of surprise,' he said. 'You can take as long as you like to get ready now.'

Before she could reply Mack's voice blurted out through the speakers again.

"Oh and yeah, remember there's a hundred grand for the man who kills The Red Mohawk."

Baby suddenly felt scared again. It didn't sound like they would even make it out of her room, let alone the building. 'They're going to kill you!' she said. 'There's loads of them, and they're armed. They'll kill us.'

'No they won't. My first plan of escape has been compromised, that's all.'

'Oh no. What was the plan?'

'We were going to make a run for it and I was going to kill anyone who got in our way. We can't do that now.'

Baby couldn't hide how worried she was. She knew what Mack and his men were capable of. 'So what are we going to do now?' she asked.

'Plan B.'

'What's Plan B?'

'We're going to walk out slowly and I'm going to kill *everyone*.'

Baby stopped tying her shoelace. 'Seriously?'

'Seriously.'

Baby thought about her friends in The Beaver Palace. There weren't many, but there were a few, like Chardonnay. 'You don't have to kill the other girls,' she said hopefully. 'They're not a threat to us. And some of them are my friends.'

'Okay, I won't kill the girls. Unless they're armed.'

'Great.'

That was a relief. A huge weight off Baby's mind. She wasn't keen on any of the killing, but some of the girls in The Beaver Palace didn't want to be there any more than she did.

'Do I have time to grab some things quickly?' she asked.

'Like I said. Take as long as you want.'

'I'll only be a minute.'

Baby finished tying her laces and jumped up off the bed. She grabbed her eyeliner and lipstick from her dresser and threw them into a pink handbag, which she tossed over her shoulder. She was just getting her Dirty Dancing DVD from the player when there was a loud bang at the door. It startled her and she spun around.

The door came crashing open and two burly security guards burst in. The Red Mohawk was expecting them. He punched the first guy full in the face, knocking him back against the wall. It surprised the second guy, and before he could react he felt the full force of one of the Mohawk's boots crashing down onto his right kneecap. Baby heard the sound of his knee shattering. It was like a wooden table leg snapping in half. The Red Mohawk twisted the stricken guy around by his head and then smashed his face into the wall. Almost immediately a third henchman charged into the room, straight into a crunching fist punch similar to the one the first guy had received. Baby hadn't been counting, but she was pretty sure all three henchmen were taken down inside less than five seconds. The Red Mohawk dragged the last guy a little further into the room and shut the door again behind him. All three henchmen were lying in a heap on the floor.

'Wow,' said Baby, unintentionally out loud. 'Are they dead?'

'Yeah. I had to take them down quick so I used the Hallenbeck technique.'

'What's the Hallenbeck technique?'

'Bash the nose up into the brain. It's an instant kill. For special occasions. You ready to go now?'

Baby slipped the Dirty Dancing DVD into her bag and took one last look around the room. She had lived in that room for as long as she could remember. Not one single fond memory came back to her until she spotted her Dirty Dancing soundtrack CD on top of the stereo next to the empty case of the soul compilation CD that Reg had picked out. There was no sense in having the DVD without the accompanying soundtrack. She ran over and grabbed it and slid it into her bag.

'I've got everything, I think.'

'Okay. Stay close to me at all times if you can. That way I can protect you.'

'What if something happens and we get split up?'

'Go where you hear some music. I love to kill when there's music playing. Find music, you'll find me.'

'Okay. But you know some of these henchmen are armed, don't you? I saw a bunch of them earlier. They've got guns.'

The Red Mohawk placed one hand on the door and prepared to open it. Before he did he pointed at his mask and made one final remark.

'Don't let the smile fool ya. I'm not as nice as I look.'

Forty Eight

The ride along in the back of Randall's pickup truck was a bumpy one. On more than one occasion Munson's entire body bounced up into the air. At times he feared he might be making regular appearances in Randall's rear view mirror. All the alcohol he had consumed during the day had now left him feeling dehydrated. And his stomach wasn't coping well with all the bouncing around. The strong cup of coffee he'd had back at The Alaska Roadside Diner had worked its magic but it was now working its way through his system and his stomach was churning.

He had his handgun clenched tightly in his right hand, ready to point it and use it if any unwelcome visitors peered into the back of the truck.

After a short drive the truck came to a stop. Munson didn't dare stick his head up to take a look at where he was. Instead he kept his focus on the night sky and concentrated on listening for any voices.

'Hey Randall,' a male voice called out. 'I'll open the gates for ya. Come on through.'

Randall leaned out of the driver side window and shouted back. 'The cops are on their way Ned. Got reports that The Red Mohawk showed up here earlier disguised as a doctor. Did you let him in?'

'Are you fucking kidding?'

'No. You seen a doctor?'

'Yeah. I let a doctor in about half an hour ago.'

'Well then you let The Red Mohawk in!'

'Shit. What the fuck?'

'You're damn right, *what the fuck!* Benny's been trying to ring through to warn you guys about it, but nobody's been picking up the phone. Have you heard anything from inside?'

'Like what?'

'Like people being chopped up with meat cleavers. What the fuck do you think?'

'No. I ain't heard nothing. I'll radio through to Mack. Oh hang on.' Munson heard the sound of a walkie-talkie bursting into life. He couldn't make out exactly what was said, but it sounded like something serious was going on. If Joey Conrad really was in the building, then it sounded like he'd thrown off the doctor disguise and started slicing up henchmen.

'Okay Randall,' yelled Ned. 'I'm opening the gates. I'd better come in with you though. This sounds serious.'

Munson heard the sound of a pair of large electric gates grinding open. He rolled over onto his front with his gun at the ready. He prayed that Ned, whoever the hell he was, decided to get in the front of the truck with Randall, rather than in the back. His hopes faded quickly when he heard Randall, just a few feet away from him, leaning out of the window.

'Hop in the back,' Randall yelled to Ned.

Fuck.

The truck rolled forward a few feet before Munson saw a pair of hands appear on the side border not far from his head. The face of a scrawny guy in his early thirties with unkempt brown hair appeared. He didn't spot Munson lying down right in front of him in the dark. He hauled himself up onto the border of the truck and threw one leg over. It wasn't until he was almost face to face with Munson that he actually noticed him. He landed on his side in the back of the pickup. His eyes opened wide with shock at the sight of another man lying there in wait for him. There was an awkward moment as both men remained motionless staring at each other. The moment ended abruptly when the truck accelerated forward and bounced upwards with a judder. As it landed back onto the ground, Munson fired his gun.

The bullet didn't have far to travel. It moved barely ten inches before it burst through the chest of Ned. Munson almost felt like he should apologise, but it in all honesty it was just the latest in a long line of shitty things he'd done to people he'd only met that day. The guy's facial expression changed instantly. The muscles in his face dropped, he looked absolutely gutted, like he'd just opened a Christmas present and discovered it was a dead rat. A second later he exhaled his last breath and his face thudded into the bed of the truck.

Up front Randall slammed on the brakes. 'Goddamn! What the hell was that?' he shouted out, peering out of the driver side window again to see what the noise was. 'Have I got a flat?'

Munson didn't waste a second. He rolled over and up onto his knees. He pointed his gun at Randall's head. The off duty cop saw the barrel of the gun first, then looked up and saw the face of Munson bchind it.

'It's not your day,' said Munson.

Randall never got a chance to respond. Munson fired his gun again. Even though he wasn't firing from great distances it was good to know he could still hit his target dead centre when he needed to. He hadn't fired a gun in anger for a long time, so it was a relief to still have the skills. This time his bullet flew straight between Randall's eyes. His head flew back and blood sprayed out through the back of his skull.

Two seconds later his dead body was slumped in the front seat of the truck with the remains of his head hanging out of the window.

Munson jumped out of the truck. Behind him he saw the large electric gates that the truck had just crawled through. He was inside the grounds of The Beaver Palace estate. The main building was right in front of him at the end of a gravel driveway. There were a couple of security guards dressed in black rushing inside the building through the front entrance. Unfortunately they closed the main door behind them.

Munson took off his jacket and tossed it into the back of the pickup truck. Even though he didn't have a black T-shirt like the other security guards, he was wearing a black long sleeved shirt so he'd blend in better with that than the jacket. He'd move more freely too. And having just fired off two shots from his handgun he didn't have much time.

He ducked down and hurried towards the entrance with his gun at the ready. As he approached the large wooden oak door at the front of the building he was wondering how he would get inside. He crept up the two steps to the front and pulled on the door handle. It didn't open. The door was locked from the inside.

Shit.

Munson took a few steps back. He contemplated heading around the back of the building to find another way in when suddenly the sound of gunfire filled the air. There was one almighty shootout going on inside The Beaver Palace. And a lot of screaming.

Forty Nine

Baby followed the Red Mohawk out of her room and down the corridor towards Clarisse's reception desk. All around them it was pandemonium. Girls were running around screaming, doors were slamming. Music was blaring out from one of the rooms. Baby recognised the song. It was *Cry of the Celts* from Michael Flatley's *Lord of the Dance* musical. She'd heard it numerous times before, and never liked it.

Up ahead, behind the reception desk she saw Clarisse. The receptionist had her back to them. She was bent over and looking into a plant pot. And she wasn't wearing any underwear. Baby tried not to focus on the sight of her bare ass sticking up in the air. There were more important things to see. *And hear.* Most notably the sound of more security guards charging down the stairs by the side of the plant pot Clarisse was inspecting. The rattling of their boots pounding on the steps was quite unnerving. It sounded like a herd of buffalo.

Baby stayed behind the Red Mohawk, keeping one hand pressed gently against his back. It wouldn't hurt to stay within touching distance. She was convinced it was the safest place to be. He crouched down on one knee and reached both hands inside his red jacket. From within it he pulled two handguns. Fairly big fuckers they were too, she noted as she crouched behind him. There was something about this guy that instilled confidence in her. They were hopelessly outnumbered by Mellencamp's inexhaustible stream of henchmen. By rights escape from The Beaver Palace should be impossible at this point, but Baby had her own serial killer. A knight, not in shining armour or on horseback, but wearing a Halloween mask. She couldn't help but think, somewhat inappropriately, that he was incredibly fucking cool. And he was hers.

'Are you gonna shoot them all?' she asked as the sound of the henchmen bounding down the stairs grew louder.

'When the time is right,' he replied, his guns trained on the staircase.

'When will that be?'

'Now.'

As the knees of the incoming henchmen appeared charging down the stairs, he opened fire with both of his heavy-duty handguns. Baby planted her hands over her ears and watched on in awe as seven or eight pairs of legs snapped in half on the stairs as a myriad of bullets exploded into them, ripping them apart. The upper bodies of a bunch of unfortunate henchmen came tumbling down the stairs. They bounced and rolled to the bottom where they landed in a huge pile. Next to them, Clarisse was still bent over with her ass in the air. Only now she also had her fingers in her ears. When the gunfire stopped she pulled her fingers out and stood up. She turned around and saw Baby hiding behind the masked killer, peering over the top of his red stripe of hair at the carnage he had created. Clarisse's jaw dropped open. She stood gawping at them for a few seconds before she came to her senses.

Whatever Clarisse was looking for in the plant pot (and Baby suspected it was her underwear) she gave up on it pretty quick. She made a run for it instead. In a blind panic she attempted to race up the stairs only to catch her foot on one of the dead henchmen. She tripped and fell face first onto the pile of dead men. It provided yet another unwelcome view of her ass as she struggled to get up, but she was soon on her feet again and escaping up the stairs, screaming for all she was worth.

The Red Mohawk stood up. 'This way,' he said heading for the corridor that led to the elevator.

Baby hurried along behind him, doing her best to stay within touching distance and out of sight behind his hulking frame. When they reached the elevator he pressed the button in the wall to call it down. Behind them, Baby heard someone shout. 'There they are!'

Before Baby could react, Joey Conrad's arm came across her. He hauled her around behind him and squared up to whoever had shouted out at the other end of the corridor. 'Get down,' he said.

He pointed his guns down the corridor and opened fire. Baby crouched down behind him in a ball with her hands over her ears. The last wave of gunfire had practically deafened her and she had no desire to hear any more at such close range.

She closed her eyes and waited for the gunfire to come to an end. The noise went on for five or six seconds before it went quiet again. She pinched her eyes open and peered down the hall. In amidst a plume of smoke she saw yet more dead henchmen. She heard the Red Mohawk replace his guns in their holsters. A ping from the elevator followed. She turned around in time to see the doors opening. Their carriage had arrived.

But it wasn't empty.

There was a large man inside the elevator. Baby froze and stared upwards as the huge figure of Mack bounded out of the lift. She wanted to shout out to warn her masked rescuer of what was to come, but she was too late.

Mack hooked an arm around The Red Mohawk's neck from behind. He hauled him back into the elevator with him. Baby watched open-mouthed as Mack squeezed his huge hands around the Mohawk's neck and slammed him up against the wall inside the elevator. The lift doors closed abruptly, ending her view of proceedings and leaving her all alone once more, stranded in a corridor in the Booty Parlour. She watched as a dial above the elevator doors indicated that it was moving upwards again.

Baby's plan of escape was suddenly in tatters. She was undecided about what to do. Wait until the elevator came back down, or make a run for the stairs?

Find some music.

It was possibly the dumbest idea she could think of, but it's what she'd been told to do if she got separated from Joey Conrad. The *Cry of the Celts* music was playing in one of the rooms near Clarisse's reception desk. Baby turned and ran back towards it, not really sure what she was expecting to happen.

Fifty

Munson peered through one of the windows by the side of the front door to The Beaver Palace. There was a reception lounge inside with a set of double doors at the far end. As he was staring through the window he saw a figure charge into the lounge through the double doors. It was a woman and she was headed for the front entrance, screaming her head off.

He could have hugged her because her timing was impeccable. She flung open the front door and raced out of it and down the front steps. Munson leapt across to obstruct her. She crashed into his chest and stared up at him. She screamed in his face. Munson looked her up and down. She was wearing a black lacy bra, but absolutely nothing else. He grabbed her by her arms. She continued screaming and struggled to break free but he was far too strong for her.

'What's going on in there?' he yelled, loud enough for her to hear over her own screaming.

'The guy in the mask, the Red Mohawk, he's inside! Let me go!' She attempted to wriggle free, her sights set on Randall's truck at the end of the driveway, but Munson refused to release his grip on her and instead hauled her back towards him.

'I'm looking for a girl named Baby,' he said. 'Is she in there?'

'Baby?'

'You know who I mean.'

'Baby. Yeah, she could be dead. The killer was in her room. I just saw him come out. That's when I ran.'

'Where's her room?'

The woman continued to struggle in vain to try and break free from Munson's grip. 'Let me go!' she screamed.

Munson let go of one of her arms and pulled his gun from its holster. He pointed it at her face. 'Where's Marianne Pincent?' he growled.

The woman stopped struggling and stared first at the gun and then up at Munson. Then, as if suddenly realising she was missing her underwear, she placed her free hand between her legs to cover her modesty, before answering him. 'She's downstairs. Through the reception lounge. Head down the stairs in the next room and it's the first door on the right. She's probably dead though. Don't go in there.'

Munson looked the woman up and down. 'You should really put on some pants,' he said. Then he let go of her arm and watched her run towards Randall's truck.

Randall's face was no longer hanging out of the side of the window because it had slid back inside. The naked lady grabbed the handle on the truck door and pulled it open. Randall's dead body fell out on top of her, knocking her to the floor and pinning her down underneath it. She screamed again although this time the dead body on top of her muffled her high pitched yelling.

Munson took a deep breath and stepped inside the main building. He was greeted by the sound of many more women screaming, and the sight of them running for their lives in all directions. It served as the perfect distraction for him to find his way downstairs to Baby's room. He hurried through the reception lounge, checking in all directions for a girl with a blue birthmark.

All around him was chaos. The sound of men and women of all ages crying and shrieking filled the air. From somewhere downstairs he heard a lot more gunfire and some music from a Michael Flatley show. Munson carefully made his way through to the room where he'd been told the stairs were. He saw a staircase on his left. It led down to where most of the noise was coming from. He stopped in his tracks at the top of the stairs. Down at the bottom he saw a pile of dead bodies. Someone had killed a bunch of henchmen. He had a pretty good idea who that someone might be. With his own handgun at the ready he made his way down the stairs. As he neared the bottom he saw a young girl in jeans and a red sleeveless shirt running along a corridor towards him. She had a blue birthmark on her face. It was the girl from the photo on Fonseca's phone. Their eyes met and they both stopped in their tracks.

'Are you Marianne Pincent?' Munson shouted above the din.

She looked surprised, but replied quickly. 'Yes.'

'I'm Jack Munson. Your *Uncle Jack* from a long time ago. I'm with the FBI. I've come to get you out of here.' He held out a hand. 'Come on. Quick, there isn't much time!'

Fifty One

Silvio Mellencamp leant back against his desk and took a sip from his giant glass of cognac. He stared at the door and listened to all the chaos coming from the other side. People were dying downstairs. There was a heck of a lot of screaming going on and a great deal more gunfire than he had expected.

He hadn't had any reason to be afraid of anyone for as long as he could remember. But this psychotic Red Mohawk nutcase had given him some real cause for concern. Mellencamp's town B Movie Hell, *his own goddamn town,* had been taken apart by this guy, in less than a day. And the fucking nutcase was somewhere within the four walls of The Beaver Palace.

Mellencamp had locked the door to his private study the minute Selena had left. It had been over two minutes since he'd sent his best henchman, Mack downstairs on a seek and destroy mission with a bunch of others. He'd expected to hear maybe one or two gunshots and for that to signal that the whole episode was over and done with. But the sound of gunfire just kept coming. That could only mean one thing. The Red Mohawk wasn't dead yet. Every second that passed made him more nervous. He found himself staring wide eyed at his door and wondering who would arrive to see him first, Mack or The Red Mohawk? A loud knock at his door made him jump.

'Who is it?' he called out.

'It's Jasmine. Selena said you wanted to see me.'

'Oh, hang on.'

He breathed a sigh of relief and walked over to the door, swilling his cognac around in his glass as he went. He turned the key in the lock and opened the door inwards. Jasmine was standing outside in a bright red basque with black stockings and a pair of high-heeled stiletto shoes. He looked her up and down and gave an approving wink. Even in the face of mortal danger, he could appreciate such a fine form. He ushered her inside and closed the door again, locking it and then checking to make sure it wouldn't open. Just having Jasmine in the room with him calmed him down immensely. She didn't seem in the slightest bit panicked by all the noise coming from downstairs. And he knew that once she started performing fellatio on him she could take *his* mind off anything. Even mortal danger.

He turned around to find her leaning against his desk. She was checking her nails.

'Did you bring the oven glove?' he asked.

'Was I supposed to?'

'Yes. Didn't Selena tell you?'

'No. But she did say that she'd heard the Red Mohawk was in the building. Is it true?' she asked.

Mellencamp pulled a face. 'What do you think? Can't you hear the gunfire?'

'Oh, is that what that is?'

'Yeah. Mack and the boys are down there dealing with him now. But don't worry, you and I are perfectly safe up here.' He opened up his dressing gown and waved his cock at her. 'Let's do something to take our minds off what's going on downstairs.'

'Don't you want to wait until you know it's safe?' Jasmine asked, ignoring his waving penis.

'For fuck's sake! Not you as well?'

'What do you mean?'

'Selena. She couldn't shut up for five minutes. That's why I called for you. You're my favourite girl, Jasmine, because you know to take my mind off anything. So do me a favour, get down on your knees and keep your mouth shut. No wait a minute, I mean keep your mouth open, but don't speak. That Selena girl was chatting to everyone instead of doing what she was supposed to.'

'She's just friendly.'

'Well friendly can wait. You're lucky I called you up here. This is the safest place to be in the whole building. The door's locked, so no one's getting in. So as a thank you, the least you can do is get down on your knees and quit with all the questions!'

Jasmine didn't do a great job of disguising her displeasure at what she was being ordered to do. She'd already serviced his cock, balls and ass twice that day. Three times in one day was rare.

'Don't look like that,' Mellencamp sneered.

Jasmine lowered herself to the floor and crawled towards him on her knees. She knew just how to get Mellencamp going. He liked a lot of the other girls but no one knew how to caress his balls like Jasmine, and her blowjob technique was unequalled. The cleverer girls had all worked out that giving good head to the boss meant giving *lots* of head to the boss. Jasmine either hadn't worked it out yet, or just didn't know *how* to give a bad blowjob.

For the next couple of minutes as he sipped from a glass of cognac and looked down on Jasmine's gorgeous dark hair, he forgot all about The Red Mohawk. *Damn*, this girl was good. She really could take his mind off anything.

He was in the process of guiding her left hand around to his asshole when there was another loud knock at the door.

'Who is it?' he called out.

'It's Mack.'

'Excellent. Did you get that guy?'

'Yeah I got him boss. Broke his neck in the elevator.'

'Great stuff! You're a legend Mack. Come on in. I'll get Jasmine to make you some sandwiches.'

He pulled his dick out of Jasmine's mouth and pushed her head back. 'Wait here a minute, sweetheart,' he said.

'Have I really got to make sandwiches?' Jasmine groaned.

'Hey! Remember what I said. When you're on your knees, I don't want to hear you speak. You hear me?'

Jasmine nodded. She looked like she wanted to complain but she had the good sense to keep her thoughts to herself.

Mellencamp unlocked the door and pulled it open. Mack was standing in the doorway.

'Come on in buddy,' said Mellencamp. He stepped back and waved Mack in. 'I'm just in the middle of a blowjob. You can tell me everything while Jasmine finishes me off.'

Mack stayed outside. 'Boss, I can't see.'

'What?'

Mellencamp peered around the door. He looked up at Mack and to his surprise he saw blood pouring down the giant henchman's face. He looked closer. Both of Mack's eye sockets were empty. Blood was streaming out of the two gaping black holes where his eyes had once been.

'WHAT THE FUCK!'

Mack suddenly dropped to his knees. Mellencamp took a step back. 'Mack? *Mack?*'

Before he could ask Mack what had happened, the giant thug fell forwards. His face thudded into the carpet that he had accidentally pissed on earlier in the day. He had a meat cleaver sticking out of his back, right between his shoulder blades. It was embedded in a good three inches deep.

Mellencamp looked around the door and spotted the meat cleaver's owner standing behind Mack. For the first time he found himself face to face with the masked madman who had been terrorising his town. Mellencamp backed further away from the door. The Red Mohawk stepped into the room. He leant down and yanked his meat cleaver out of Mack's back. And he took a long stride towards Mellencamp.

222

'Wait. Wait!' Mellencamp pleaded, back-stepping with great haste as he tried to talk his way out of trouble. 'I've got money. If it's money you want, I've got all you need. You can come work for me. Name your price.'

The Red Mohawk didn't respond verbally. He continued walking towards Mellencamp, with his blood-stained meat cleaver in his hand.

'I'll give you a million bucks right *naaaa-aaagh....*'

Mellencamp's foot knocked into something on the floor behind him and he toppled over onto his back. He had tripped over Jasmine who had been kneeling on all fours behind him. His head banged against the floor and he dropped his glass of cognac, spilling it over the carpet. He was too out of shape to get back up quickly. Instead he looked angrily across at Jasmine and yelled at her. 'You stupid bitch! Why didn't you say something!'

Jasmine got up off her knees and stood up straight. She looked down at him. 'You told me to keep quiet when I was on my knees.'

The Red Mohawk walked over and stopped alongside her. Jasmine wisely backed away from him towards the desk.

'You're free to go,' the Mohawk said to her. 'I'm here for him.'

'Are you going to kill him?' Jasmine asked.

'Any minute now.'

'In that case…' Jasmine took a look down at Mellencamp. His dressing gown was wide open. His legs were splayed apart and he was on his back in a defenceless position. She took a run up and swung her right foot at his balls. The toe of her shoe caught him right where it hurts. His testicles damn near went right up inside his stomach. The expression on his face changed from terrified to agonised in a single frame. He closed his eyes and howled in pain. Before he could get his hands down to cup his aching balls, Jasmine followed up the kick with a hard stamp from her stiletto heeled shoe. The bottom of her heel dug down deep into his scrotum, right between the balls. She twisted it round hard, a full ninety degrees. It triggered a rather strange crunching noise. Mellencamp winced and cried out like a baby.

'You ungrateful bitch! After all I've done for you.'

Jasmine allowed herself a self-congratulatory smile. 'Suck on that!'

'Are you done?' a voice behind her asked.

'Oh yeah.'

Jasmine turned and walked past The Red Mohawk. She strutted out of the room with a confident stride normally reserved for dancing to a Beyoncé song.

Mellencamp grabbed a hold of his balls and rolled over onto his side, wincing in pain. The shadow of The Red Mohawk loomed over him. The masked killer reached down and grabbed him round the throat. Mellencamp looked up into the black eyes behind the yellow mask. By now B Movie Hell's infamous crime lord was too afraid to speak. He was crying like a bitch and his balls really hurt. He also had a feeling he'd just done a shit into his best dressing gown.

The Red Mohawk lifted him up off the floor. He spoke in a gruff voice. 'Bad news,' he said. 'No quick death for you.'

Fifty Two

Baby high-stepped her way over a string of dead bodies as Jack Munson dragged her up the stairs with him to the ground floor. He'd said he was her Uncle Jack from a long time ago. She didn't remember that, and she wasn't sure she could believe him. However, she'd never seen him in The Beaver Palace before so he probably was from out of town. And based on the movies she'd seen, he really did look like an FBI agent, albeit one wearing casual grey trousers and a black shirt. Maybe he *was* her Uncle Jack? It didn't really matter in the end, because he had her hand in a firm grip and he had a gun. That was just about all the convincing she needed.

The Beaver Palace had turned into an absolute madhouse. There were people everywhere in various states of undress. Screams, shouts, gunfire, and the click-clack of marabou covered stilettos bounced off the walls from every direction. On the plus side the music seemed to have stopped. There was no more *Lord of the Dance* nonsense impeding on proceedings.

When they reached the top of the stairs Munson hesitated and looked around. Baby stared at the elevator doors in the corner of the main hall. They were still closed on this floor. She wondered what had become of the Red Mohawk. Even though Munson had said he would get her out of there, she couldn't help but think her chances of getting out alive would improve greatly if she had her own masked serial killer with her.

'Come on. This way!' Munson yelled dragging her over to the double doors that led into the reception lounge. He charged through them with her tagging along behind. They were greeted by a sight that made Baby's heart sink. The front door of the mansion was wide open. And storming through it into the entrance lounge was an army of armed riot police, dressed from head to toe in dark blue clothing with matching helmets. Benny Stansfield (who stood out prominently because he was wearing a beige suit) led them in. Munson stopped dead in his tracks and Baby clattered into the back of him

Benny Stansfield pointed a handgun at them, holding it in both hands. The group of armed officers behind him, most of whom had machine gun rifles followed suit.

'Drop that fucking gun, mister!' Benny yelled over the din.

'Shit,' Munson muttered under his breath. Then he shouted out to Benny. 'I'm not going to shoot.'

'I know you're not, because you're gonna bend down slowly and place that gun on the floor, or I'm gonna shoot *you*.'

'Okay, okay.' Munson eased his grip on his gun, holding it by the handle with two fingers. He leant down and placed it on the floor. He stood back up and raised his hands to show he was surrendering. Then he whispered quietly to Baby. 'Don't panic.'

'You're Jack Munson, I presume,' said Benny, keeping his gun aimed at Munson's chest.

'You know you're never going to get away with this,' Munson replied.

Benny ignored him. 'Where's Mellencamp?' he asked.

Munson held his arms out with his palms facing upwards. 'No idea,' he said. 'I've never met him. Wouldn't know what he looks like.'

'Baby?' said Benny, turning to her. 'Where's Silvio?'

'I don't know. Upstairs in his office probably,' she replied.

Benny gestured to some of his men. 'You two check upstairs.' He pointed at a couple of others. 'You two go downstairs. The rest of you stay here with me.'

Without questioning the order, two of the riot cops hurried past Baby and Munson and headed down to the brothel area via the stairs, pushing aside one of the girls who tore past them, screaming her head off. Another two cops charged up the staircase that ran along the wall and up to a balcony directly above Baby's head.

Munson called out to Benny. 'Look man, I'm FBI. You're making a lot of trouble for yourself here. I've already informed my head office of what's going on in this town.'

Benny had been watching his men hurrying up the stairs. When Munson finished talking he glanced over at him as if he hadn't heard anything he'd said. 'Jack,' he said with a smirk. 'It is Jack isn't it?'

'Yes.'

'Here's the thing. I don't give a fuck what the FBI knows. This is B Movie Hell. We make our own rules here. If Mellencamp wants you gone, and I'm almost certain that he does, then you're gone. And probably so is Baby.'

'We can come to some kind of arrangement you know,' said Munson. 'We're on the same team.'

'No we're not. You're a dead man walking. But you two aren't even the reason we're here. I want to know what happened to the doctor who showed up here earlier? Is there a fucking doctor in the house or what?'

Munson shook his head. 'I don't know what you're talking about.'

'I'm talking about a serial killer called The Red Mohawk who showed up here disguised as a doctor. Where is he? Or is it you Mr Munson? Are you the guy that's been walking around in a mask murdering people in my town?'

'Obviously it's not me,' Munson retorted.

'Obvious to you my friend. But not to the rest of us. If anyone shows up here we can just tell 'em we shot you because you were The Red Mohawk.'

'That would work,' said Munson. 'If it weren't for the fact that my boss already knows the identity of The Red Mohawk. You guys may not know, but I do and so do my superiors. You try to frame me for the murders and they'll throw you in jail. Fuckhead.'

'*Fuckhead?* Did you just call me *fuckhead?*'

'Yes I did.'

Benny raised his gun a few inches and outstretched his arm, hinting at the possibility he might fire it at Munson. 'That's not very nice,' he said.

Munson grinned. 'You know, I just realised something,' he said.

'What?'

'You've never shot anyone before, have you? You're stalling because you don't really want to shoot me.'

Baby wished there was something she could do to help. She looked around the entrance lounge for anything that she could use as a distraction or a weapon. To her surprise, she spotted something within seconds. Her only problem was how would she get to it? There were six riot police, including Benny, and they were all pointing guns at Munson. She took a small step away from him. No one seemed to notice, or care. There was a sofa to her right. It was the sofa she and Chardonnay had been sat on earlier before Mack had stormed in and dragged her downstairs. She needed to get to it.

She took another step towards it while Benny and Munson continued to trade macho insults and play mind games with each other. One of the riot cops behind Benny looked like he was watching her, although it was hard to know for sure because his eyes weren't visible through the visor on his helmet. His rifle seemed to be slowly moving in her direction. She took one more step towards the sofa and planted her hand down on the arm of it.

'What are you doing?' the riot cop asked, pointing his rifle directly at her.

Everyone's attention was drawn to Baby.

'I was shot earlier,' she said. 'I'm feeling faint.' Without waiting for anyone to tell her otherwise, she slid onto the sofa and sat down.

Benny kept his gun trained on Munson but shouted out to her. 'Don't you fucking move from there, Baby!'

'Okay.'

'Munson. You get down on your knees.'

Baby watched Munson drop to his knees. Benny edged towards him, his gun now pointed directly at Munson's head. He was planning on shooting the FBI agent in cold blood, Baby was convinced of it. It was time to put her plan into action. She picked up the remote control for the television. On the screen in front of her, she could see the frozen picture of the packed Coyote Ugly bar. Chardonnay had paused it earlier when threatened by Mack. Baby hit the PLAY button on the remote. On the screen Maria Bello's character shouted out via a megaphone -

"Okay, let's give a big Coyote Ugly welcome to LeAnn Rimes!"

The riot police were startled by the shock of the shrill voice from the TV. They started pointing their rifles wildly, while swinging their heads around trying to figure out why LeeAnn Rimes had decided to come to B Movie Hell. Benny stopped edging towards Munson and turned around to see what was going on. 'What the fuck?' he said, a confused look on his face.

The other riot cops zeroed in on Baby and the TV. On the screen the sight of LeAnn Rimes and the Coyote Ugly girls dancing on the bar and singing *Can't Fight the Moonlight* greeted them. For a few seconds they all watched the television in fascination, before Benny shouted out again.

'TURN THAT SHIT OFF!'

Baby pointed the remote at the TV and pretended to press a button. She shrugged. 'It won't turn off.'

'For fuck's sake!'

The distraction clearly worked. Benny now seemed to be caught in two minds about shooting Munson. He raised his gun and then immediately lowered it. He shook his arms, as if loosening them, and raised the gun again. He did this a few times before he seemed to eventually psych himself up and take aim with some genuine purpose. Baby's breath caught in her throat as Benny's finger began to squeeze the trigger.

In the end he hesitated for just a second too long. Without warning, an object the size and shape of a football came flying over the balcony above his head. Benny saw it just in time. He caught it in his arms just before it hit him in the chest. It almost knocked his gun out of his hand. He stared down at it. *Everyone stared at it.*

It was Silvio Mellencamp's head. It looked pale and shrivelled and there was a vast amount of blood seeping out of the bottom of it.

'SHIIIIT!!!' Benny dropped the head on the floor. It rolled away from him towards Baby. It came to a stop on its side. Mellencamp's tongue slid out of his mouth and licked the floor, while the whites of his eyes gazed up at Baby.

Benny staggered back. He had blood on his hands and down the front of his beige suit. He stared up at the balcony. His comrades all pointed their guns upward to see who or what had thrown Mellencamp's head down at them.

Something else came flying over the balcony. A much larger object. This time it was the body of a man. A riot cop. It was one of the two guys Benny had recently sent up to Mellencamp's office. Benny reeled back out of the way. The body landed with an almighty thud on the floor, scattering the other cops who all jumped out of its way. Baby felt the ground beneath her feet shake. There was a groan from the body that had landed on the floor in the middle of everyone.

'He's still alive!' someone shouted.

'What the fuck's that in his hand?' someone else mumbled.

'A grenade.'

'Shit.'

A small grenade rolled out of the fallen cop's hand. It flashed brightly and made a loud hissing sound. A huge swathe of smoke poured out of it, spreading quickly in all directions, filling the room almost instantly. Baby heard a great deal of coughing and spluttering as everyone tried to back away from the smoke.

What followed next was a barrage of gunfire from above. Baby dived over to the corner of the sofa to get as far away from the middle of the room as possible. The gunfire was thunderous. The riot cops began firing back blindly from within the cloud of smoke that had engulfed them. Baby placed her hands over her ears and tried to focus on LeAnn Rimes and the Coyote Ugly girls. She could barely see them through the smoke, and it now looked like they were dancing along to a chorus of gunfire and screaming rather than *Can't Fight the Moonlight*.

It quickly became hard to breathe and as the smoke engulfed her, Baby began coughing, which just made it even harder to catch her breath. She put her hands over her mouth and nose. Her eyes were stinging.

Eventually about two thirds of the way through *Can't Fight the Moonlight*, the gunfire died down and LeAnn Rimes voice became audible again. Baby heard a few groans from within the dissipating smoke. She looked back to the middle of the room, her eyes streaming with tears from the smoke. It was hard to see anything. But then suddenly a man's hand grabbed her by the arm and hauled her up from the sofa.

He dragged her through the smoke and towards the front doors. She stumbled over a couple of bodies on the floor but carried on, desperate to get to the fresh air outside. Whoever it was that had hold of her hand, he seemed to know where he was going. She could feel the air clearing a little with each step. Her lungs felt like they had closed up completely. But then suddenly she felt fresh air on her face. Her rescuer dragged her further clear of the smoke and into the cold air outside.

Baby opened her mouth wide and tried to suck in as much oxygen as possible. It made her cough and she doubled over as she attempted to get her breath back. The man who had pulled her out kept a tight grip on her left arm. After a couple of deep breaths she straightened up again and looked upon the face of the man who had helped her out of the building.

It was Benny. He pulled her in closer to him, his arm wrapped around her waist. His body pushed up against her back and he pressed a gun against her temple.

'You're coming with me,' he said. 'Make one stupid move and you're dead.'

Fifty Three

Benny had his arm wrapped tightly around Baby's waist. He was backing away from the front entrance of The Beaver Palace, dragging her with him. Baby kept her eyes focussed on the front door of the building, hoping to see the Red Mohawk make an appearance through the smoke that was billowing out from the reception lounge. There was definitely someone still alive in there because every few seconds a gunshot would ring out, although it sounded like whoever was firing was deep inside the building.

Benny was clearly panicking. He kept alternating between pointing his gun at Baby's head and the front door. His breathing was erratic and hinted at some genuine anxiety. In fact, Baby considered the possibility that he was actually more nervous than her, even though she was the one with the gun against her head.

When they were halfway down the drive Benny whispered into her ear. 'My car is parked just over there. When we get to it, you get into the passenger side. Don't do anything stupid or you'll regret it.'

Baby decided to try and play on his anxiety. 'The Red Mohawk has come to take me home,' she said. 'If you take me with you he'll come after us. Leave me here and he'll forget all about you. Why don't you just make a break for it?'

'The Red Mohawk came take you home?' Benny sounded surprised. 'Who is he?'

Baby didn't get a chance to answer. The silhouette of the Red Mohawk appeared in the middle of the smoke just inside the Beaver Palace. He strode out through the doors until he was clearly visible and the smoke was filtering out behind him. He was holding a gun in his right hand. He stopped and aimed it at Benny and Baby.

Benny pointed his gun at him and shouted. 'Stop right there!'

The Red Mohawk had already stopped so it made little sense for Benny to shout the instruction, a further sign that he was in over his head.

The Red Mohawk kept his gun trained on them. It looked like he was lining up a shot at Benny's head.

'Hold on just a goddamn minute!' Benny shouted. 'Just listen will ya? I'm not going to hurt the girl. Just put your gun down and let me and her get out of here. But if you fire even one shot at me, I'll kill her *and you*. And it'll be your fault!'

'Shoot at me,' the Red Mohawk replied, daring Benny to back up his words with action.

'What?'

'*Shoot at me*. From that distance you'll miss.'

Benny stopped pointing his gun at the masked psycho and instead pressed the barrel against Baby's head.

'Don't fuck about!' he snarled. 'I'm calling the shots here. You place your gun on the ground or I shoot the girl. Do it now. No sudden movements.'

The Red Mohawk didn't move or show any sign to indicate that he was considering doing as Benny instructed. The delay made Benny even more nervous. He pushed the barrel of the gun harder into Baby's temple. Baby held her breath and tried not to move a muscle. Was this how she would die?

'Put the gun on the ground and lie down!' Benny yelled. 'You've got three seconds to comply or I'll shoot her. One…. Two….'

The Red Mohawk finally reacted. 'Okay,' he said. He raised his left hand to signal to Benny to stop counting. Then he bent down to place his gun on the ground. Baby closed her eyes and winced, fearing Benny was about to fire a shot at The Red Mohawk.

BANG!

She heard the gunshot loud and clear. She even felt the bullet whistle past her ear, missing her by less than an inch. Benny released his grip on her and she heard his gun clatter onto the gravel by her feet. She opened one eye and saw Benny crumple to the ground in a heap by her side. He had taken a bullet to the face. His head hadn't exactly exploded, he just had a hole right in the middle of his forehead with blood dribbling out of it. His eyes had rolled up in his head and his tongue was hanging out.

She stared back at the Red Mohawk. He was still bent down, resting on one knee. But standing in the smoke behind him, pointing a gun at her was Jack Munson. A darker shade of smoke was rising up from the barrel of his gun.

Baby took a sharp intake of breath as she realised that Munson had taken a very risky shot.

'Oh my God,' she mumbled. 'I don't believe you just did that!'

'It's okay,' said Munson, lowering his gun. 'I make that shot ninety-nine times out of a hundred.'

Fifty Four

Joey Conrad took off the Red Mohawk mask and dropped it onto the ground by his feet. He ran his hand through his thick dark hair, which had matted somewhat under the mask. 'Good to see you again Jack,' he said.

'You did good Joey,' said Munson. 'A little excessive for my taste, but you got the job done. That's what counts, I suppose.'

'Yeah.'

Munson looked down the driveway at Baby. She hadn't moved since he'd fired a bullet through the forehead of Benny Stansfield. 'You okay Marianne?' he called out.

Baby nodded. 'Can you call me Baby?' she replied meekly. 'I'm not ready for Marianne just yet.'

She looked cold, standing there in the night air in just a pair of jeans and a sleeveless red top. Joey Conrad walked over to her. He took off his red leather jacket and draped it around her shoulders. 'Here, this'll keep you warm.'

'So what now?' Baby asked.

'I'm taking you home,' he said. He stroked her hair and smiled.

Baby looked into his eyes and smiled back nervously. 'Thanks for everything,' she said.

'No problem. You were worth it.'

Munson called out to them. 'I can take her home.'

Conrad turned around. 'This is my first proper mission Jack. The objective was to rescue Baby and take her home. Let me finish it.'

Munson hesitated. He looked at Baby and knew she wasn't really in the right state of mind to make any kind of decision. Her world had been turned upside down in a matter of hours, and it was obvious that she was clinging to the one thing she knew would keep her safe. Ironically, it was Joey Conrad, the guy who had spent the last twenty-four hours walking around town in a Halloween mask murdering everyone he met.

'Baby, are you *sure* you're happy to go with him?' Munson asked, just to make sure he was reading the situation correctly. 'I can take you if you like. It might be a little more discreet if nothing else.'

'It's okay,' she said. 'No offence but if I go with Joey I'm pretty sure I'll get out of this town in one piece.'

Munson snorted a laugh and shook his head, amused at the irony of the situation. 'Sure thing, just promise you'll say hello to your father for me, when you see him.'

He bent down and picked up the Red Mohawk mask. It was heavier than he expected it to be. It was so grotesque; even now with no one wearing it, it still looked horrible. He tossed it to Joey Conrad. 'You should keep this,' he said. 'You might need it again sometime.' Conrad caught the mask. 'I hope so,' he said.

Munson dusted himself off. All kinds of debris from the smoke and gunfire had settled on his shoulders and in his hair. 'I'll clean up here,' he said. 'You two should hurry up and go. You can get out of town without anyone knowing you were ever here. That asylum is going to have to report you as missing soon, Joey. And the minute they do, the whole fucking country is going to be looking for you. You gotta get her home before they get to you.'

Joey Conrad walked up to Munson and held out his hand. Munson shook it firmly and Conrad smiled. 'It was good to see you again, Jack.'

'You too.' Munson paused for a moment before adding a compliment he thought his former trainee would appreciate. 'You would have been a great soldier.'

Conrad pulled a small metal object from a pocket in his black jeans and pressed it into Munson's hand. 'Here,' he said. 'I snagged this from Mellencamp's office.'

It was a shiny mirrored zippo lighter. Munson had used a zippo to burn down a crime scene once before. At least this time he wasn't racked with guilt about doing it.

Munson was distracted by the sight of his reflection in the lighter for a moment, until Baby called out to him. 'Will I see you again when I get home?'

He looked up and gave her a reassuring smile. 'Probably not. I'm planning on retiring. I think I'll live the quiet life somewhere where no one will find me. Especially your dad.'

Baby ran up to him and planted a kiss on his cheek. 'When I meet him, I'll tell him how great you were.'

'Thanks. Now get the hell out of here.'

Joey Conrad put his arm around Baby's shoulder and led her down the driveway. They stopped briefly by the dead body of Benny Stansfield and Conrad picked the dead cop's car keys from his jacket pocket. Munson stood and watched the bizarre sight of the two of them walking off down the driveway towards Benny's car. Sweet young Marianne Pincent, the girl he'd known when she was just five years old, was walking off into the sunset in a red leather jacket that was way too big for her, accompanied by a man who had recently escaped from an asylum and inflicted a massive killing spree on a small town. And yet, when Munson looked at them and saw Conrad with his arm around Baby's shoulder, and her leaning against him, it made him kind of envious.

"It's a fucked up world," he thought to himself.

He looked at the zippo lighter in his hand. It was time to burn down The Beaver Palace and its evil history.

He headed back inside the building and searched through a few of the rooms on the ground floor for flammable liquids. The best thing he found was a drinks cabinet in one of the dining rooms. He poured as much liquor over the floors, stairs and furniture as he could and started setting fire to any sets of curtains he came across.

When he was sure he'd started enough small fires that would eventually spread and set the whole place ablaze, he hurried back out to the front lounge with the last remaining bottle of alcohol he'd snagged from the drinks cabinet. It was a bottle of his favourite rum.

He unscrewed the lid and took a sniff. He didn't even feel the urge to take one mouthful. He savoured the smell but then without a moment's regret he poured the contents all over the sofa in the lounge. Every last drop of it.

He flicked open the zippo lighter once again. The flame lit up immediately. The lighter was hot in his hand where he'd been repeatedly using it. He tossed it onto the sofa. A huge whoosh went up and flames spread quickly across the floor. Munson felt a huge surge of heat engulf him. He backed away and turned to head back out into the cold night air. He'd taken barely two steps towards the front door when he heard a woman's voice scream out from the balcony above him.

'Help! I'm up here!'

Munson spun around and looked up. Standing on the balcony at the top of the stairs, looking absolutely terrified was a beautiful young woman with long dark hair and gorgeous creamy brown skin, wearing a red basque and black stockings. The raging fire was blocking off her route down the staircase.

Shit!

'JUMP! I'LL CATCH YOU!' Munson yelled, positioning himself below the balcony.

'Jump? Are you fucking nuts?'

She was clearly panicked and not thinking straight. Fortunately, years of training and experience meant that Munson knew exactly how to calm down a hysterical prostitute in a house fire.

'What's your name?' he yelled up to her.

'Jasmine.'

'Okay Jasmine. My name is Jack. I'm a government agent. Throw yourself over the balcony and I'll catch you. Don't worry, I've done this a million times. I won't drop you.'

Jasmine seemed to forget her predicament for a moment. 'A government agent?' she gawped, her face showing signs of genuine interest. 'Like James Bond?'

She was either in shock or as daft as a bag of cheese. She was seconds away from burning to death and yet she had taken the time to ask him if he was like James Bond. It was endearing and ridiculous in equal measure. An abrupt and reassuring answer was required.

'I'm *exactly* like James Bond,' Munson yelled. 'Now *fucking* jump for *fucks sake!*'

Jasmine's face lit up at the news that he was *exactly like James Bond.* She vaulted over the balcony without hesitation. Munson steadied himself and caught her in his arms, cushioning the fall by bending his knees. As soon as he had hold of her she wrapped her arms around his neck and kissed him on the cheek. She had a beaming smile on her face and seemed oblivious to the fact they were surrounded by raging hot flames. Munson attempted to put her down but she tightened her grip around his neck and looked into his eyes.

'I always wanted to be carried out of a burning house by James Bond,' she said.

'It'll be quicker if I put you down,' said Munson. 'Then we can run out together!'

'I can't run in these heels.'

Munson looked at her shoes. She was wearing a stupidly high-heeled pair of stilettos. And even though there were six foot high flames and burning bodies of dead cops all around them, he noticed that she also smelled really good. *Oh what the hell*, he decided. *Every man should carry a crazy hooker out of a burning building at least once in his life.* He hurried towards the front door with Jasmine in his arms. She wasn't heavy so it wasn't too much of a hardship. He dashed through the front door and into the cool air outside. Parts of the staircase and ceiling were beginning to fall apart behind him. As they raced down the driveway they heard a series of loud explosions from within the building. The Beaver Palace was collapsing as it lit up the night sky.

Eventually Munson stopped and put Jasmine down. She steadied herself on her high-heels while he bent over to catch his breath. Carrying Jasmine from the flaming building, while exhilarating and heroic in an ego-boosting kind of way, was also very tiring for a man of his age.

236

'Who started the fire?' Jasmine asked, staring back at the burning mansion and dusting herself off.

'Does it matter?' Munson panted.

'It does to me. I work there.'

Munson straightened up and rubbed his back, which was beginning to ache. 'You don't have to work there any more. You can go home now.'

'That *was* my home.'

'Well then you can start a new life somewhere else now.'

'With *what?* Everything I own is going up in smoke!'

'Trust me. You're better off.'

'So where are you taking me now?'

Munson stared back at the burning building. The heat coming off it was immense even from forty metres away. He considered the fact that without the fire Jasmine might be freezing her ass off in her underwear.

'Would you like my shirt?' he offered.

'No. I want somewhere to live. Where are you taking me?'

'I don't know. You'll just have to find somewhere. It's not my problem.'

Jasmine put her hands on her hips and stamped one of her stiletto heels on the ground. 'I know you burnt the place down. You owe me a home *agent man!*'

Munson rubbed his forehead as he tried to think of a way to appease her. Before he had a chance to come up with anything, Jasmine started clapping her hands together. '*Look, look!*' she squealed. 'I think the top floor is collapsing in! This is so cool. I've never seen a building burn down before. Have you?'

Munson stared at Jasmine and struggled to mask the bewildered look on his face. This girl was batshit crazy. But he found it oddly endearing. She was gorgeous too, which he considered might possibly be clouding his judgement. As he watched her clapping her hands together wildly at the sight of the fire, he felt his cell phone vibrate in his pocket. He pulled it out and saw he had an incoming call from Devon Pincent. He put the phone to his ear.

'Hey Devon.'

'What's happening?'

'Your daughter is on her way home. We got her out. She's in one piece.'

'Holy shit.' Pincent's voice almost cracked momentarily. Munson smiled as he considered how emotional his old friend must be feeling. True to form though, Pincent held it together and carried on. 'Is she there with you now?'

'No. Joey Conrad is taking her home. He really came good. Those years of training finally paid off. Operation Blackwash is a success after all.'

Pincent let out a huge sigh. Munson guessed it was from relief on a number of fronts.

'Thanks for helping out on this,' Pincent said. 'I appreciate it. How much mess is left over? Can we cover it up?'

Munson looked back up at The Beaver Palace burning to the ground. He cast a sideways glance at Jasmine who had stopped clapping and was standing so still, that she was clearly listening to his conversation without trying to look like she was doing so. He turned away slightly. 'I've torched the evidence. Only thing is, half the town knows I was here. It won't take a genius to know I was involved in all this shit.'

'I'm way ahead of you Jack. Get out of town and get yourself to Andrews Airport, double quick. I've got you a private plane that'll take you to Romania. I've set you up with a real smart apartment there.'

'Romania? What the fuck? Why Romania? Why not the Bahamas?'

'Because there's something in Romania I need you to look at. Another job if you will. Only this time you won't have to kill anyone. And I've set some money aside for you.'

'Romania though? Romania is a shithole. Why would anyone want to go there?'

Jasmine piped up with an answer. 'The Danube, the Carpathian Mountains, Peles Castle, the Black Sea Resorts.'

Munson covered his cell phone with his hand. 'What are you on about?' he asked in a furious whisper.

'Romania. You asked why anyone would want to go to Romania. I just gave you a few reasons.'

'How do you know so much about Romania?'

'History Channel. Ooh look, the chimney's collapsing!'

Munson shook his head. Jasmine was once again transfixed by the sight of the burning mansion. *Crazy woman.* He stopped covering his cell phone and returned to his conversation with Pincent.

'Do I have any options other than Romania?'

'Not right now,' Pincent replied. 'Look. I need you there for a few months. Do this one thing for me and you'll be set for life. I'll find you a spot in the Bahamas after, I promise.'

238

Munson pondered the offer. It didn't sound like he had much of a choice. He needed to skip the country and lie low for a while. And it sounded like the Romania trip was the only option at short notice. 'Will I need my passport?' he asked.

'No. You won't be going through customs.'

'Hang on.' Munson lowered the phone and looked at Jasmine. 'You're homeless right?' he said.

'Yeah.'

'And you seem to know a lot about Romania.'

'More than *you* by the sound of it.'

'You any good at cooking breakfast?'

Jasmine tilted her head to one side and smiled at him. 'I can warm up a good sausage in the morning,' she said with a wink.

Munson rolled his eyes and sighed. 'How'd you like to come to Romania with me?'

'I thought you'd never ask.'

Munson put the phone back to his ear. 'Devon. Make sure there's room for two on the plane.'

'Will do Jack. And good luck. Sounds like you're gonna need it.'

Fifty Five

Getting out of B Movie Hell hadn't been as tricky as Baby expected. She and Joey ditched Benny's squad car a mile away from The Beaver Palace and hopped into Joey's yellow and red stock car that he'd abandoned by the side of the road earlier. The stock car was so cool and Joey drove it really fast.

A cop car that had been parked at the end of the bridge preventing anyone from leaving town, scarpered quick-sharp when its driver caught sight of the Red Mohawk's stock car hurtling towards him across the bridge.

From there it had all been plain sailing. The drive across the countryside was something Baby had never experienced before. They listened to her Dirty Dancing CD on a loop for the entire trip. Joey Conrad seemed to appreciate the music, and for the first time in years, Baby felt like a normal person.

For the first few hours they swapped stories about their lives in The Beaver Palace and Grimwald's Mental Asylum, frequently one-upping each other with their tales of craziness and oppression. Eventually, Baby began to feel tired and somewhere in the middle of telling him a story about her friend Chardonnay's fascination with leopard print clothing, she fell asleep to the sound of *She's Like The Wind* by Patrick Swayze.

She slept for what felt like days. It had been a deep sleep. A contented sleep, the likes of which she hadn't had since childhood. The fear of being woken and forced to perform sexual acts with strangers was gone. No one could harm her while she slept next to Joey Conrad.

When she woke, the car was parked. The Dirty Dancing CD was playing. She blinked a few times to make sure she was awake and not dreaming about Patrick Swayze as she had done so many times in the past. She heard Bill Medley and Jennifer Warnes singing *Time of My Life*. This was no dream though. She was still in Joey Conrad's car. She smiled when she thought about the fact he had continued to listen to her favourite CD even while she was asleep.

She looked across at his face. He wasn't wearing his mask. He was staring ahead through the front windscreen. He looked like he was deep in thought about something.

'Where are we?' she asked.

He hadn't noticed that she was awake. He looked at her and smiled. 'You're back home.'

She rolled her neck around to unstiffen it and stared out of the window. He had parked up outside a detached house in a quiet suburban neighbourhood. There was a white picket fence around the perimeter of the house and a tarmac pathway that led up to the front door.

'This is it? I live here?' She didn't recognise the place at all.

'I think so. I'll wait in the car while you go see if anyone's in.'

Baby sat upright and rubbed her eyes. 'Are you not coming with me?'

'I can't.'

'Why not?'

'I have to go. There are other missing people to find. And other Silvio Mellencamp's to kill.'

She looked into his eyes and cast her mind back to her first few encounters with him. He had sliced up Arnold at the diner, along with a couple of other guys who had tried to restrain him. The next time she saw him was when he had reappeared in her room and chopped Reg the chef to pieces. Then he had gunned down all the henchmen in B Movie Hell. He had done those things while wearing his yellow mask and the red leather jacket, which he was now wearing again after briefly lending it to her.

'Before I go, could you do one last thing for me?' she asked.

'What?'

'Put the mask back on.'

He smiled again, as if he could read her mind. 'Okay.' He reached over to the back seat of the car and grabbed the thick yellow rubber mask. He slipped it on over his head and adjusted it until his eyes were able to see clearly through the holes. Then he looked over at her again. The mask was as hideous as ever and a constant reminder of everything Joey Conrad was capable of. Baby drank in the image of it, from the red hair and black eyes, to the yellow skin of the skull and right down to the evil grin. She never wanted to forget it.

'Go on. Time to get out' he said. 'You'd better hurry. I've got to keep moving. The cops are after me, you know.'

'Will they catch you?'

'One day, yeah. They'll catch me.'

Baby unclipped her seatbelt and leant forward. She ran her hand through the strip of red hair across the top of his mask and then leaned in and kissed the hideous yellow and black teeth on the mask. Joey Conrad's mouth was on the other side of the rubber. She felt him kiss her back. For years she had dreamt that a Prince Charming would come to her rescue and that they would kiss and everything would be all right. In her dream Bill Medley and Jennifer Warnes were always singing *Time of My Life* in the background. That dream had finally come to fruition, only Prince Charming looked nothing like how she imagined. But she would never forget him.

She pulled away from the kiss and reached for the car door. As she opened it she hesitated. 'Will I ever see you again?'

He turned the key in the ignition on the car and stared up at the road ahead. 'You'll see me on the news one day.'

'Then will you promise me something?'

'It depends.'

'I want you to keep my Dirty Dancing CD and whenever you hear *this* song, will you think about me?'

He stopped staring at the road and looked across at her. She couldn't tell for sure, but she had a feeling he was smiling beneath the mask. 'Sure.'

Baby picked her pink handbag up from the floor by her feet and climbed out of the car. She closed the door behind her and leant back in through the open window. 'I'll never forget you,' she promised.

He nodded. She smiled at him one last time, then turned around and took the first nerve wracking steps towards the front gate of her father's house.

****

Joey Conrad watched Baby walk tentatively up the path to the front door of the house. She pressed the doorbell and stood nervously waiting for someone to answer. Five or maybe six seconds passed before the door opened inwards. A man in his early fifties in a grey suit stood at the door. Conrad recognised him. It was Devon Pincent. Pincent took one look at the young woman on his doorstep in the blue jeans and red sleeveless top and his face instantly lit up into a beaming smile.

He stepped outside and grabbed his daughter. He threw his arms around her and squeezed her tight, as if he never wanted to let her go. Baby responded in kind, throwing her arms around her father for the first time since she was a five-year-old child. From his seat in the car, Joey Conrad could hear Devon Pincent weeping like a child as he hugged his daughter. He was pleased for Pincent, his old mentor, but deep down, for selfish reasons he felt just a little bit sad. He'd only known Baby for a short time, but already she was the best friend he'd ever had. He'd miss her. Devon Pincent was a lucky guy.

242

He'd been watching Pincent and Baby hug each other for little more than ten seconds when he heard the sound of police sirens behind him. As they grew louder, the sirens drowned out the Bill Medley and Jennifer Warnes song. In his rear view mirror The Red Mohawk saw two police cars screeching around the corner, heading towards him. He twisted a knob on the CD player and turned the volume up to the max.

It was time to hit the road.

The End

The Red Mohawk will return in *The Plot to Kill the Pope* (June 2016)

Printed in Great Britain
by Amazon